ON FIRE

HOW TO SET YOURSELF ON FIRE

A NOVEL

JULIA DIXON EVANS

DZANC
BOOKS

5220 Dexter Ann Arbor Rd.
Ann Arbor, MI 48103
www.dzancbooks.org

Library of Congress Cataloging-in-Publication Data

Names: Evans, Julia Dixon, author.
Title: How to set yourself on fire / Julia Dixon Evans.
Description: First edition. | Ann Arbor, MI : Dzanc Books, [2018]
Identifiers: LCCN 2017036657 | ISBN 9781945814501 (softcover)
Subjects: LCSH: Granddaughters--Fiction. | Family secrets--Fiction.
Classification: LCC PS3605.V3657 H69 2018 | DDC 813/.6--dc23
LC record available at https://lccn.loc.gov/2017036657

First US edition: May 2018   MAY 11 2018
Interior design by Leslie Vedder

Printed in the United States of America

10   9   8   7   6   5   4   3   2   1

"In the end we had pieces of the puzzle, but no matter how we put them together, gaps remained, oddly shaped emptinesses mapped by what surrounded them, like countries we couldn't name."

—Jeffrey Eugenides, *The Virgin Suicides*

ONE

IT'S THE THIRD MORNING of a wildfire to the east and everyone's used to the smell by now. Still, I've been awake for hours and my brain seems to crawl inside my skull, equal parts anxious at and tired of the smoke. Every wildfire season, when a thick blanket of ash hovers between the fire and the ocean, I wonder if I'm far enough from it, if this concrete grid of hundred-year-old suburb will repel fire the same way it repels me. Maybe fire will feel right at home here, the same way I do. Every wildfire, I feel safe and I don't feel safe. I care and I don't and this is my California. From the concrete walk of the courtyard, I count the ants in twos as they rush across the tops of my shoes, two, four, six, dozens, hundreds, too many to possibly all know where they're going. There's nothing out here for them, just sidewalk cracks, lifeless plants leaning against the walls, cheap patio furniture, my neighbor's ashtray, the low-hanging lone-liness heavy in the air. I wonder what the ants know that I don't.

Greyish-orange skies yield to heat already and I hear my neighbor start up a Skype call. It's barely six.

"Hello, Vinnie," a woman says. His ex. She lives on the East Coast somewhere with their daughter, Torrey. I know all this because his place is so close to mine. I've listened to Torrey grow up on the other side of these video calls. I'd feel more like the creeper I am if Vinnie weren't so obnoxious and unconcerned with being loud at 6 a.m. I'd feel more like the creeper I am if I knew how fathers were supposed to be with their daughters.

"Sarah," Vinnie says. Clipped. "Where's Torrey?"

"She'll be down in a minute. We *have* to discuss next summer, though."

"For the love of God, it's November."

He says this the same way he says *What's happening* when we meet at the mailbox. The thing with Vinnie is, he doesn't get louder. He never shouts. He has one volume.

"These things take serious juggling, and if you're not willing to step up and plan—"

"Oh, don't give me that."

"I'm just saying. All her friends are going to summer camp here. Maybe this isn't the right year for her to come to you."

"Sarah, I'm going to pretend you didn't say that."

I can hear him moving around in his apartment across the tiny courtyard that links our two miniscule buildings. He must be in the kitchen because I don't see movement through the single window. I shake off my shoes but the ants just reassemble. Some guy from the building behind our courtyard shouts, like he always does, "How about you shut the fuck up, Daddy?" but Vinnie ignores him, like he always does.

I try to remember the last time I slept.

"Hey, Dad," Torrey says on the other end. "I scored a goal this weekend!"

"Oh yeah?" Vinnie says, and I feel a weird fondness for his sudden shift in tone. "That's so great."

I tune out. I realize that it's unfathomable to me to be on either end of that kind of conversation. Of that kind of relationship. I am not a father. I am not a daughter. I am not my father's daughter.

I brush the ants off with my hands and go inside. I almost slam the door, but I find myself not wanting to make a bad impression on a girl on the other side of the country. My phone rings, but it takes me a minute to place the noise. The last time I heard that ringtone was when I picked it from the settings.

It's my mother. *Run*, I think, like there's another fire on the other side of the phone.

I let it ring. After a minute, she calls again.

"Hi, Mom," I say.

"Sheila," she says. "It's Mom."

I lean against the cabinet in my kitchen, really just a corner of the single room I live in.

"Hi, Mom," I say again.

"When's the last time you visited your grandma?" she asks, the *your* placing guilt squarely on my shoulders.

"Uh, last week?" I say. It was probably a month ago.

"Well," she says, and she takes a deep breath. I can tell she feels important and serious. She lives for this shit. And I understand the 6 a.m. call. "I think you should visit her as soon as possible."

Hang up, I try not to say out loud. *Run run run.*

TWO

MY GRANDMOTHER IS VERY old, and tonight, she'll die in her sleep. But right now, she says, "I have something to tell you, sweet girl."

She's wrinkled—shriveled really—but she still looks like me and my mother. We each inherited her wiry blond hair and bony knees and shoulders. My grandmother's hair is grey now, neck-length. She looks away, her chin down, and she doesn't look happy but she also doesn't look afraid, and that's how I've always known her. Her papery hands clutch a small shoebox to her stomach. She holds it tight, like it's hardwired into her blood. I try to keep my eyes off the box. It's a child's shoebox, and I know without question that the shoebox is sixty years old and once housed something of my mother's. I don't know what shoes my mother wore as a kid. The shiny Mary Janes she forced on me when I was very small? Lace-ups? Miniature penny loafers? I doubt my mother was the type to scuff the toes or wear down the soles into rubbery shreds, like me.

"History always repeats itself," my grandmother tells me. Or maybe she says, "History never forgets," or maybe that's just what she'd always say at Christmas, at the dining table, her forearms resting on the red poppy-covered tablecloth, whenever people were arguing about something pointless. We'd all laugh because we wanted her to be funny. Nothing is funny now.

I smile at her. I'm something between vaguely uncomfortable and curious and I shove my hands beneath my thighs so I have something to do besides grab the shoebox. I want to egg her on.

"Yeah?" I ask. She's never been much of a talker and neither have I. It's not uncommon for us to sit here in silence for the entirety of a visit. I both love this and feel like I'm failing her.

She closes her eyes and nods her head, once, twice, and then leans it back against the stack of pillows propping her up. I can already tell I'm not going to get much more out of her.

The room oppresses me. It's too big for just a twin bed and two wicker chairs. I don't think about my grandmother, the way she has always been there for me: loving, but a few steps away, and I don't know if that distance was me or her. I focus on very recent history, my second appointment with a therapist in many years. I think about the prescription tucked into my wallet, which I'll never get filled. This room is too big for my tiny grandmother, tiny not really in size but in the way she doesn't take up space. When I was younger, she'd be sitting with us at our house, right in front of me, and still sometimes I would wonder where she'd gone. In an assisted-living facility, an old woman shrinks more than ever. She looks like she's somewhere else, like she's never belonged here in the first place.

"Okay, Grandma," I say. "What do you mean?"

Then she asks me to leave. She says, "Go now, sweet girl. Not today. I'm tired. I'll tell you tomorrow."

It's quiet in the courtyard outside my house. The sun is about to come up, the chilly air full of marine layer and morphing from black to grey to golden-grey. I haven't slept much at all tonight. I shiver, sitting on my front step, but I had to get out of the sweltering heat of my house. My neighbor's ashtray perches atop his green plastic patio table. I could probably reach it if I stretched—pick up the discarded cigarette stubs and see what was left of them. When I hear movement inside his place a minute later, I stand up, silent, and slip back inside without thinking. Without thinking why I don't want anybody to see me. Without thinking why I don't want to see anybody.

I dial Jesse's number, the number of a man I knew so well but who never knew me at all. When I was a teenager, doing this sort of thing with boys, I'd have to stop before I got to the last number so the call didn't go through. But it's a touchscreen now, and I can dial all the numbers, see them stretched out like a sentence. I like the way the numbers look all in a row. Sometimes I type the numbers a dozen times over and it's beautiful, a plea: *You'll never know how good we could be.*

I have his number typed all the way out when my phone vibrates and the screen switches over to an incoming call. My mother.

"Sheila?"

"Hi, Mom," I say.

"It's Mom," she says. And then, "She's gone." Just like that.

"Oh," I say. Just like that. It's not as breathless as I hoped.

"Did you see her yesterday?" she asks.

"No," I lie. I wonder why I lie.

When I get to the nursing home, my grandmother's body is gone and the room is packed in tidy boxes. I open them all, carefully at first, tucking everything back in place and trying to restick the tape, but before long I get impatient. I tug box lids until the corners bend, and things don't fit back in after I ratch through each box. I want the shoebox.

When my mother arrives, I'm sitting on one large box and rummaging through another, and she makes a face—pulling her chin back toward her neck and scrunching her eyebrows. If I tried that, I'd look foolish, but she manages to look graceful. She seems startled to see me, but I cut her off before she can ask me something like: *What are you doing going through all of your freshly-dead grandmother's boxes like this?* And then: *Have some decency,* she'd add.

"Hi," I say. "Just checking all these." I don't really want to give her time to respond. "Did Grandma leave out a little shoebox?"

She glances to the side before she answers. "What shoebox?"

Two weeks ago, I started getting nosebleeds. At first I panicked. I read websites about how to treat nosebleeds and combed through the hashtags. There's always pictures. Not of the nosebleeds but of their happy lives, despite a bloggable medical issue. Their children are well-adjusted. Their houses are nicer than mine. They are better at photography. They are better at social media. They are better at living with nosebleeds.

"Less stress, more salt," my doctor suggested. A pause, then: "Have you ever thought about psychiatric treatment?" I laughed and he said, "I didn't mean it like that," with his hand on the doorknob, and I wondered if they taught him to act like a bad boyfriend in medical school or if he was born with it.

By now, I've stopped panicking. I stop trying to treat the nose-bleeds. I like the way the blood feels as it leaks from my nasal cavity into the back of my mouth. I like the way the blood looks as it drops onto Jesse's letter. There's just the one letter. It's not even addressed to me.

A tiny drop falls onto Jesse's salutation. *My dearest love* is now blotted with my cells and plasma and it's almost like he loved me too.

———

When my mother is at work, I let myself into her house. It's unusual for me to be here alone, but I am here enough otherwise. She's lived in this place my entire life, opting, for private reasons, not to leave as her family dwindled from three to just us two, to finally one. I never go upstairs anymore. A small part of me wants to see my old room, to sneak up there, and an even smaller part imagines her coming home while I'm upstairs. I imagine her face as she notices me in here, holding her accusations on her tongue, her withered nostalgia, her *I wish we were still close* and *Whatever happened to the two of us* and *Look, it's just us, just like the olden days. Do you want some tea? Some Prosecco?* And I imagine her face as I walk past her, down the stairs, and leave without telling her why I was in the house, without giving her any answers to the questions she would never have the balls to ask me. But today I have other plans.

It's not hard to find the child's shoebox because it's sitting on the countertop beneath a small stack of paperwork from the nursing home and the mortuary. I stuff the box in my purse. It fits, but one corner of the lid tears and I feel I've disrespected my grandmother and my mother, not because I'm snooping but because the shoebox lived so long without being damaged, until me.

I don't leave a note.

The shoebox sits untouched on my coffee table. Frontline is on PBS, and I'm masturbating.

The lone window in this tiny house is closed and the volume is up, but across the small courtyard, I can still hear Vinnie Skyping with his kid and his disgruntled ex-wife. I hesitate every time I hear the twelve-year-old girl, because it sends me down a mental rabbit hole.

Vinnie is insufferable when he's talking to his ex-wife, but I sort of like him when he talks to his daughter. She's quiet, often bored, sometimes absurd. I think she thrives on saying the things her parents are expecting her to say the least. Vinnie is sweet with her, patient in a way he and the ex are not with each other.

Last summer, when Torrey was out here for two weeks visiting her dad, I stayed inside as much as possible but could hear every word they'd say to each other.

"You can't just write Pop-Tarts, Dad," Torrey had said.

"Listen, this is the most detailed grocery list I've ever made. The only time I've ever used capital letters." I could hear the smile in Vinnie's voice. I was on the couch in my tiny place, lying with my head flat on the seat and my feet up on the armrest, a portable fan pointed directly at me.

My father, when he shopped, never used grocery lists. He'd meander the aisles, navigating by feel. Half the time he forgot the ingredients for dinner. But he'd always buy the treat foods—the Pop-Tarts. The things with capital letters.

"You gotta write strawberry Pop-Tarts," Torrey said. "It's important."

"Whatever you say, champ," Vinnie said. "Strawberry it is. All the other flavors are terrible."

"Well," Torrey said. "Let's not get carried away."

Vinnie just laughed. He just seemed genuinely happy to be making a finicky grocery list. Charming. Vinnie was and is charming with Torrey. And I'm consistently impressed with his ability to chin up and not only call his ex but look at her on a video call. I'm impressed, and then quickly sad. My father couldn't even muster up a phone call. And then, past the sad, I'm pissed. Stop. I grasp a breast in one hand, squeezing, lifting.

"Look, I'm not going through this again!" Vinnie shouts.

"Vincent, don't do this in front of Torrey," Sarah the Ex says.

Frontline is a rerun, which is fine because nostalgia is all I have room for. They're doing a montage of evening news program sound bytes about Obama's first term. My hips shift. I press harder.

I close my eyes. They're showing a clip of a White House press conference. I'm so fucking close I can feel it low in my gut, spreading.

"I'm not doing *anything*," Vinnie says. "Let Torrey choose how she wants to spend her *own* goddamned summer!"

Nancy Pelosi says, "*I call it the dance of the seven veils. I'm going to be there, and then I'm not, and I'm going to be there, then I'm not, now you see it, now you don't,*" and she sounds insane.

"Stop it!" Torrey finally says, angry, and it's the first time in a long time I've heard her at a pitch above apathy. "I don't want to go to any dumb summer camps."

I'm angry, too, as I come, because it's not even any good.

THREE

When I finally open the shoebox, PBS is still on, but it's the weird late-night stuff. Vinnie is sitting in the shared courtyard, smoking and playing phone Tetris with the sound on. I breathe deeply, his expunged smoke satisfying the nicotine addiction I never properly kicked. I consider Vinnie's hygiene, the way he dresses, the way he doesn't seem to take care of himself, the way his hands look so worn, so used. I breathe deep again.

My fingertips twitch to hold something, to fidget with a cigarette. I rub the edges of the shoebox lid, its cardboard softened with age, more cloth than paper, and I think about my grandmother's skin, how it didn't look soft. She looked hardened, wooden, etched. I lift the lid.

It's letters. The shoebox is full of letters, more than I can even begin to estimate. Small ones, the personal envelope size that nobody uses anymore. Only one of them has a stamp and a postmark. The stamp is unfamiliar. The postmark is faded but still clear: SAN DIEGO. MAY 13TH, 1950.

The address is in cursive and I smile. I've forgotten how to write in cursive, forgotten how to write letters to anyone, the days long gone since the carefully folded notes in fourth grade, since I could keep a friend long enough to compose and fold a note. This letter doesn't have a name, just an address. My grandmother's address—the house she moved into as a nineteen-year-old newlywed. The house she lived in until a few short months ago, when her illness and my mother's unwillingness to handle it justified live-in care. The return address on the back flap doesn't have a name.

I feel no remorse, no invasion of privacy when I open it. I feel mostly blank, with just a thin layer of excitement. I have no idea what to expect, but for a split second I catch myself imagining evidence of some great fortune or royalty. I laugh, just one huff of an exhale through my nose, because it's about as likely as anything else.

> *Dear Mrs. Baker,*
>
> *I am writing with great regret to inform you that your young daughter's doll, which is quite large and realistic and therefore worrisome at first, has met its demise at the mouth of my terrier. I believe it was thrown into my back yard on Thursday the 10th, as our gardens back up against a shared fence. I do not believe it is in anyone's best interest to return the doll to you or your daughter. It is a morbid scene. There is no longer a head. Please allow me to purchase a new doll for your daughter. If you would kindly inform me of where the doll was purchased, I can rectify the situation immediately. I will not rest until an intact doll is returned to your young child, so please do not protest, and please reply immediately, either by post or a visit around the block. Otherwise I shall be required to continue sending letters or trying to reach you until I can remedy this.*
>
> *Sincerely and regretfully,*
> *Mr. Harold C. Carr*

Mr. Harold C. Carr's return address was one street over from my grandmother's. That child was my mother. My mother's doll. There's some karmic injustice about this that makes me hate my mother a little less. It's not even like she has been a monster to me, and here is a humanizing tragic toy loss. Maybe imagining her headless doll gives my pity something to hook into, sixty something years gone. I forget to wonder why this letter mandated a carefully guarded shoebox clutched against my grandmother's sunken frame. I forget to wonder what my grandmother was going to tell me. I open the next letter and Vinnie hacks up cigarette smoke, the Tetris music still blaring.

"Vinnie," I say.

"Yeah?" he says. He's croaky still.

"Need anything?"

"Nah," he says. He spits on the ground of the shared courtyard. I consider his hygiene. I eye his cigarette butt.

"Okay," I say. "How're things?"

I feel a little awkward as I stand there while he finishes coughing.

"Good, I s'pose. Just trying to kick this cold."

He stands up. His white ribbed tank top is yellowed at the armpits and neckline. His sweatpants are too low on his hips and his waistline is pale and hairy. He holds out the cigarette box to me, and I decline and I want to hate him. His fingertips are weirdly stained and callused. I want to ask him what he does for a living but I'm afraid of making him say *nothing*.

He doesn't return the "How're things?" He doesn't say anything else. The Tetris music is still playing on his phone and the shapes have long since piled up.

"Well, all right then. Just checking on you."

I go inside. I turn off the TV. I close the windows, despite the heat, despite the thickness of the relentless October night, post-wildfire, still terribly dry though I somehow sweat instantly. I count the envelopes in the box. Three hundred and eighty-two. I start to read and by one in the morning I have to open the windows again.

At two in the morning I get another nosebleed and I quietly curse when a drop gets on one of my grandmother's envelopes. It doesn't feel subversive or surreptitious or thrilling like it did on Jesse Ramirez's letter. It just feels like a mess. Like I'm ruining something.

The sky starts to brighten just after six and I'm still not done reading.

FOUR

JESSE RAMIREZ, THE UPS driver who delivered to my old job—my last semblance of stability, my last attempt at doing this, at functioning—dropped his letter, presumably accidentally, on a warm morning one October, one of many mornings I'd watched him walk away. It was the first time I touched anything of his, when I slowly approached the sidewalk after he'd gone, my eyes fixed on the dropped envelope. The letter was a little bit older than that October, so he must have been carrying it around. Maybe he wasn't ready to send it yet. I knew I should either give it back or keep it. I knew unequivocally that I was not going to send it. It wasn't in an envelope, no name, but clearly it was his to send, not his to receive.

I kept it folded up for three weeks before I read it. That delay is my most noble accomplishment.

There's a line on the first page I trace over with my fingers so often that the paper has started to bunch and fray, little specs of worndown pulp as clingy pieces of papery lint.

There's a line on the second page that I wish I could never read again. It has no pulpy lint.

There's a line on the third page that I've copied out thirty times and counting in my own handwriting in a small book: "*You and I were able to briefly be the most beautiful thing in the world, the kind*

of beauty that without you, I would never know existed," I wrote. He
wrote. I wondered what it was like to know something so incompre-
hensible. I wondered if he was making shit up.

I wondered if I'd recognize the point when you pass over into
that knowledge. Was it arbitrary? Was it obvious? Is it obvious when
you realize that now you know something exists that you didn't know
yesterday? And is it measured in days? Do people notice this immediately, or months later? Is it only when the letters are written, the
broken-hearted letters?

Rather than longing to feel something so powerful myself, I
mostly just wished someone felt that way about me. I didn't feel any
shame that I didn't necessarily wish to feel that way too.

Jesse Ramirez didn't know me at all.

"Try this," the therapist said, ripping off a piece of paper. I read not
the words but her office's letterhead at the top of the small notepad.
Her first name was Mabel and she seemed fifty years too young to be
a Mabel. She seemed too young to be more educated than me. "It's
the mildest medication, given that your symptoms seem so mild. You
won't need to worry so much about side effects."

I hated her for calling me mild. I hated how she could posit to
measure feelings on a chart, in a table, with a thermometer.

That afternoon, and then the next afternoon, I dutifully took
two total doses and then no others. I'd sit and read blogs about the
miscellaneous afflicted taking their multitudes of pills a day, but I
couldn't bring myself to take one. Was I scared of finding out that
the drugs would help and then, if they helped, that I had something
that needed helping? Was I scared of finding out that the dose would
help, so therefore my condition *was* mild? As desperate as I was to
have something wrong with me, quantifying it would unhinge me.

I didn't show up to the next appointment. Or the next.

She called me three months later. I folded Jesse's letter smoothly, sealing the Ziploc bag properly before picking up.

"How's it working, Sheila?" she asked.

"Fine," I said.

"Great! And the dosage was okay from the get-go?"

"Yeah," I said. Fully aware that I should have been more specific with this lie. Act like you actually wanted this, I tried to tell myself. "No problem with the dosage. I feel like a different person," I said.

My therapist is the only person I'll ever tell what she wants to hear.

I don't want Jesse's letter to get mixed up with my grandmother's letters, my new obsessions. It's different only in size. The content is startlingly similar, like maybe Harold C. Carr had some futuristic time and space-bending skills and is now a thirtysomething Latino UPS driver. Jesse's is a large, heavy sheet of printer paper. Probably not recycled. I fold it up, a perfect trifold, and put it in its dedicated Ziploc. I open my nightstand drawer, empty. It's always empty, except for this letter. I close the drawer. Ritual.

Tonight, I open it again. I lift out the baggie. I handle it a bit, feeling the smoothness of the plastic in my hands. There's a little air in the bag. I open it and unfold the letter. Then I put it back and quickly walk away. I leave the room, I leave the house, I leave the complex. I don't even look at Vinnie when I walk past him smoking in the courtyard. I don't know where I'm going. I don't have anywhere to go.

The first time my father stormed out, I hid at the top of the stairs, eavesdropping from behind the smooth oak veneer of the banister.

Not that there was anything to see or hear. My parents were quiet when they fought. Their anger ran piping hot beneath the surface, lava never erupting through the planetary crust. The plates move, the earth burns, but I never even heard a boom.

I think I knew this wasn't just my dad going out to the store or to work in the garage. Not from anything he said, because all they did was look at each other, clipped goodbyes in low voices that carried a marriage's worth of shorthand. I could tell by the way my mother leaned against the wall in the small corridor between the kitchen and the front door. She faced away from me, the side of her forehead against the powder-blue fleur-de-lis wallpaper, her graceful shoulders slumped. I was only eight years old but I knew this was different.

He didn't come back for two days, and when he did, their re-union was as subdued as his leaving. Quiet. Still.

Those two days, my mother filled my time to the brim. I had no space to ask about my father, about why I was feeling like the sky could open up and steal me, about why I was feeling like nothing was as fun or as tasty or as easy as before. I think that was the first time I ever felt sadness, its force and comprehensiveness, its stun.

The second time my father left, a few years later, he was even quieter and I didn't know it was happening. By then there were no battles, no fire beneath their earth's crust, just a marriage more war-torn than warring, crumbled concrete in an ancient city street. The second time he left, it was for good.

FIVE

THE SHOEBOX TORMENTS ME. If I squint I can almost see my grandmother's thin hands wrapped around it, reedy finger bones pulling it close. It reminds me that I am not entirely sad about her death. It's not like we were incredibly close. She was an old woman, after all, in a different world, a peaceful, composed life. She always seemed so detached from me and from my mother, in that mentally compromised sort of way, but now I'm thinking maybe all along she was so sad.

I wonder if she blamed my mother, the child, anchoring her to the home on the wrong side of the fence.

I wonder if she also blamed me, because I am a part of my mother in the same way that my mother was a part of her. It's confusing, this ancestry of pain and blame.

My phone rings. My mother.

"Sheila. It's Mom."

"I know," I say.

"How are you?" she asks.

"You know, fine, I guess?" I pause. She also pauses. "How are you?"

"I'm okay, all things considered."

My mother likes to add "all things considered" at the end of her sentences in some sort of verbal martyrdom. I hate it, for the same reasons all daughters hate the harmless things their harmless mothers do. But the death of her own mother seems to be the one time it actually fits.

"Yeah."

"Were you over here yesterday?" she asks.

Lie. I should lie.

"Yeah." I don't lie.

"Oh. You didn't mention it."

"Well, you weren't home."

She doesn't respond right away. I take pleasure in the way she must be agonizing over how to bring up the shoebox.

"Okay, then. Just wondering. I thought there might have been a burglary or something."

I could throw her a lifeline. I could ask if anything was missing, give her a way of bringing up the shoebox.

"Nope, just me."

"Okay," she says. A pause. "Well, are you coming tomorrow?"

"God, Mom. Of course."

"I know," she says. "I'm sorry," and she seems flustered. It isn't often I see her like this, tripping over her words. "I didn't mean it like that."

"It's okay. I'll be there. Want me to pick you up?"

"That'd be nice. I suppose we have to ride to the graveyard in the hearse."

It occurs to me that we are my grandmother's only living relatives. This, *this* is the thing that makes me sad. This is what sets my grief on its rightful course. I grieve not for the lack of this woman in my life, but for her shitty legacy. One daughter. One granddaughter. Worse, it's me. The awareness of this, the comedy of it, the misguided pressure, causes a noise to escape my throat that sounds like a wail, a choked-back sob.

"Oh, honey," my mother says.

I want to laugh, but I think it will be better for my mother to imagine her daughter grieving like a normal person.

"I'm okay, Mom. I'll see you tomorrow."

I hang up first. I kick the shoebox under the bed. And then I grab it and open it again. I spread the first year of letters out across my bed. Some of them are undated. One day I swear I will know these letters so well that I can line them up based only on their contents, but for now I leave the undated ones in their own small pile.

"Hey, Torrey." I hear Vinnie's "inside voice" across the courtyard.

I'd get up to close the window but, for one thing, I enjoy listening to Vinnie's Skyping, and for another, I have Harold C. Carr's letters spread out across my knees and shins.

"Hi, Dad," his daughter says. Her apathetic quiet is no match for the way sound carries between Vinnie's house and mine.

"How's school going?"

"Ugh, *fine*, Dad."

The silence is long and followed by mumbled, mostly indecipherable conversation. I start to read the next letter.

Dear Mrs. Baker,

I implore you, please let me know the exact make and model and place of purchase for the child's doll my terrier so frighteningly decapitated. I am committed to writing to you each day until this matter is resolved. I hope you either respond quickly, or that you enjoy receiving daily letters from a desperate man.

Sincerely,

Harold C. Carr

Postscript: Your sunflowers look lovely. They have just this week poked their heads above the fence line. I can see them from my writing desk right now, as it looks out over my own backyard.

"Torrey," Vinnie says, and though I hear him clearly, his voice is so quiet. "I miss you so much," he says. I wish I'd been listening better.

I slither out from under my blanket of letters, taking care to rearrange them in their rows and columns. I manage to push closed the window above my bed. I take off all of my clothes and lie down on the floor, on the small rug right next to my bed. I put my cheek down on the ground, against the little bits and pieces of lint and brittle, stray long hairs and crusty stuff. I wish I had vacuumed. I wish I took better vitamins and had better hair. I fall asleep even though it's early evening, and I sleep, eyes crusted shut, mouth foul from not brushing or flossing, until dawn. The dawn smells so different when it's woken to, than when it's reached after a night spent sleepless. It seems cleaner, colder like this. It's been forever since I woke this early, since I slept so well.

SIX

IT WAS LATE SUMMER. It was three years ago but it's supposed to be over by now. It's not supposed to have been three years since I held a regular job. I'd left the job thinking I just needed to try something different, because church work, even secretarial church work, is not for the weak, and I am the weak. Temp jobs are for the weak—jobs I can leave when things don't work out. It's not supposed to have taken me a matter of days to get used to the idea of never working a steady job again. It's not supposed to have been three years of living in a rundown, pre-gentrification corner of a neighborhood on the wrong side of downtown, in this tiny shack with a tiny concrete courtyard, ants and green plastic patio furniture the only decor, because I can only afford California slum rent on my spotty income. It's not supposed to have been three years of asking my mother for money. It's not supposed to have been even one day of asking my mother for money, but the worst habits, once forged, are the hardest ones to kick.

It's not supposed to have been three years since I was happy. I almost don't remember it. I almost don't believe I ever was.

That day, three years ago, I wore an old black dress, borrowed from my grandmother years prior. Late summer is always the worst heat and the dress clung to my sweaty thighs when I stood up from my desk. But I stood up, just in case he decided to do more than drop off the mail.

"Oh, thank you," I said. *Next time*, I cursed myself, *next time say something smarter.*

"You're welcome. How are you today?" he asked. He showed his teeth in a wide smile, white even right up to the upper back edges of the canines, along the gum line.

"I'm okay," I said, my heart racing. *Ask him how he is. Ask him. Maybe just say "And you?"* But I didn't.

"Well, it's a lovely day. Let's see. We have a few things here."

I was a church secretary. It was the best job I'd ever had, the best job I'd ever given up on, all thanks to my mom's neighbors, the Reverend and Mrs. Spike.

It was the stuff out of a soda commercial, secretaries and hunky deliverymen. He wasn't even that hunky and I certainly wasn't much of a secretary. But he had very white teeth and a crooked smile. He always looked a day behind in shaving and it made me wonder if he was hairy all over. Sometimes I thought about him naked while I sat in the blue-walled office building adjacent to the sanctuary. I could see a Jesus from my desk, many Jesuses.

"You're new here, right?" he asked.

I shrugged. *Speak. Time to speak.*

"I've seen you around. I like your dress," he said, and he turned around.

"Hello? Oh, sure. I can hold."

Click, garble.

"Yeah, hi. I'm still here. So, I was wondering if there's any way to find out the name of one of your delivery drivers?"

Mumbled, jaded words, hardly listened to.

"Oh, no, I understand. It's nothing like that. We're St. Peter's Church. Yes, on Euclid."

The tenor of trust, tentative.

"Mm-hm. Well, perhaps I should explain. You see, and please keep this confidential, but he mentioned some, you know, concerns? Some unfortunate health problems with his family. And everyone here loves him, you know, and the church elders have all voted to provide him with a monetary gift. It's just a small check. We'd like to write it out to him in advance so he has no choice but to take it." I worried I was pushing it. I thought of Mrs. Spike, her holy voice. The way kindness oozed from every word. "And of course, we would love to be able to put his name on our prayer list."

Uncertainty. She was a secretary, probably, just like me.

"Sure. I can hold again. And again, thank you so much."

I felt no remorse. I was a little turned on.

"Yes, hi. I'm here. Oh, that is wonderful. Hold on, let me get a pen."

I smudged black ink on my fingers fumbling the cap.

"Okay, ready. Mmhm, Jesse, J-E-S-S-E? Yes, Ramirez? With a Z? Z, okay. Thank you so much. Oh, a mailing address? Wow, that certainly would make things easier. If you're sure? You're right. I'd better get his phone number as well. Thank you so much! God bless you."

I hung up the phone and walked out the door. It was 6 p.m. I was supposed to take notes in a church meeting at seven, but I had already forgotten. I drove, my mind startlingly clear, straight to Jesse Ramirez's house.

It only took a few days, but eventually I had his schedule down, and that freed me up to get back into a routine at work. They had been asking questions. Concerned, worried. Offering to pray. It was better for everyone that I was now able to compartmentalize my time with Jesse into manageable units.

It was in October, on the forty-third morning of watching him leave the house, that I saw him drop the letter. The air felt thick but it seemed like I was floating, full of air, but almost like I didn't need air in the first place. I stepped, somehow, forward, toward the letter, and picked it up. I took it home. It was as if there were no other options. I had no other options, the letter had no other options, and Jesse had no other options.

SEVEN

BEING AWAKE AT DAWN means I have four hours to kill before the funeral. I look up at my bed from my spot on the dirty floor, but for today, today especially, I want to keep my grandmother's letters neatly arranged. I wonder what it would be like to have this shoebox if my grandmother was still alive. It's not exactly that I'm wishing for it. I don't exactly miss her. A part of me that is both very lazy and a little generous is glad she is dead. Her life wasn't amazing. She lived a non-life for such a long time, shushed away in a too-big room with wicker furniture and attendants who spoke like cheerful preschool teachers. And before that, a long decline into then-undefined sadness. It was tedious for my mother to be around her. It was tedious talking to my mom about her. I can't help but recognize the relief in this for both of the women in my life.

I open the closet. It's hard to miss it, that dress. The one I was wearing the time Jesse spoke to me.

I pull it out of the closet and run my fingers over it. I wish it were silk, something romantic, something notable, but it's not. It's polyester or worse. But then I remember the way silk smells. The way silk would predictably show the sweat in the crease below my breasts, the crease under my butt, and along the line of my seatbelt after driving. The sweat will be there anyway, but at least it won't show. It's my grandmother's polyester dress. She gave it to me to borrow one Christmas when I was eighteen but I never returned it. "Just keep it, Sheila," she said. "It doesn't fit me. That's not a dress for an old woman."

My mom will probably clutch her chest in that prescribed way when she sees me wearing it, the way mothers are supposed to press against their hearts when they see their daughter wearing an heirloom dress on funeral day. She will react with a whispery gasp, "Oh honey," and I will take pleasure in manipulating it out of her: the secret undermining of my mother.

She won't know that I picked it because it's Jesse's dress. Maybe he didn't even really notice the dress, maybe it was a knee-jerk compliment, but I have to have something to believe in. I have nothing left of me and him, nothing except for a dress and a letter. Our relationship is entirely inside me and these objects. I'll wear it, the dress, not because of my grandmother, but because it's a sacrament, a host, and maybe one day it will transubstantiate into something real between me and a man who doesn't even know me. And even if it doesn't, I'll take the host anyway.

By 7 a.m., I hear Vinnie come outside of his house for a smoke. I'm still naked or I would go outside and sit with him. This instinct to be around Vinnie surprises me and annoys me at the same time. I fill up a bath with the hottest the water will go. The bathroom window is closest to where Vinnie sits anyway, so I open it. It's too high for him to see in.

"Morning, Vinnie," I say.

"Hey," he says.

I step into the bath and the water stings.

"Vinnie?"

"Yeah?"

"What do you do?"

"What?"

"Like, for work? A job?" I ask. As I lower my body in, the scalding heat on my cunt makes me want to exit and reenter the water over and over again.

"Oh. Well, I'm between jobs right now."

"Like, literally?"

Vinnie doesn't answer right away.

"I'm waiting for my next order."

"Order?"

"I'm going to go inside now."

"Today's my grandmother's funeral," I say quickly.

"Oh. Sorry, kid."

"I'm not a kid."

"Just sorry, then."

It's not like I ever know what to say when someone dies. It's not like I can expect that out of Vinnie.

"It's not your fault," I say suddenly. That makes me laugh. "Unless you murdered her."

"Jesus, Sheila."

I sink my head all the way under the water and open my eyes. My hair, dark with wet, fans around my face, long seagrass against a steadying tide. I wonder if Vinnie is talking. The world is a wall of heavy noise. I want to take a big breath exactly as much as I want to stop breathing. Underwater it looks as if the roof is starting to cave in.

I float up and gasp for air.

EIGHT

My mom is predictable.

"Oh, honey," she says. She only calls me honey when she's feeling good about her motherhood. When she feels like this is how it's supposed to go. "I love you in that dress."

I try not to wonder where her insecurity comes from. For thirty-five years, have I made her feel like she needed to work to get to that place, how it's supposed to go between mothers and daughters? Do I hold all the power? She's the one being a mother, and just waiting for me to hold up my end of the bargain and be the daughter? I wonder: if the tables were turned, and I was waiting around for her to be the mother, would I cling to every motherly moment, or would I walk away? I think my mother probably has an idea. I think she assumes I would not wait around. And therein lies the power. And the shame, and the pity. I recognize my mother's insecurity as my doing, but am powerless to stop it. With great power comes great powerlessness for me, always.

"Are you ready?" I ask. I take a deep breath, steeling, and then, a morsel of daughterhood tossed between us, a peace offering: I smile.

"Not quite," she says. "Come in for a sec."

A second turns out to be fifteen minutes. I stand in my childhood living room and pick at the stupid shit my mother keeps on the mantel. I close my eyes and remember the way it was when I lived here, when my parents were still married. Right in the middle, they had an eight-by-ten wedding picture in a silver frame. It was an awkward picture, totally staged, with just the two of them, a bunch of flowers, and the kind of smiles people smile after they've been told to smile all day. I always thought it was too big to just be propped up on the mantelpiece.

Now, my dad is nowhere in the house. My mother left his things in their places for a year. I'd hear her at night, angry whispers into the phone, negotiations, accusations, and then fewer of those phone calls until, eventually, silence, darkness. Even the dark stopped calling. When I'd ask about him, she'd withdraw with a sullen look that unnerved me, so I learned not to ask. I never asked if they were ever officially divorced. I never asked if she ever saw him again. I never asked what happened. She never changed her last name, but almost exactly a year later, she took down the eight-by-ten wedding picture. She took down his moth-eaten Merino wool sweaters, hanging neatly in a row of beiges and greens on his side of their small closet. She packed up the shoes he didn't take with him. She packed up his paperwork, the jars of sandwich-cut pickles she used to keep for him, the pizza cutter, his set of German beer steins, his college t-shirts. She packed it all up and I do not know what became of it because I never wanted to ask. One day, will another granddaughter receive another old box of remnants—of junk—from a life that didn't work out? All the ways we bequeath our failures.

My father walked away from an already small family and left it even smaller. If my mother ever heard from him again, she never volunteered it. When I was younger, a teenager, I'd still smell him on strangers in the grocery store, on teachers and other dads who must have used the same deodorant or lotion, something clean and masculine, but also a little bit sweaty, the difference between sniffing a brand-new tube of deodorant and smelling it on a body after a day's use. Now, at thirty-five, twenty something years since I last smelled my father, I don't even know if I'd remember the scent of him. I've forgotten even that.

On my mother's mantle now, there's a picture of her as a child, with my grandparents. My long-deceased grandfather looks pissed off, which is exactly how I remember him. My grandmother isn't looking at the camera. I always assumed that people in the old days were too poor to take lots of pictures and sink money into film and developing, so they had one take and one take only. But now I've read the same letters that my grandmother read. Now I wonder if she was just looking away the whole time. I wonder if that's how she survived.

As children, my mother and I both had the same chin-length blond hair. The same long nose. The same dimples. It almost hurts how much she looked like me. I want to be as different from her as possible and she wants to be as close to me as possible.

"I love that picture," she says, standing in the doorway.

I pick it up and hold it closer. I now look so much more like my mother than I look like my younger self.

"Ready?" she asks, like she was the one who was waiting.

"Yeah."

In the car, she talks the whole time.

"I'm not sure if they got the music right," she says. "I mean, we sent them her list, but they never said that they got it."

She pauses.

"Yeah," she says, like I had asked. "Your grandma planned it all out."

I turn left.

"She planned it shortly after your grandfather died. She was so annoyed by the service the church put together for him."

I stop at a red light and I watch the clock. It takes forever. Four minutes. I shake my knees and keep my elbows locked on the steering wheel.

"He died so suddenly, you know."

I don't even nod. He's a blip on my radar.

"Well. So she planned everything out for herself in advance. She had a little list."

I turn right.

"The readings, the flowers. She wanted only sunflowers."

"Sunflowers?" It's the first thing I've said this whole drive.

"Yes. Isn't that strange?" she says, but it's her voice that's strange. I can't read her. "I remember we used to grow them every year when I was a little girl, against the back fence. But one year we stopped, and I swear I have never seen a sunflower in that woman's hands since."

I turn right again.

"I think it's the dementia. She'd forgotten that her favorite flower was always a tulip. That's what she had in her bridal bouquet. That's what your grandfather used to get her for their anniversary every year." She's nervous. She's something.

"Forgotten?"

"You know how these things are."

"No," I say. "No, I don't."

My mother, it seems, has maybe never read the letters in the shoebox. I feel, for the first time, what I consider might be actual, real grief at the thought that this woman, my grandmother, wanted to honor this massive piece of her heart, this secret life.

"Well, I got one arrangement with sunflowers. But everything else is mixed. I only really remember her liking other flowers, so I got some with those, too." She pauses and leans her head on the window. I wonder if she's leaving an oily headprint on the glass, the kind of smudge I'll never get around to wiping clean. "I need to honor the memories of the rest of us, too."

I almost pull over but remind myself not to overreact.

"So," I say, forced casual. "You didn't follow her instructions?"

"Well, she had dementia! You do the best you can, all things considered."

I take a deep breath. It sounds like frustration. It sounds like a sigh.

"Listen, do not judge anything here. You don't even know the half of it," she says, and her voice is thick with warning and something like panic.

I remind myself that my mother does not know that I have the shoebox. My mother does not know that I know about the letters. That I know about Harold C. Carr.

As much as I want to stick it to her right then, I hold back. I turn left into the church, my grandmother's church, and for the first time I wonder if Harold C. Carr is still alive. Does he know she died? Would he have come? I glance to my mother as I park the car. She looks uneasy: eyes closed, jaw tight. Maybe she has read the letters after all. Maybe she knows everything. Maybe she knows exactly what she's doing.

NINE

THE SERVICE IS SHORT. I spend the time staring at the lone sunflower. At least it's in front, in the arrangement that sits on a fake Grecian pillar. The column is small and probably made of painted styrofoam. I imagine the old church ladies picking it up with one arm.

I close my eyes during the eulogy and don't really recognize my mother. She uses kind words. She sounds peaceful and nostalgic. She speaks of my grandmother's marriage to my grandfather, a man I don't really remember. She speaks of a strong love. When she says, "They're together again now, after so many years apart," I open my eyes. I feel oppressed by my grandmother's marriage on her behalf, two generations later.

I think of Vinnie. I think of Torrey. I try to imagine my mother as a twelve-year-old girl, being raised in two homes, her parents arguing over summer camps. This was not the life she had, and this is possibly why she guards this secret. She wants the picture of happiness for her family. Or maybe she just wants the picture of happiness for herself.

She's still talking but I stop listening. I know I'm obvious when I swivel my entire body around and scan the crowd behind me. I look around like I would recognize Harold C. Carr from the pain and injustice on his face. But most everyone looks bored. Some old ladies have hankies to their eyes. More people are looking at me than at my mother.

"And, this is why, to me, today is not so much a day of mourning as it is a celebration," my mother says, such a cliché. "A celebration of a wonderful, happy life."

This time I laugh out loud.

After the service, as my mother gets into the car, I abruptly turn around. I walk straight back into the church, past the priest, past the milling guests. I go right up to that fake pillar and pluck the single sunflower out of the hideous vase. A woman approaches me, perhaps to protest, but I have never moved with such purpose in my life and I like to think I am intimidating.

I return to the car. I get in and slam the sunflower on the dashboard.

"Fuck the tulips," I say.

As I drive away, the full-color reflection of the sunflower obscures my safe view of the road. My mother looks out the side window.

"Fuck the tulips," I say again.

I hear a sniff. I do not grant her the courtesy of looking in her direction.

At the burial site, I lean against the car the whole time. I do not follow the crowd across the grass to the portable shade tent. I do not stand next to my mother above my grandmother's grave. I wish I still smoked. Now would be a perfect time to smoke. Instead, I clutch a cut sunflower, wearing an old dress, and I must look so angry, so detached. I feel outside of myself. This was never a moment I envisioned as a child. Nobody plans out the dress they wear or the flowers they'll hold at their grandmother's funeral. Nobody plans how mournful they'll appear to outsiders: Will I be riddled with grief? Will I look over it? This is not an occasion I practiced or held any expectations for. I wonder if instead of thinking I look angry and detached, the other people here just think I'm very, very sad.

The car is dusty because it hasn't rained since May—nearly six months—and I realize I'm probably dirtying up my dress. These relentless summers: we cannot light campfires and we cannot water our lawns and we cannot lean angrily against our cars. I focus on the act of keeping still, of not rubbing more car dirt on me. It's easier than thinking.

As the burial ends, I plan to take the sunflower over to the grave. Other people toss flowers down into the grave. It seems like the right thing to do. But my drive for the dramatic gesture has waned. I just want to get the fuck home. I just want to get away from my mother. I just want to take off this dress.

I put the sunflower back on the dashboard. I don't slam it this time. I don't say "Fuck the tulips." I don't speak to my mother for the rest of the drive, and with each turn, with each stoplight, I feel more shitty about that.

The drive home from my mother's house, my childhood home, though just fifteen minutes, is less familiar to me than the drive from my mother's house to church. Still I feel like I could make my way anywhere from that house with my eyes closed, so I do close them, just for a few seconds, and lock my elbows at the steering wheel. I could feel my way home if I were brave enough. I open my eyes. The streets are grids of concrete and dying lawns. Old houses in patchwork: one restored to glory and the next rotting to the ground, and as I get closer to my house, there's more rot, more dead lawns. I drive past my grandmother's old house, stranded between my place and my mother's. It looks tiny but pristine, like always. At home, I forget about the sunflower and leave it on the dashboard.

The next morning, when I head to the car to go to work, another temp job I've barely started, the sunflower is pungent and lilted. Dead. I don't get in the car. I just go back in the house.

TEN

I DON'T SHOW UP for work. It's Thursday. I call the temp agency. My next move depends on which agent takes my call.

Once I was naïve enough to think that I'd be assigned an agent all of my own to help me navigate the complicated and demeaning temporary employment landscape, like a grown-up high school guidance counselor. In truth they don't write any prose in my file, any sparkling insights on their dealings with me, suggestions for my future, their hopes and dreams. And in truth, neither did any high school guidance counselor. Just lists. Jobs performed. Qualifications. Terminations. Reference phone numbers. Payments. I get whoever answers.

I hate to break it down in such a gender-biased way, but:

If a man answers:	If a woman answers:
"So, I'm really scared to say anything, and, like, I don't want to make any formal claims…" I trail off. "Yes?"	"So, I'm afraid to say anything, but…" "Go ahead," she says. I can tell she's tired of everyone who calls.

"Well, I just am not comfortable working for Clayton Sanders."

"Oh, I'm sorry, Sheila. Do you mean you're trying to say you were —"

"I just feel like it's a toxic working environment. I don't want to go back."

"But you don't want to make any formal statements or press charges?"

I summon my sweetest, most clueless voice: "No, I just wish I had never worked there. I don't want to cause any problems. I just…" I pause. I sniffle a little. It's a good thing he cannot see the look of total apathy on my face. "Please may I have another placement? I'll wait if I have to."

"I, um." I pause for dramatic effect. "Have you ever heard of endometriosis?"

"Oh, honey."

They hang up with a vague promise of work next week. I don't care. I cherish the long weekend, and surely my rent is cheap enough to survive a little longer on unemployment.

Vinnie's out in the courtyard already. When I get a look at his face, I feel actual fear. Because he looks terrified.

"Shit, Vinnie. You okay?"

He looks up, startled. "What?" he says.

"I said, 'Shit, Vinnie, you okay?'"

"Oh, yeah, no."

"I can tell." I sit down. A part of me starts to feel less bad for him. Then I remember I didn't exactly feel bad for him in the first place. That same part of me is going to stop asking him if he's okay. That same part of me stops caring if he answers, and that's what makes me feel like shit.

"Sheila?" he says.

I don't answer. I watch him twirling the plastic ashtray. It makes little ellipses just above the table, little orbits.

"My ex, Torrey's mom, she was in some sort of freak skydiving accident. She's in a coma."

Oh God, I think. And that's what I should have said out loud. Instead, I say, "Who even skydives?"

Vinnie, God bless him, takes my question seriously.

"Well, she was on some kind of date, I guess."

"Oh, right. I bet they both had it checked in their OK Cupid profile."

"What? Had what checked?"

I pick a tiny scab off the boniest part of my shoulder, right on the point. There's a white dot left behind, camouflaged on my freckled shoulder. "You know, skydiving."

"Right. Well, I guess something happened with the plane? They jumped when they thought they were at elevation, but something was broken? And the plane wasn't high enough? They didn't have enough time in the air."

"Wow."

"Yeah."

"So then what happened?" I ask. I quickly cover my mouth with my hand, uncovering some fresh decency.

"Well, God, I didn't ask all the details. They're not going to tell me shit."

"Oh, yeah, good point. Can't you ask Torrey?"

Vinnie, to his credit, stares me down. He could have killed me with that look. "I'm not going to ask my twelve-year-old daughter to find out the exact details of her mother's—"

"—Yeah, I know. I didn't think it through. I'm just a sucker for the gore."

"Sheila."

"Yeah?"

"This isn't gore. This is a woman. This is my ex-wife. Once I thought she was the finest person in the whole world, so even at this point she's still pretty far up there on the list."

"That's admirable. I thought people hated their exes. Like, by default."

"Well, believe what you want to believe. I loved her so much once upon a time. And she's a good mother to Torrey. That's really all I want from her."

"Is she gonna make it?" I say, feeling like an asshole.

"It doesn't look good."

This is not how I expected this conversation to go. I expected to feel a little bit of glee in knowing that his tedious custody battles and long-distance Skype fatherhood would come to a close. Vinnie is a good man.

"You're a good man."

"Shit, Sheila. Don't make me cry."

"Sorry." I am sorry. I really do not want to see Vinnie cry.

Vinnie has *The Today Show* on in his house. I can hear every fucking word Al Roker says about coats and fall fashion, which he is not really qualified to be explaining, and we, across the country, many microclimates away, stuck in our endless summer, are not really qualified to be listening to. I recognize Al Roker's voice without seeing the screen and I hate myself for it.

"Will you have to go out there?"

"That's not a good idea."

"Why? Doesn't Torrey need you? She needs someone. She can't, like, cook dinners or drive herself places!"

"Hey," he says. "Calm down."

"Okay."

"Well," Vinnie says. I feel like I'm about to learn so much about him. *Why are your fingers so stained, Vinnie, and what is that smell in your house, Vinnie.* "Sarah's parents are there. They take care of Torrey while she works anyway."

"That's nice. Don't you think she needs her dad?"

"Fuck."

And there it is: Vinnie is actually crying. It's horrible. I don't want to watch. He doesn't even look as sloppy today as he usually does, he almost looks beautiful in the strong morning light, but there's something so terrifying about him crying. I want so badly to go inside.

"I know she needs her dad," he says. "I'm just not welcome there. It'll cause more problems than it's worth. She'll come here soon enough once…you know."

"Once?"

Vinnie gets up and goes into his house. His movements are quiet and un-Vinnie-like. The door doesn't even audibly click when it closes.

Oh. Once she dies.

My feelings right now are strong, big. Mostly I'm just very glad I am not Vinnie. I am sad for him and I am afraid of his grief.

I don't go inside. I sit out there in the warm October sun until the tops of my feet get sunburnt. I hear the *Today Show* credits music. The TV turns off. There's the sound of the remote clattering on Vinnie's coffee table. Does he even have a coffee table? I hear nothing else.

If I were Vinnie, I might be in a fetal position on the couch or maybe even the floor. I am not Vinnie, but I sit there, in the sun, in my unemployed leisure, and silently grant Vinnie permission to curl up and cry.

ELEVEN

HER HANDWRITING WAS ALWAYS tall and tidy. As a small child, I could easily read her greetings on birthday cards when other senders did not pay as much heed to a new reader's sensibilities.

Happy birthday, my dear Sheila, she'd write. *I'm sending a dollar with your mother. Buy something sweet, like you.* Then she'd sign it, still tall and still tidy but also looping. A sort of easy-reader version of a signature. *Love, Grandma Rosamond.*

But I don't want to think about that. I don't want to think about the other things she had written in her long life.

It's easier to think about Harold C. Carr.

It's 4 a.m. but I'm out of bed. It's hot in the room. I don't want to read the letter that unsettles me, the one I've read forty times already in the last twenty days. The one with his answers. Answers to questions that my grandmother had to ask. The one that makes me imagine a matching stack of letters somewhere else, inked out in my grandmother's hand, with my grandmother's questions.

I go back to near the beginning instead.

> *Dear Mrs. Baker,*
> *Things are getting desperate. I am also most regretful that I left the aforementioned mangled doll in my garden. I should*

*have removed it. However, I fantasized that you would come
to visit me, or peek over the fence, and we would talk about
it. Perhaps we'd laugh about it! I would show you the exact
crime scene. I wanted to keep the scene intact, just in case. But
I learned my lesson, and now there is barely a shred of evidence.
The next time this sort of thing happens, I will be sure to keep
my meddling dog away from the crime scene. Terriers have no
respect for these kinds of things.*

*I'm afraid this will be my last written correspondence before
I'll have to knock on your door. You have left me with no other
options. I will buy you and your daughter another doll, so help
me God.*

*Since today is Friday, and I will see to it that this letter is
personally delivered in your mailbox by lunchtime, I will give
you until Tuesday to respond, either by dropping a letter in my
mailbox or poking it through a hole in the fence. Perhaps you'd
even prefer to use the United States Postal Service? I believe
Tuesday will be plenty of time for either option. And on Tuesday, after the post has been delivered to our neighborhood, I'll
pour myself a cup of strong coffee, sit in my kitchen and drink it,
perhaps with a biscuit or a piece of banana bread from Zucker-
mann's market on 33rd, and then I will walk around the block
to your front door.*

*I just need to know where to buy a replacement doll. And I
just need to apologize in person. It is quite a dreadful thing, the
guilt of a decapitated doll on one's conscience.*

Sincerely,

Harold C. Carr

*Postscript: After three straight days of letters to you, I dare-
say I am not looking forward to this four-day silence. I'm not
entirely sure I will obey. Perhaps you ought to expect reminders.*

This is the letter that makes me root for Harold. I imagine my grandmother as a young woman, and the smile on her face as she'd read this. I forget to notice if it makes me smile, too.

I have a headache. It's been two days straight. The headache is right behind my eyes and at the base of my skull. My sinuses hurt. I'm relieved that it's all symmetrical and even because tumors wouldn't be. I'm relieved because when there's no pain I can pinpoint, I don't understand why I'm in pain anyway. I'm relieved because a headache means something real. I feel wetness on my face. A nosebleed. I feel neutral about this. Neutral to good. I think of that therapist, telling me my symptoms are mild, and I wonder if maybe the nosebleeds and the headache make up for that. I think: I would absolutely trade the way I feel all the time for nosebleeds all the time. It's been weeks since my last nosebleed, since before the funeral. Instead of pinching my nose or finding a tissue, I bring my right hand to my nose and form a cup. The blood moves slowly, though it feels like it's thinner than normal blood, mucous-laden watery blood.

Five minutes pass and the nosebleed seems to stop on its own. My hand isn't very full, but I pour it into a chipped porcelain teacup that's been sitting on my nightstand for two days now. The blood covers a sticky layer of evaporated old tea and honey.

Across the room, my one-room studio, there's a small stack of papers on the countertop. A picture of my mother and me from over thirty years ago. I'm four, maybe five, and my hair is atrocious, golden but scraggly, thick and all over the place. My mother is very pretty, and I can see it on her face that she knows this. She's poised. She's always poised. That kind of confidence is usually admirable in a woman. But with my mother, I just want to see right through her.

I bring the picture to the bed and pick up the chipped teacup. The ornate handle is shaped like an ear, but otherwise the cup is completely plain. I touch the bottom corner of the photograph to the blood and goopy tea left in the teacup. Nothing happens at first. But then, after a few seconds, the picture starts to change. It darkens in tiny increments from the corner upward and outward. It doesn't get red or bloody yet. It just gets a single layer darker, fuzzier. The photograph thickens, the paper fibers separating slightly at the edge. And then the color starts to change. By the time the fluid reaches the edges of our photographed heads, the teacup is drained and our matching hair is half orange-pink, half yellow.

I put the teacup back on the nightstand. I prop the photograph against it to dry.

TWELVE

"Torrey's coming out," Vinnie says. He's sitting on his hideous faded green lawn furniture, nestled in our shared concrete not-lawn.

"Oh, for a visit?"

He lights a cigarette. "No."

"Oh," I say. "*Oh*."

"Yeah."

"When did it happen?"

"Last night."

I didn't hear any phone calls, I feel like saying, but I don't. I don't say anything.

"The fucking boyfriend sent me a goddamn email," he eventually says.

"Oh, shit."

I wonder, though, if I would've done it differently than the fucking boyfriend. The more I think about it, I realize I'd probably make someone else contact Vinnie. Actually, the more I think about it, the more I kind of like it, this idea that I'd hold a great tragedy in my hands, a little responsible and not responsible at the same time. I'd probably send an email.

We stare at each other for an indeterminate, awkward time. This is a good time for someone to offer condolences, grief, support, anything. But all I can do is coexist with him between our houses.

"The funeral's on Tuesday," he says when his cigarette burns all the way out.

"When do you leave?"

Vinnie laughs and it feels a little cruel. "I'm not going," he says.

This isn't my business. "You should go."

"I've told you, I'm not welcome there."

"I don't care about any of *them*," I say.

"I don't need it. I can deal with this on my own," he says. "I'll say a goddamned prayer or something here."

"Vinnie, I'm talking about Torrey."

Vinnie picks up the cigarette and a tube of ash falls off the end. If he actually tries to smoke that, there's a good chance he'll singe his lips off.

"If I were Torrey," I say, looking away, out through the fichus trees, out to the street, "I'd always hate you for not going."

"I'm sure she has a long list of things to hate me for," he says.

"Don't add to the list just because the list is there," I say, and I feel too wise and it's unsettling. I don't like understanding this; I don't like knowing what it means for a dad to be gone. "That's an asshole move."

Vinnie shrugs. He doesn't understand people, this goes without saying. He certainly doesn't understand twelve-year-old girls.

"Listen, my dad sucked when I was twelve. Well, when I was every age."

I can feel the nicotine addiction deep in my bones, crawling beneath my fingernails. I want to pick up Vinnie's stubbed-out cigarette and rub it over my lips and breathe in deeply until I choke on it, hacking up ash and blood and snot. This is the way my father still ruins me.

"But the times when he pulled through? I remember those just as strongly as the times he sucked."

"Yeah?"

"Yeah. I'll never forgive him for lots of things. But for some of the time, those times he came through for me, I'll never, ever forget those. Fly out there for the funeral and just be whatever Torrey needs."

Vinnie starts peeling the filter off of the finished cigarette. I feel something like hate for him, or maybe it's respect. His fingertips are stained a pale purplish brown. It's not nicotine; it's not from smoking. One day I'll ask him.

"What's your dad's deal?" he asks. "Where is he?"

"My dad is nowhere," I say.

The morning of my confirmation, the bishop removed his tall hat and handed that, then his staff, to Reverend Jenny, then turned to me and asked *Do you reaffirm your renunciation of evil?* And I said *I do*, and then he said *Do you renew your commitment to Jesus Christ?* And I, the bride, said *I do*, and I forgot my next line so the bishop had to feed it to me. I glanced back at the pews, my mother sitting there alone. No dad. I checked the back to see if he was standing awkwardly in the door. *...And with God's grace...?* the bishop prompted. *And with God's grace I will follow him as my Savior and Lord.* And then when I went home, freshly minted as an eleven-year-old mature member of the church, my father still wasn't home, and he never came home again.

I never went back to church. It's not that I blame my father. It's not that I was unable to be faithful without my father backing me up, because he hardly ever backed me up in the first place. It's just that I gave up on so many things that afternoon and church was the easiest. Church was the first to go. Well, the second, I suppose. First was my dad.

THIRTEEN

WHILE VINNIE'S GONE, I collect his mail for him. He's gone for two and a half weeks and doing this job is the most important thing I've done in a while.

His mail fascinates me. His official first name is Vincent. I like that, and I try saying it out loud a few times. He seems to get a lot of checks, payments. There's one returned letter with one of those invalid address stickers over the label, and, peering through the glassine, it looks like it's some sort of invoice.

I wish he'd left a key with me. If I had a key, I'd spend one hundred percent of my time inside Vinnie's place, scrutinizing whether the construction is completely identical to mine and looking in every tiny corner of his house, in every drawer, in every cabinet. I'd leave no stone unturned. I'd sleep there. I'd eat whatever food he left in the fridge. I'd wash my face in his sink. I'd bleed into his toilet. I'd scrub the cracks in his floors. I'd watch broadcast television in his living room. I'd bring my grandmother's letters.

He calls ten days into it and asks me to open one of the envelopes. I'm giddy but it's a total disappointment. Just a man's name, a few vague line items (full: $600, base: $50), and the address to Vinnie's place.

"Do you work out of your house?"

"Not entirely, that'd be impossible!" he says, like it's obvious.

"Do you have an office?"

"Well, I've never really referred to it that way," he says, distracted. Now is not the time to play the guessing game about his career. "Hey, I'm coming back in a few days. Torrey too."

"Torrey?"

"Yeah," he says. In his voice I can almost hear the way he's sitting, slouched, fingering an ashtray. I wonder if he also has a green plastic lawn chair out there.

"She's moving here? Like, permanently?"

"Yes."

"Are you going to stay in your place?" I ask.

Vinnie laughs. "Yeah. I'm staying in my place."

"How is that even possible?"

"It's a lot bigger than yours."

Now is not the time to ask him how much he pays in rent.

I hear a voice near to him, Torrey, and she says "Dad," and then it's illegible, and it sounds like Vinnie muffles the mouthpiece with his hand and says, "Of course, Tor, hang on."

"Sheila, yeah, well, we'll be back on Saturday."

"Okay," I say.

It doesn't really sink in.

I watch *Antiques Roadshow* with the sound off. The closed captions are malfunctioning, stuck on the local station announcements and a bunch of dashes. The Keno twins, their sandy blond hair rustling with every gesture and nod, are appraising some sort of wrought-iron lamp, or maybe it's a plant stand. It's so quiet. I miss Vinnie's noise, his smoke, his stupid phone games. Maybe I just miss something to be annoyed at.

Just as I start to feel incredibly lonely, the twins share a laugh and a knowing look. Someone the next building over starts cooking onions. The oil was clearly very hot before they slid the onions off the cutting board. It's loud and sputtery, and instantly fills the block with that pungent sweet smell, and it makes me so hungry. I want to be fed. My mother always hated cooking onions, so the smell is not nostalgic for me. It's not a smell of home. It's a smell of somewhere else, something else, someone else. It's a smell of longing. It's a smell of lacking.

I pour some cereal.

It's value reveal time, and I watch the guest closely, a plainly dressed woman in her seventies. Her hands tremble. This is my favorite part, when they try to act like they don't care about the money. Note the nonchalance before the number is given, and then, with few exceptions, they go to great lengths to maintain their nonchalance. Sometimes they get stupidly excited and do something embarrassing for their family watching at home, but for the most part they try to be cool. But the thing is, there's always a slip. That moment when the number is revealed, there's either a wash of disappointment or a wash of greed, and it absolutely delights me.

My phone rings but I don't look away from the screen as they reveal the amount. It's greed. It's quiet and it's small but it's greed. I wonder what she has to feel greedy for, at that age. Or maybe she went her whole life banking on this one piece of folk art furniture to fund her retirement or endear her heirs.

The phone rings again.

"Hi," I say, hoping to skip the—

"Shelia? It's Mom."

"Yes."

"What are you doing tomorrow?" she asks.

"Hm," I say, as if I have to think about it. "Let's see."

Antiques Roadshow is over now. It's a split screen with the credits rolling and Mark Wahlberg, muted, saying probably the same thing he says every day.

"Why?" I ask. "Do you need help with something?" The last thing I want to do is tell her I'm not going to work.

"Well, do you think you could take a long lunch or something? We haven't done that in a while."

I laugh. Her voice is fake and nervous.

"Sure, Mom."

"Okay, great. Shall I pick you up at work? Where's your assignment these days?"

"It's okay, I'll come pick you up. I can take two hours if I want." The lies come so easily with this woman, it's almost troubling.

With the next three letters in the series, I can almost get inside Rosamond Baker's mind during the weekend before her first meeting with Harold C. Carr. Because there are three letters. Three—one for every day my grandmother still did not respond to him. Which means my grandmother waited until the exact last moment to respond to Harold C. Carr. I can pretend, I can pretend to be her. I'd sit in a corner, somewhere in the house that allows me a tiny view of my back fence. Maybe I could even see a sliver of Harold's roof. I'd check for movement in between the fence slats. I'd hold his letters. I'd not show them to my husband.

> *Dear Mrs. Baker,*
> *Just saying hello. I hope you have a lovely Saturday. I hope you spend it busily writing out the exact manufacturer of your daughter's doll.*
> *Sincerely,*
> *Harold C. Carr*

Dear Mrs. Baker,

It's a lovely Sunday morning here. How's the weather where you are? I wonder if you get different low pressure systems around the block. I look forward to hearing from you soon. Enjoy this weather, unless it's raining there.

Sincerely,

Harold C. Carr

Dear Mrs. Baker,

Your daughter's crying woke me up in the night. I am not saying that to incite pity or shame or to have you worry about waking the neighbors. I just wish to let you know I am concerned about your daughter, and about your likely sleeplessness. Is she ill? Does she need a doctor? I happen to know of a moderately good and moderately handsome one who lives very near to you.

Hopefully it was just a bad dream. I remember bad dreams as a child. I remember being only willing to scream. I hope she is not terribly sad about her doll. I imagine it would have helped provide solace to a distraught dreamer. Except in its current headless condition, of course. At present, it would have made for a much darker night for you all.

That said, I hope you are well enough rested. And if you are able to, please do take care of writing back to me, or come knock on my door. Tomorrow's the day! I daresay I am looking forward to meeting you.

Sincerely,

Harold C. Carr

FOURTEEN

"So," my mother says.

She looks at her plate. She looks at the ceiling. With her fingertip, she draws vertical lines in the condensation on the outside of her water glass.

"You know how you asked me the day your grandma passed away…"

"Asked you what?" I say. I know without doubt what she's getting at.

"You asked about a shoebox?" She draws horizontal lines now, a little condensation grid.

"Oh."

"I can't seem to find it," she says.

"That shoebox?"

"Yeah. What did Grandma tell you about it?"

"Nothing," I say.

"How did you know about it, then?"

I pause. This is unfair of me. I'm fully aware of it as it happens. I can guess what my mother is afraid of, of people finding out that her own mother was an almost-whore. That her own family was a sham. But if it were me, I wouldn't give a shit. Let people find out. Let people marvel in the mystery and the drama. It's better than a sham, a staged picture on the mantelpiece.

Or maybe she just doesn't know how to tell me. How to bring it up in the first place. Maybe she doesn't want to think about it at all.

Right now, my mother is so small. She's broken down into little pieces.

Things I don't know: whether it'd comfort her to discuss this with me, to have to reveal a secret I don't even know if she has known her whole life; if she knew about Harold all along, or if she learned about him when she acquired the shoebox from the assisted-living facility mere weeks ago; if, at age four, she knew her neighbor, this man; whether she has read the letters; has she never, ever read the letters; if I'm the only one—just me, my grandmother, and Harold C. Carr—in on this too-late secret.

In a fit of great humanity and terrible dishonesty, I say, "Grandma told me she wanted me to have them, that she'd tell me about them the next day, but that she wanted to be buried with them. Then she died before she got the chance to tell me about them."

My mother gasps, an exaggerated noise.

"So when I went to your house, I got the box to take care of that for her."

"Sheila! You should have said something."

"Well, you didn't ask."

She looks away.

"So I put the box in her coffin."

"WHAT?" she shouts.

"I SAID I PUT IT IN HER COFFIN." Everyone in the restaurant turns to look at me. God, I wish I had a cigarette. I wish I was smoking inside this fancy restaurant and the people would have that to judge too.

"Goddamn it, Sheila, be quiet."

"Well, I did."

"Okay," she says, and it's hard to tell, but there's some relief there.

"Is that bad?" I ask. I bite at the splitting skin around my thumbnail. I feel a little bit like an asshole and a little bit like a child. I could laugh.

She sighs. Her shoulders heave. "No, honey. It's not bad."

I look away.

"It's for the best," she says. "It's something that needed burying."

I pretend to not have heard her.

My mother pays the check. The stuff we don't say to each other hangs between us like bricks, a hundred bricks, hitting the ground with a smack as each minute passes and she doesn't ask. I don't offer. She's the bricks and I'm the one stacking them into a wall.

She never asks me if I opened it. She never asks if I've read the letters.

FIFTEEN

I'M SITTING ON THE front step rereading a small selection of the letters when Vinnie and Torrey arrive in an airport taxi. It's getting late. The sky is a mixture of orange and grey.

My instinct is to hide the letters, but it's too late. I try to act natural. I just don't want anyone talking to me.

"Hi, Vinnie," I say.

Torrey looks nothing like I remember her from a year ago. It's that age where every day she's a new person. I remember being twelve, vividly, painfully.

"Hi," he says. "You remember my neighbor Sheila, right, Tor?"

"Yeah," she says.

I have it in my power to disappear and make this less awkward. I feel like a good person for this. "Well, I need to get inside," I say. I try some sort of concluding stretch move with my arms as I stand up, which I probably learned from television. "Nice seeing you again, Torrey."

Nonetheless I listen to them through the open window. I feel restless, so I clean the edge of where the floor meets the skirting board with an old toothbrush. Being on my hands and knees with a bucket of soapy water reminds me of my grandmother on my father's side. I never saw Grandma Rosamond, my mother's mother, cleaning. Her house was always immaculate anyway. My father's mother, though, was always cleaning and never getting ahead of it. I'd help, when my family would take trips up the coast to visit them, when I was younger, when my dad was still a part of our family, when a dad was a thing I had. My mother would get angry about bleach spots on my clothes. I learned to love the smell of bleach. I'd take deep breaths until I felt a chill inside my ribcage. Maybe that was when I learned how best to spite my mother.

"Here's your room, Torrey," I hear Vinnie say. "Sorry it's nothing much."

"It's fine, Dad," she says, though her voice is quiet and hard to decipher. "I like it."

I don't even have a bedroom. Vinnie must have two!

"We can go get stuff for you if you want. I don't know what you like. Posters?"

I laugh, and then I quickly cover my mouth with my hand. I taste Dr. Bronner's peppermint soap.

"No, Dad, no posters. This is fine."

"I want you to make yourself at home," he says.

"I will. I don't need posters to be at home."

By the time it's dark and silent outside, I have scrubbed every corner of my little shack. My fingertips are red and starting to blister. My cuticles will smell like peppermint soap for three days.

The clocks change tonight. I crave the longer night, the feeling of the day closing sooner, the way I believe those things happen without anything really changing. Time doesn't change, the night doesn't really change. Just the clocks, but I devour this shift anyway.

There's movement outside. It's quiet movement, not the oafy elephantine movement of Vinnie. I'm feeling brave. I'm feeling like a woman with very clean floors. I feel like if there is ever a time to hang out with a twelve-year-old girl, it's now.

"Oh, hi," I say as I push through the screen door. "I didn't know you were out here."

"Do you, like, smoke or something?" she asks.

"No. Not anymore. Do you?"

She laughs. "God, are you clueless?"

"What? I'm trying to treat you like a person. It's a natural progression of the conversation."

"No, I don't smoke," she says. "I'm a kid?"

"Very well, then. That's a good choice. It's a filthy habit. You should tell your dad that."

"My dad is sad. He's not going to stop smoking anytime soon."

"Sad?"

"Sad dad," she says in a mocking voice. "I need to write that down."

"Are you some sort of teenaged poet?"

"I'm not quite teenaged."

"So just a poet?"

She lifts a single shoulder in some sort of extra-effortless shrug.

I smile. How precious, I want to think. There's something not precious about her. Something that tells me if she isn't just being a jerk, I'd actually want to read her poetry. It wouldn't suck.

"So, your dad is sad?"

"Duh. My mom died." She picks up a piece of the gravel landscaping and rolls it between her finger and thumb.

"What makes you think he's sad?"

"Dude. It's Sheila, right?"

"Yes."

"Well, Sheila, he's mopey."

"He's always mopey."

"Well, you're probably right. But my mom left him a few years ago. I don't think he was exactly fine with it."

"That's so *Parent Trap* of you. Every kid thinks their parents are better off together."

"I don't think they were better off together, lady."

"Well, in your defense, he did tell me he still loved her in a certain way."

"Really? When was that? You and my dad have deep conversations or something?" She looks rightfully incredulous.

"Just the once. It was actually a really remarkable thing he said. I was surprised."

"What did he say?" she asks.

"He's probably listening."

"Well, tell me anyway," she says. I love the smile on her face as much as I'm a little afraid of it. She seems so much smarter than me.

"He said something about how he once thought she was the finest person in the entire world."

Torrey closes her eyes and presses her mouth shut, her lips two thin lines.

"Then," I continue, "he said that sort of thing doesn't change much. She's still up there on the list. Or whatever."

I'm almost ready to go inside, to give her some space, to escape the heaviness myself, when she finally speaks again.

"What's the deal with you and my dad, anyway?" she asks.

"There's no deal."

"Why do you get along so well? You don't seem like you'd get along well with anyone."

"I actually don't know. That's a good question," I say.

Torrey smiles and leans forward. "He's really great, though. He's weirdly great."

"Weirdly great," I repeat just to hear how it sounds.

"But you don't know any more about how he's doing?"

"No," I say. "We don't talk much. We just…exist well. In vicinity."

I sit there for twenty minutes, a grieving twelve-year-old by my side in what is the most comfortable silence of my entire life. I don't ever remember being so happy to have someone nearby, and that makes me incredibly sad.

SIXTEEN

I'M SMALL. MY MOTHER'S age when Harold knew my grandmother. One Saturday, early spring, we sat in our backyard, overwhelmed with weeds because California had already endured a dozen mini springs since fall.

"You never play with her," my father said. He wore shorts and loafers, which is how I knew it was a Saturday.

I'd never specifically noticed. My childlike self-centeredness just assumed all grown-ups were tedious bores who got off on ignoring kids. My mother, though, looked ready to snap.

"You don't know anything about me," she said.

Suddenly they were both attentive to me, handing me toys in the unlearned way of people who never played. Both of them, arms outstretched with an offering: a doll or a block, me grabbing at neither. Until my father put his down, stood up, and walked inside.

My mother shook the doll once toward me, and I took it.

"Let's feed your doll some of these nice weeds," she said, a cheeriness I never bought. She grasped a handful of broadleaf clover in her palm, violently pulled at them, and then sprinkled them with surprising tenderness at my doll's feet.

SEVENTEEN

THE NEXT MORNING IS the first morning with the hours askew, and it feels too late, like the middle of the day, like I've missed something already. I sit in the courtyard on one of Vinnie's faded green plastic lawn chairs. Torrey is in the other, stretched out with her head swung all the way back to the wall, eyes closed. She looks insanely long and lanky, more like a boy than an almost-woman. I wonder if it's sick of me to long for the waistline of a twelve-year-old girl. I wonder if it's sick of me to wonder if Torrey appreciates her own waistline. I wonder if she's even sexual yet, because I was starting to understand it at that age. I see a pimple forming in the crease around her nose and I feel better and snap out of it. The table is the same green plastic as the chairs, cracked at the corner. One leg is loose, dangling like an extra limb. Vinnie's ashtray rests on the intact side of the table, full and pungent.

"Hey," I say.

Torrey opens her eyes and lifts her head slightly, then closes her eyes and puts her head back. That's going to be her only salutation.

"You know, I never really liked my mom," I say, and I put my feet on the table.

Torrey sits up. "God. That's an awful thing to say to me."

"What? Doesn't that make you feel better?"

The table is not going to be sturdy enough to hold my feet. I put them down. I'm angry that in a conversation with a twelve-year-old girl, I'm somehow the awkward one.

"No!" she says. "That's like…that's like telling someone whose mom just died that they're *lucky*."

"Well," I say. "That's pretty much exactly what I was saying."

Torrey lets out some sort of preteen sound.

"My dad warned me about you."

I laugh. "Vinnie?" I laugh again. "*Vinnie*. Warned you? About *me*?"

"God, why are you even out here? Did you come out here to try to talk and, like, bond with me and shit?"

I don't answer. Because, yes. Yes I did.

"Just leave me alone," Torrey finishes.

She puts her feet up and the entire table falls. The plastic ashtray bounces as it casts cinders all over the concrete slabs between our doors. I feel victorious for a second, like I won the awkwardness war. Then I feel shitty. In the face of this feeling, my strongest desire is to go back inside and close the doors and windows. I remember why I do not keep friends, why I can't keep friends: I can't stick around beyond this phase, when it's not as easy as that first meeting, when I doubt everything I say, everything they say, every expression on my face, every expression on their faces, and it's the summer after eighth grade again and just when I think I have a "group," the other moms plan a father-daughter camping trip to the mountains. "You can come anyway, Sheila," they said to me the day before they left, weeks and weeks too late to properly invite someone camping. Just in time for a pity invite. Just in time to let themselves off the hook. "You can share my dad for the weekend," they said, but they didn't look me in the eye, or maybe they did but I wasn't looking them in the eye. I'd never look them in the eye again.

I didn't even want to be Torrey's friend. I just wanted a *moment*. Any initial inspiration to be a good person, to be some sort of support to this strange, sad girl, it's all gone.

"I'm sorry," she says.

"Torrey, don't be sorry," I say. "I'm the asshole."

"I know," she says. "Oh my God!" she adds. "I didn't mean it like that! I don't think you're an asshole."

Suddenly she's not even twelve anymore. She slaps her hand over her mouth and her eyes go wide, like a young child. I remember the last time she was out to visit Vinnie, a year ago. Eleven is so different from twelve. She seemed much smaller then.

"No, it's okay. I am."

She leans back and rearranges herself in her original position, the crown of her head flush to the bumpy stucco. It doesn't look comfortable or comforting but I try it, too. The wall is prickly on my scalp, but it's not worth the effort it'd take to lift my head back up. I feel momentary pride in understanding a preteen girl.

"Tell me about her," Torrey says.

I laugh.

"God, you laugh at everything me or my dad says. Either we're really funny or you have mental problems."

I laugh again. "That time you were funny."

"Great," she says. Sarcasm is an admirable trait in any child. I reward her with a laugh.

"No," I say. "You don't need to hear about my mom. She's just a normal mom. It'd piss you off to hear about our problems. Tell me about *your* mom."

The silence between us is fragile. I hear a toilet flush inside. It makes me think of Vinnie sitting on the toilet for the entirety of this conversation, taking a shit. Vinnie's shits historically reach the courtyard with their stench. Sometimes even if I'm indoors, I have to close the windows against them. I brace myself for this one but it doesn't come.

"I mean, I've never met her. I just used to hear all of Vinnie's Skypes with you and she was there. I guess I've heard her voice a few times. She seemed so much nicer than your dad."

"You need to learn to stop talking."

"Well, it's true. I mean, Vinnie was always a raging prick when he talked to her."

"Like I said."

"I always liked Vinnie when he talked to you," I say.

"It's so weird that you eavesdrop on him," she says, but she's smiling.

I tilt my head toward her.

"You kinda look like your dad when you smile."

It's Torrey's turn to laugh.

"No, I'm serious. A less old, less ugly Vinnie."

"Thanks."

"You're not going to talk about your mom, then?" I ask.

"No."

"Okay. I can tell you a fucked-up story about mine, if you want."

"Go on, then. Nothing can make me feel better or worse," she says, and I marvel at her wisdom. I wish I had half of it. I wish I understood that feeling now, in my thirties, never mind as a kid.

"Let me pick a story."

"Oh, you have more than one?"

"Of course. My mother is crazy."

"Are you crazy?" she asks.

"Yes, but not like her. I actually think it was her own mother's fault. I just found out that my grandmother had this, like, unconsummated affair for basically her entire life."

"I don't even know what you're talking about."

"Never have kids, Torrey, is what I'm saying."

She laughs. "I'm too young to think about that," she says, like it's a practiced line. Like the teachers at whatever ultra-progressive school she went to back east fed the little girls some specific drivel when they were caught playing dolls or house.

I take a deep breath, and I feel like a moron for taking a deep breath to steel myself. It doesn't even work.

What would I say about my mom to a daughter who has just lost her mother? I think about when she sat with me on the stairs after my dad left the first time, temporarily, and she must've been so sad but she didn't take care of her own sadness, she took care of mine, but I hated what had happened so much that I couldn't separate it from her. I couldn't stop blaming her. She made me a warm drink, honey and lemon in hot water, comfort food, and nothing tasted the same. What did blame and hurt taste like?

Or the time he left for good, that morning, she came to my Confirmation and smiled, dressed in linen, transparent red plastic-framed sunglasses in the church courtyard, greeting the other mothers, greeting the bishop, her arm around me. I was annoyed by how proud she acted, how fake it seemed. The next day I was angry that she hadn't told me about my father. Even then, I think I knew I would've instead been angry at her for ruining my Confirmation day. Under the silent gaze of Torrey, of a girl already proving herself to be smart and kind and weird, I couldn't come up with a single memory that showed my mother as batshit crazy. The only things I could come up with showed that it was all my fault.

"Did Vinnie tell you that my grandma recently died?"

"No," she says. "I'm sorry."

"It's okay, you don't have to be sorry," I say. "It's just important if you want to know more about my mom."

"Sheila, I don't know if I want to know more about your mom," Torrey says. She has a bit of dread in her voice.

"It's not that bad. Don't worry. It's mostly just a story about my grandmother. Right before she died, like hours before, she told me she wanted to give me something, this ancient shoebox. But she said it could wait until the next day."

"And then she died."

"Yeah."

"So, did you get the shoebox?"

"Well," I say. "I had to sneak in and steal it from my mom's house."

"That's terrible! You're dysfunctional."

"I know. But in the box were hundreds of letters. Letters from a man who wasn't her husband. Letters of increasing intimacy."

"Ooh."

"I know. I'm glad you see it that way, too. My mother, apparently, doesn't."

"How's that?" she asks.

"She seemed really stressed to have lost track of the box," I say, and I sit up straight and shift the chair a bit so I'm facing her. The plastic legs scrape against the concrete and I worry for a split second that I look too intense. I try to apply some nonchalance to my face. "I think she's paranoid people might find out. She wasn't gonna tell me what was in the box, or who the letters were from."

"Well, I guess that makes sense," Torrey says.

"Anyway, I had to lie to her."

"I bet you're really good at telling really good lies," Torrey says. She still has that childlike ability to say something incredibly innocent and offensive. It's hard to be angry when it's so true.

"Yeah, well, I have my talents."

"What did you tell her?" she asks.

"I told her I found it, but that I put it in the coffin and it got buried with Grandma. But it's really still in my house."

"Oh, shit," she says. "You still have the letters."

"Yeah."

"Yeah."

I feel a fire inside, a spark. I'm almost certain this is a terrible idea.

"Wanna read them?"

EIGHTEEN

"Whoa."

"I know," I say.

"This is the last one?" Torrey says.

"Yeah."

"Well, obviously, I guess. But I wish—I mean, I just want him to change his mind."

I don't say anything. I don't disagree.

That night, I read them all again. Every single letter. Five hundred and eighty-two. Sleep never happens. I always sleep somehow, even if it's a nap at four in the morning. Five hours into reading, I close my eyes, but all I hear is Compline, a holy rite, a remnant, leftovers from who I used to be. In the darkness, I even see the print of the prayer book, a strongly serifed font with tall, round capitals.

"*Guide us waking, O Lord, and guard us sleeping; that awake we may watch with Christ, and asleep we may rest in peace.*"

It was repetitive, but never repetitive enough for me. It was always a little disappointing that the line was only repeated at the very end of the brief service. I wanted it over and over again. Right now I let it repeat a dozen times, maybe more, until I cannot bear to keep my eyes closed any longer. My fingernails dig into the skin on the opposite elbow, my arms cross beneath my breasts, my shoulders hitch up. And then it's the opening supplication, and I'm whispering it, and I don't love church and I don't love God, but I can't stop myself.

"O God, make speed to save us.
O Lord, make haste to help us."

Unguarded, unsaved, unhelped, I do not sleep.

Torrey's not there the next morning. We've had two mornings of sitting together and I was getting used to it. I thought we had a pattern going. A habit. A thing.

Vinnie comes out instead.

"Vinnie," I say with a nod.

I'm trying out green tea. It looked like the best decision on the shelf, the most life-improving. Vinnie lights up to smoke. He looks well rested and I distrust him for it.

"Where's Torrey?" I ask.

"It's 9:30 on a Monday. She's at school."

Oh. "Since when does she go to school?"

"Since she was five?" Vinnie says.

I realize it's a dumb question.

I roll my eyes and fake a serious voice. "I mean, is this her first day at her new school out here?"

"Oh, yeah."

"That's gonna suck," I say.

"I wouldn't be so sure. Torrey's a good kid. Other kids love her," he says. "They always do."

How do you know that, I want to ask. *How do you know anything about a girl's social life, much less a life lived somewhere else.* I wonder this because my dad is nowhere. I wonder if he ever pretends to know me, too. I wonder if he ever pretends I'm a good kid.

"She's not like you, Sheila. She's not like me. She's good with people."

I laugh. "I'm great with people."

It feels like I'm a kid again, waiting for the mail. I sit all the way over to the side of the step, so I can see the rusty-gated entrance to our shared courtyard. I try to remember. Middle school gets out at two thirty? Maybe three. I need something to do.

NINETEEN

THERE ARE ANTS ON the front step, again, still. Sometimes when I watch them, I'm impressed. I can't help humanizing their systems, their shared work, their collaboration, the purity of their social order. Their ability to exist in nearly every place on Earth. Their ability to evolve. Their ability to do all the things I can't. There's no purity in my social order. I can barely exist in one room in one house.

I squat at the bottom of the step with a kettle full of boiling water like my grandmother taught me. I pour the water slowly and watch as their little bodies curl up when they're scalded to death. Or maybe they drown first. I think about whether I would notice the burning water against my flesh as I drowned. Or maybe the feeling of my skin bubbling up and peeling off would mask any sensation of drowning. Maybe it would be an interesting way to go.

"You're good with her," Vinnie says.

I jump a little. I didn't know he was right behind me. Usually Vinnie moves like a goddamn elephant. He is never where I don't know him to be.

"No," I say. "No, I'm not. I'm terrible with her."

Vinnie doesn't answer right away. I turn around and sit on the front step, facing him. The kettle is hot through my jeans when I rest it on my lap. I count in my head. One, two, three, four, five. It starts to feel good. Six, seven, eight, nine. Too hot. I move the kettle. I'm a coward.

Vinnie picks at a callus on his palm. He has a whole row of these calluses, right at the base of his fingers, but this one is half off. He picks some more and pulls it completely off. He twirls the amputated callus between his thumb and fingertip for a few seconds until it's some sort of balled-up, once-human pellet and he flicks it to the ground. I watch it come to rest right next to my river of drowned, scalded ants.

"Yeah, well," he says. A shrug. "No one ever knows what's good for them when it's right in front of them."

He lets that hang in the air. I pick up the kettle and pour more water on more ants and surreptitiously aim for the callus. I watch it float down the tiny rivulet of ant carcasses and finally disappear in the soil next to the step.

"It's good for her to talk to you."

I hear his feet shuffling back to his door, and then it creaks open, then clicks shut. I don't look up. I keep watch on the dead bodies at my feet.

TWENTY

"So where are the rest of them?" Torrey asks.

Her voice startles me awake. This is the shittiest place I could doze off for an afternoon nap, sitting on my doorstep with my cheek against the rough stucco. I assume I look horrific, with the wall's indentations red on my cheek like a vicious pox. Torrey really must be good with people after all, because she doesn't say anything about it.

"The rest?"

"The letters," she says.

"There's over three hundred of them! We read them all." I try to act like I don't know there are exactly three hundred and eighty-two. I try to act like I don't know what she is talking about.

"Surely you've thought of the *others*."

I rub my cheek. I can feel the stucco embossed there.

"Yeah," I say.

"Yeah. The other half."

I'm about to stand up. Or go inside. Or ask Torrey about her first day of school. But then she says: "What was she like?"

"My grandmother? I don't know, really."

"But you must have been close."

"As close as we could, all things considered." I kick at the wall. "*Fuck*," I mutter. "I sound just like my mother."

Vinnie comes out. "Hey, Tor. How was it?" He doesn't wait for her answer before he adds, "And stop teaching my daughter how to curse."

I glare.

"What are you doing?" he asks.

Torrey opens her mouth to talk but I interrupt.

"I'm just teaching your daughter about star-crossed lovers. It's worse than the F word."

He looks like he's thinking of something to say, mouth closed and pursed to one side, but instead he just goes back inside.

"Sheila, we don't even know if they're star-crossed!"

"First of all," I say. "We? And of course they are. Look at his letters. They reek of a reciprocated love."

"Well. I have nothing to do right now. Nobody expects the new girl to do any homework."

"And?" I ask. But I'm smiling.

"Let's go. Whatever we can't find online we can find in the library."

"Torrey, you think I haven't tried looking this shit up?" I'm not sure why I say this. I haven't looked anything up.

"So, you have tried?"

I don't answer right away. "I googled a bit."

"Try harder. Come on. I'm good at this stuff."

"How can a twelve-year-old be gifted at stalking?"

"My mom taught me how. We ran our own little background checks on any guy she met."

"That…" I pause. Is it okay to badmouth her recently deceased mother yet? "That's kind of dysfunctional."

"Whatever. First we find out when the house was sold."

"What house?"

"Oh my God. Keep up, Sheila. Harold's house."

———

I feel a bit of relief when a prior sale date on Harold's old house matches up with Harold's final farewell letter. Sometimes I wondered if it was all fiction. It might have been my grandmother's opus, a work of art, a game of hide and seek for future generations. Mixed somewhere in the relief is disappointment, because that kind of work, that kind of craft, would have been astonishing. But despite this almost-relief, I start to panic. It's a dull ache, starting in the top of my gut, kind of esophageal. Then it's in my chest, thick and heavy. The air is poisoned; I can smell and taste it. The ache is a trap, a lock, a temperature vice in the back of my throat. My eyes feel heavy with unfocus but also like they're going to float out of my head—my entire head could float away, eyeballs first, then scalp, then everything else.

"Torrey, go home," I say. I brace both hands against the desk.

"What?"

"Go home. I need you to go home."

She looks crushed. She leaves, quietly. I lie down on the floor

It takes twenty minutes for me to get up off the floor. I only bother so I can get to the toilet and throw up, weak and slow. Vomit gets caught in the back of my nose. The last time I threw up was the night my grandmother died, before I knew she died, so it's not like it was connected. Finished, I lean back against the cold iron edge of the bath. My chest still hurts. My hands still shake.

I crawl to my bed to lie down again and nothing changes. I take a letter out of the shoebox. It's a hard one to read.

> *Dear Rosamond,*
>
> *My. It was such a pleasure to meet you. I will assuredly still purchase a new doll for your daughter, despite your insistence that I not. But not yet. First, I wanted to write to you. Would you think of me as silly if I were to walk to your home to deliver this letter before I left for the toy shop this afternoon?*

You are incredibly kind and forgiving. Not just in the things you said to me, but I can see it in your eyes. Even your hands look gentle. Oh, it was such a pleasure to meet you. Perhaps you might come to the back fence one afternoon to drink a cup of tea and share a conversation?

When you came to my door to deliver your message, well, I just can't explain it. Thank you so much, for not only allowing me to redeem myself and repent for the sins of my terrier, but also for affording me the chance to converse, however briefly, with such a lovely and bright young woman. I have felt quite lonely in this part of town. Until I met you, I felt I was the only one like me.

Well. That is all. I look forward to speaking with you again. Or perhaps you could write back. It would be quite amusing to have a pen pal with a shared back fence.

Sincerely,

Harold C. Carr

It's three in the morning when the feeling in my chest and throat lets up and I decide to get in the car. I drive to my grandmother's old house. It only takes fifteen minutes in the dead of night. There's a new streetlight just to the right of her house. The light pools onto the front yard and the small stretch of grass that leads to the back. I wonder who lives here now. They have two cars in the long driveway, a Subaru and a minivan with a large dent in the side. The idea that there are new children in the house makes me hurt. I imagine a daughter, four years old, playing with a doll in the backyard. I get out of the car and sit on the sidewalk, directly beneath the streetlight.

It's Jesse Ramirez's letter that I've brought with me. Not Harold's. I don't remember reaching in my nightstand drawer to get it out of the gallon-sized Ziploc. I don't remember putting it in my back pocket. It's bent now from sitting in the car.

"Fuck," I say, at full volume.

It's not just that I'm afraid of myself for bringing this letter without noticing. It's not the idea that I perform physical tasks without remembering. It's not that it's bent after so long of keeping it nearly immaculate in the baggie in my drawer, save for the drop of my own blood—my DNA, blood cells, skin cells, the insides of me dead on my breath—soaked into the fibers of the paper, the etchings of the ink. It's all of these things. It's the fact that I am here at all. It's the fact that I didn't bring Harold's letters. I wonder if I'd feel something, holding the letters so close to their birthplace, their origin. The moment Harold and Rosamond began.

I try to think like a young mother. I try to think like the two of them. How would I act if I met Harold C. Carr? And how would I act if it were me asleep with my happy family in my new house, with my minivan and Subaru in the driveway, when I woke up to a woman sitting on the sidewalk cursing?

If I never have children, I'll never need to know.

I read Jesse's letter again. His voice was always kind, quieter than the usual cheerful delivery person. I imagine the way he might talk to a lover, even kinder, even quieter. I read the line on the second page that I never want to read again. I read it twice. It's the part that tells me exactly where I would stand if he ever noticed me again. If he ever noticed me in the first place.

"*But how.*" I read it out loud, the streetlight's beam a yellow-green cone around me, the hiss of insects, the quiet staccato of a single cricket, a nearly imperceptible buzz from the power lines. "*Can I even begin to imagine a life with someone else when they'll just occupy spaces still taken by you?*"

I read it again, slow and loud.

"But how," I tell the night, the sick way my skin looks in the streetlight.

"Can I even begin," I say.

"To imagine a life," and I stand up.

"With someone else."

I walk up the steps. Now's a good time to go back to whispering. I don't.

"When," I say, as my bare feet touch the grass in the side yard. It's wet with dew.

"They'll just occupy spaces." I walk slowly, but I speak even slower.

"Still," and I'm in the backyard. Away from the streetlight's preternatural glow, the night is lovely. The moon is at three quarters, the kind of moon where the waxing edge is blurry and smudged. There are no clouds, just a slight chill in the air and on my dew-drenched toes, signs of November in the coastal desert.

"Taken," I say as I get to the back fence.

"By you."

I stand in the dirt where the sunflowers used to grow and put both hands on the fence. I put Jesse's letter in my pocket. I think about leaving it here, about poking it through the gap in the fence, some sort of ancestral closure, but I'm too selfish. As I stand there, looking over the fence, the dawn changes the color of Harold C. Carr's old house. Then I slowly walk back through the strangers' garden, across the street, and drive away.

"History always repeats itself," my grandmother said.

TWENTY-ONE

Dear Rosamond,

It was lovely to have you over for tea this morning. You are such sunshine in my life. I'm sorry your daughter could not join us, but I suppose we would not have been able to speak so easily if you had a small child to tend to. It is indeed fortunate that you had a friend to watch her for you. I hesitate to admit this, but over the last week I have observed you a little bit. I watch from my back patio. It's charming and haunting all at the same time. Ellen seems to be at a troubling age. Lots of crying and tantrums. And it fills me with another emotion that I am only just beginning to understand: it feels like longing. I long for a child, for a family, but at the same time that life feels so far away. I cannot explain it yet. Perhaps one day I will understand it, and I hope you will be around to sit in my kitchen with a teacup and listen to my monologue on the subject.

I do hope your daughter is enjoying her new doll, or, better yet, she has not noticed a difference between this one and the former doll, may she rest in peace.

Please either come to see me again, or steal time away to come to the back fence to say hello. If I see you there, I will come and greet you.

In fact, shall we put our correspondence through the gap between the fence? It seems easier than the United States Postal Service or walking our letters around the block. I am so pleased that you have agreed to write to me. It will be enjoyable to have a friend. I shall feel silly saying this, but I already feel quite fulfilled by this endeavor, and it has only just begun.

I also acknowledge that perhaps your husband does not know that you are receiving letters from the man who lives behind you. And I acknowledge how disastrous that sounds. I admit to having heard his temper from all the way in my own bedroom at night. I would understand if you did not wish to tell him. Perhaps the fence-gap correspondence method will be more discreet. I will poke my next letter through so that it ends up beneath the small bush growing next to your lovely sunflowers.

Sincerely,

Your new friend,

Harold

TWENTY-TWO

"Vinnie," I say as I step outside. It's noon. Torrey is at school. The sun is strong for November. I smell the edge of a wildfire far away.

"Sheila," he says. He lights a cigarette. His fingertips are red and peeling. It looks like some kind of chemical irritant.

"What do you do, Vinnie? I've wondered this since the day I moved in and saw you here all day every day."

He smiles. "Well, I do a little freelance work," he says.

"You mentioned that." I can't tell if I'm angered or amused by this.

"Listen, nosy woman. I am a taxidermist."

I laugh. "Oh come on. Just tell me."

He stubs out his cigarette and rests it on the edge of the ashtray. He stands up.

"Wait here."

A minute and a half later, he emerges with a white plaster dog-like creature mounted on a long wooden base. He sets it on the wobbly table. The mouth is open and those are fucking real teeth pointing right at me. The eyeballs bulge out. I want to touch them to see if they're glass or real eyeballs preserved in formaldehyde. I try to touch my own eyeballs, but that semi-autonomic reflex lets me down.

Next, Vinnie brings out a pelt.

"It's a gray fox," he says. "Quite common, yet elusive in protected wilderness areas in San Diego County."

"Holy shit."

An hour later, I come back outside, determined. The fox is still on the green table. Vinnie is reading some sort of newsletter.

"Vinnie?" I say.

"Yes?" he says, not looking up.

"When's the last time you had sex?"

He puts the page on the ground. The wind moves it a little. The sound of paper on concrete makes me shiver. He's slow to answer. He picks up his once-discarded cigarette and relights it, and I breathe in deeply as he expunges the first smoke.

"It's been a while," he says.

"How long?" I ask. Impatient.

"Well, quite a while. It's not like I've had any inclination. Sarah's death and Torrey moving back here have been a bit preoccupying."

"How long before Sarah died?"

"Goddamn it, Sheila."

"Well, do you have any inclination now?" I ask.

He speaks slowly and carefully. "Inclination?"

"Inclination," I repeat. "For sex. Not to mean anything. Just to get it out of your system."

"What are you doing?" Vinnie asks.

"I don't know." I don't know.

"Are you serious about this?"

"Yeah," I say. I don't know.

"'Cause if you're serious, then, fine."

"Fine?" I laugh. "You're so agreeable all of a sudden."

"It's easy to be agreeable when your neighbor suggests a no-strings-attached thing with her oaf of a neighbor."

"Don't call yourself an oaf, Vinnie. It's a turn-off."

"I call it like I see it."

"You're more interesting than that."

He laughs. I don't often hear Vinnie laugh. It's uncomfortable how unfamiliar it is.

"Since when am I interesting?"

"Well, look at you," I say. "You're a goddamn taxidermist."

"So you're saying I was a regular oaf until you found out what I do for a living?"

I don't answer. For as oafish as Vinnie technically is, he is razor sharp. He is so much smarter than I ever imagined, and I feel shitty about being surprised by that.

"So you're saying taxidermy is sexy?" He points to the fox. The wide-open mouth, the exposed tongue. The bulging, glossy eyeballs.

I laugh. I'm not even sure I do find Vinnie sexy. I'm not even sure I want to have sex with him. Despite the fact that I'm about to. "Yes, Vinnie. It's the taxidermy."

He stares at me and I stare back, the fox between us, grotesque but already kind of normal.

"I'll fuck you," I say, slowly, and I can see his breath quicken as my voice changes. "I'll fuck you, as long as you bring over some sort of preserved creature to watch us."

Vinnie looks concerned.

"Jesus. I'm kidding!"

"I never know with you."

"Go home," I say, as if he's not currently leaning against his wall. "And do whatever you need to do to, like, get ready." Part of me wants to suggest a shower but even I realize it would be a terrible thing to say.

"Okay."

"Then, just come over."

"Like, inside your place?"

"Yes, Vinnie." I roll my eyes.

"Well, I've never been inside. You've never been in here, either."

I'm surprised he's noticed.

I watch Vinnie. He is not an ugly man—in fact, he's quite nice to look at. His jawline is attractive. I like the look of his strong forearms. His belly is a bit hairy but I imagine the forearms propping him up above me and it's easier to be okay with it all. We have never touched, Vinnie and me. Our coexistence survives on being in this same tiny, fenced-in piece of planet, small but with just enough elbow room. Until now, until me.

Inside, I remove my clothing. I fold my things carefully and put them back in the drawers. It's only noon. I can wear them again later.

I lie on my bed and close my eyes. I love the idea of sex in the daylight. It's been so long that I love the idea of sex at all. I push two fingertips as far as I can inside my vagina and this is how Vinnie finds me when he walks in.

"Oh hell," he says.

I don't stop, but I close my eyes. I want to be touched. I want to be alone. I want sex. I want to feel something. I want to feel someone else's something. I want someone else to feel something. I want to be left alone and to never talk to another person again. I don't even know what I want.

"What should I do?" he says.

I consider Vinnie's hygiene.

"Put your mouth on me," I say, and just like that, the very first time that my neighbor touches me at all is with his mouth between my legs. I bring my fingers to my own mouth and lean back, my head almost dangling upside down between my propped-up elbows. I don't watch.

It takes forever but it's better than anything I've ever felt.

"You're a good man," I say. I still don't look at him. "Fuck me."

TWENTY-THREE

THE LAST MAN I tried to sleep with, before Vinnie, was a man called Sloane I met while briefly temping at an engineering firm, a wishful screenwriter settling for a technical writing job. He was sweetness incarnate, everything I should have been seeking in a partner, but I couldn't handle it. Jesse was too big to me, even after I'd stopped working at the church, even after I'd stopped parking my car outside his house.

Sloane, a kind man, soft and hard at the same time, smooth and scruffy, a beard but skin that seemed almost liquid beneath my fingertips. Sloane, the kind of man I should've brought to my childhood home to meet my mother. We'd've stood there in the living room waiting for her to get ready, because she'd have to look her finest vision of grace, because she'd love him already and, with the two of us alone in the room, he'd lean close to me and he'd run his fingertips across the top edge of frames on the mantel, the same frames I'd seen a million times, the pictures I'd forgotten to be embarrassed about because they'd become background noise, wallpaper. And when he'd touch the places where all the pictures of my father used to be, would I notice? Would I even think of my father when a kind man was leaning against my hip? That's a question I knew the answer to without ever bringing Sloane home. I'd have thought of my father the whole time. He was a kind man, almost all of the time. He was kind when it didn't matter. Sloane was kind, too. Would Sloane always be kind?

We were only together a short while. We'd have sex in his bed, under white sheets, and he'd tell me I was pretty and tell me all the things I made him feel. I never said anything to him about how he made me feel. "You're so quiet," he'd say. "I like it. It's kinda mysterious."

I wished I knew what wasn't enough about him. I wish I knew then that nothing would have been enough at that point in my life. Each morning, leaving his house, I'd feel sick and uneasy. Equal parts being in the wrong place with the wrong man, and being so unfair to Sloane, a kind man. It was easier to stop showing up to work.

After Vinnie leaves my house, I feel remarkable. I don't feel sick. I don't feel uneasy. I feel easy. Things I've never felt before.

The next morning is better than I expect. Torrey is awake early. She sits on the steps with her pink and white Jansport backpack between her feet, the straps hooked over either knee.

"Morning, Sheila," she says.

"Morning. You're up early."

"Not really. This is about when I always leave. You're the one who's up early."

"That's true. Although I haven't gone to sleep yet."

"That's troublesome," she says. I wonder how much of her language comes from her own brain and how much comes from reading old-fashioned books.

"Teenagers are troublesome."

"I'm not a teenager."

"You will be soon." I smile.

"Hey, Sheila?" she says. Brief panic: she is going to ask me if I had sex with her dad.

"Yes?" I say. I look at the ground.

"Can we go to Harold's new place after school today?"

I don't look up. I feel a tightness in my limbs, a tension, like restlessness and paralysis at the same time. It's fleeting but I fixate. I don't even care if Harold has moved. I don't care where he lives, what he's like. My biological functions had thirty-five years of doing their thing, surviving mostly, before I knew about Harold Carr, before I knew about my grandmother, about these letters, about the possibility that this thing, the way I've memorized 382 letters, might pass me by.

These letters, my grandmother, Harold, all of it, maybe they are birds, wild birds, and maybe they never really landed on me at all.

"So," she continues. "You know how we almost had it the other night?"

I breathe in. I lift my shoulders, up, down. A roll of the neck. Snap out.

"The location?" I ask.

"Yeah. Well, I figured it out. At least, the next place he moved."

I don't say anything for a few minutes. I want Torrey's school bus to pull up. I want this conversation over. Torrey doesn't seem to consider the fact that Harold might very well be dead.

"Not today, Torrey."

I watch her face carefully. There's a strange urge to backpedal, to make her feel better.

"I just need a bit more time," I say.

"I know."

"You do?"

"Yeah," she says. "You're weird. You do things weirdly." She shrugs a little and picks up her pink and white Jansport. "I'm okay with it."

I laugh and feel a bit manic. "At least someone is."

————

That afternoon, there's the slow rumbling of the engine, the puff of air from the air brakes, and the squeaked swing of the automatic doors. Shuffling, sneakered feet running up the path, the forced click of the latch and the broken metal gate's drag on the concrete. Torrey is home from school. I close the window the second I hear the bus pull up. I hide inside my house. I read the next letter, the *one*. The first one that mentions my grandmother's replies.

> *Dear Rosamond,*
>
> *Thank you. Thank you, thank you, thank you. Your letter arrived properly through the fence. Your penmanship is striking. It's not as feminine as I expected. I am tempted to take it to one of those newfangled handwriting analysts to see if he can tell me what you think of me just based on the slope of your I's. I beg your pardon. It is not gentlemanly to tell my neighbor that I am curious of what she thinks of me!*
>
> *I hope it is not an insult to say your penmanship is not feminine. In fact, I find that alluring. It strikes a strange contradiction. You are femininity incarnate in person. You're a gentle matriarch. You dress in quite delicate fabrics. Your voice is calm and pretty. And you are indeed beautiful, if that is not too out of line to suggest.*
>
> *I planted sunflower seeds this morning after receiving your letter. They're right there, against our fence. I imagine in a few months, we will both have sunflower beds. Although, perhaps your sunflowers will wilt before mine grow tall enough to see over the fence. If that is the case, then we shall just have sunflowers for longer, like a relay. Yours first, then mine.*
>
> *I have yet to grow any flowers, but I already cannot imagine a point in my life when I will not associate sunflowers with this back fence, with these letters, and, of course, with you.*

I look forward to hearing from you again.
Sincerely,
Harold

I jump ahead. I can't help it. Each time I've read these letters, I've read them in a meticulous order, as best as I can figure out. Even the letters without dates are starting to find their places. But today I desperately want to read ahead.

My dear Rosamond,
It is late, very late. So late, in fact, that it is early. Yet I am wide awake. I was awoken by your husband's shouts coming from your house. The source of the trouble was unclear, but I am afraid for you. I am in turmoil, feeling so powerless, when all I want is to bring you to my home and keep you here. I know this is probably not the kind of greeting you would like to receive on the morning after what must have been a difficult night for you, my sweet Rosamond. Perchance I am weak in spirit to send this to you. Perchance selfish. But I write it only out of fondness, affection, and care. I only want you to know that I care. I do not wish to add to your heavy feelings.
There is a soul out there, close to you, who wishes for peace for you, above all else. Above my yearning, my wretched and unholy yearning. Above our friendship. Above our letters. Above my love.
My dear, my love. I tell you now something that I have known a long time, but never gave it voice: I do love you.
I love you with the kind of love that will torture me for all of my days. Never have I been so pleased to be tortured.
Sincerely,
Your Harold

TWENTY-FOUR

I CONSIDER TORREY'S OFFER to find Harold's next house, and my aversion to this offer. I don't understand it myself. I'm the kind of person who walks into people's backyards while their children are sleeping. I don't know where that or where Harold falls on the stalking spectrum.

I don't want to face Harold yet. Knowing that he said such a clear farewell to Rosamond is comforting. He was so definitive in his departure. A secretive sale of the house, packing up, keeping Rosamond in the dark. He was sure that he needed to leave, or that Rosamond needed him gone, or both. I admired that, the clarity of his goodbye.

I don't want to know if Harold is dead or alive. I suspect Torrey knows, based on her research. I don't want to ask.

On my phone, Jesse Ramirez's number fills the screen but I don't remember entering it. I've typed the whole thing. The whole thing. I've typed this many times, but I've never pressed SEND before.

I press SEND.

It rings. Once. Twice.

"Hi, this is Jesse." It's been a year since I've heard his voice.

I've never actually heard him say his name. He never told me his name. The unscrupulous sucker at the United Parcel Service call center gave me his name. And address. And number. It's been years since I worked at the church, where I would be expected to see Jesse or hear his voice. It's been six months since I last drove by his house.

Six months clean, I like to think.

"Hello?" he says.

I want to tell him: "You are not the loneliest soul on the planet." I want to tell him that was my favorite line from page one of his letter. I want to ask who he wrote it for. I want to ask why he never sent it.

"Is anyone there?"

I want to speak; I can feel it in my bones.

"I'm sorry," he says. So polite. "I'm afraid there's a problem. I can't hear anything."

The screen goes black. He's hung up.

The good news: I know he's home.

I make myself a cup of coffee in the ridiculous BUNN Pour-O-Matic two-burner machine that became mine when the church replaced theirs with a much tinier pod machine. It's completely unsuitable for the size of my kitchenette's single countertop and the quantity of coffee one person consumes. I pour my fresh coffee down the sink and boil some water for my new white tea instead. White tea supposedly has more benefits than green tea. Perhaps white tea will do the trick. Perhaps I'll feel better, perhaps I'll feel things differently. I think about telling the doctor that everything is fine. I fill a tall mug, the tallest that will fit in my cup holder.

I raise the mug to Vinnie and Torrey in the courtyard but I do not answer them when they say hi. I just drive to Jesse's house.

From my parking spot, one house down and across the street, I can see his front door. I can see his living room window. And I can see his form through the window, walking around. He looks to be tidying up. I want to know what he's tidying up for. I want to know how he cut through my skin and muscles and bones and found his way into my guts, my heart, my nerves. I want to know who the fuck he is. A dark and secret part of me wants him dead and gone, but I find no solace in that. Because what if he just gets replaced? What if the second I rid myself of him someone or something else takes over? What if he's just a deliveryman who was in the terribly wrong place at the terribly wrong time? I close my eyes and try to think about Vinnie, about why it's so easy to know him. And then I panic, because what if Vinnie *is* the next thing? I slowly open my eyes.

Another figure comes into view. It's a woman. She stands near him but not next to him. They face each other. They must be talking. The silence in my car almost hurts.

And then they embrace. It's brief. They continue tidying up the front room.

Is she the woman from the letter? Or is she someone with whom he is attempting to fill the spaces, the ones he promised would remain empty?

My tea is gone. It's been three hours. I scratch my knee until bits of flaky skin stick beneath my fingernails and dust the floor of my car.

I don't want to watch this anymore.

It angers me to know that I've gone so long, six months, without driving by here, and just by coming here again I've fucked it all up. I'll be back tomorrow. And I'll be back the day after that. I know these things, clearer than anything else at that moment.

Six months clean, down the toilet.

TWENTY-FIVE

TORREY AND VINNIE ARE still outside when I get home. I wonder if they sit outside all afternoon and evening because there's a deconstructed mountain lion or something hogging the living room floor.

Torrey is reading some sort of Penguin Classic. Vinnie is playing Tetris on his phone. He isn't smoking.

"Come sit with us for a little while," Torrey says.

"Okay," I say. I look at Vinnie. I haven't looked at him since we slept together. "Give me a minute."

Vinnie looks up, nods, and goes back to Tetris. This is relieving.

I go inside, where Harold C. Carr's letters lie scattered across my entire floor. I don't remember doing this, leaving them like this. I panic a little, considering the likelihood that I scattered the letters without noticing versus the likelihood of a break-in while Torrey and Vinnie watched my front door. Still, I check them all. I count them, paranoid. Three hundred and eighty-one. There's one missing so I count again. I must have miscounted them because now there are three hundred and eighty-two and I realize I am sweating. My knee itches to the point of insanity. I look at it and see a pale, crusty patch of eczema that wasn't there yesterday. It's the size of a quarter, and as I stare at it and my vision blurs and warps, I can make it grow until it covers my entire knee, the floor, the walls, the sky outside.

It's been an hour since Torrey asked me to come sit with them. Counting letters takes time. The sun has long gone down and they're inside their own house now.

Is Vinnie panicking about our supposed no-strings arrangement? That because I didn't come outside, maybe I'm feeling awkward? I'm not awkward. At least, not about sex. Not about Vinnie. I partly want to spend the rest of the evening talking to Torrey, because she makes me feel something like hope. And I partly wish Torrey wasn't there because then I could have sex with Vinnie again.

Frontline's on. It's about drug-resistant bacteria. I'm fascinated and appalled. I wash my hands in the kitchen sink eighteen times in the first half hour of the segment, eyes glued to the screen. The eczema on my knee is getting worse. I turn up the volume while I rifle through the medicine cabinet. I check the kitchenette. On the counter is oil and vinegar and my skin's so irritated right now that I opt for vinegar. It burns. I wash my hands again, first with vinegar. Then with soap. They're red and flaky.

"...*She was a skin picker,*" the doctor on Frontline says. "*She, as do many kids, picked at her little scabs. And that was likely what introduced the staph infection.*"

I want to look up eczema blogs, but I don't. I leave the television on and go outside. Vinnie's finishing up a cigarette.

"Hey," I say.

He nods.

"Is Torrey asleep?"

"I think so. She was up early today to get an assignment done."

"Oh. Sorry I didn't come out earlier. I got held up," I say.

"It's okay," he says. He presses his finished cigarette into the ashtray and gives it a slight twist.

Frontline says through the open window, "*So you're telling me that he had these bugs and you had nothing left to treat him with?*"

"God, what are you watching in there?" Vinnie asks.

I shrug. I sit on my front step and scratch my knee, and bits of my skin drift to the concrete. I want to throw up.

"You okay?" he asks, his voice quiet for Vinnie. If Torrey were awake, there'd be a good chance she actually didn't hear that.

"Yeah," I say.

"Your knee?"

"Oh, it's eczema. I think."

"Is that why you're watching some horrible germ show?"

"I don't know," I say. I don't know.

"Well, I have some stuff you can put on it, if you want. Taxidermy is a rough business. I keep lots of salves around," he says.

I laugh.

"I'll go get something and bring it over," he says.

I wait for a minute. Then two. Then I go back inside.

A nurse is saying, "*You go into a room, and maybe there's a hole in your glove.*"

The letters are lined up on my bed, spread out. I never cleaned them up when I counted them earlier.

"*It's a very complex environment,*" says the nurse. "*Alarms are ringing.*"

Vinnie walks in.

The nurse says, "*Did I forget to wash my hands between Mr. X and Mrs. Y?*"

"Here," he says. "Let me."

And then he's touching my knee, and it's weirdly intimate and disgusting at the same time. I want to know when he washed his hands last, but he smells clean, and he's a professional, and I'm watching PBS, so surely he knew to wash his hands.

"Is Torrey asleep?" I ask, again.

"Yeah."

Vinnie undresses me. This arrangement is going well. I reach for the remote, but there's a Pfizer VP on talking about cutting research, and he's a bit handsome. He's an asshole, and he's smug, but I hesitate to turn the TV off.

"Leave it on," Vinnie says in a low, dark voice. I look at him and wonder if I misheard him. "For the noise," he clarifies. "You know. Torrey."

My hands are still raw and peeling. There are probably a thousand tiny points of entry for bacteria to get under my skin, right into my bloodstream. I look at his hands. I look at his skin. I consider Vinnie's hygiene.

When he climbs on top of me on my small couch, his leg brushes the eczema spot on my knee. I brace myself by grabbing his shoulders and my fingernails scratch his skin. He makes a noise—a moan, a gasp, something in between—and I think about his skin cells beneath my fingertips. I think of him liking this feeling. I think of my fingers, raw and peeling, covered in a thousand micro-tears and vinegar. I wonder if Vinnie's shoulders sting.

I scratch harder, just a little drag. The idea of Vinnie's blood and toxins on my skin is unsettling but it makes me lift my hips off the couch.

Vinnie pushes into me. There's a pause, there's heavy breathing. I feel intense and powerful.

Frontline says, *"It's been two years since his last operation. It had taken three surgeries and another round of highly toxic antibiotics before doctors believed they had removed all the NDM-1 from his leg."*

"Fuck," Vinnie says. "I'm a little bit out of my mind right now."

I don't answer. I don't disagree.

"Those letters," he says, breathless, a little distracted, nodding toward my bed. His movements slow but he doesn't stop. "What are they?"

I prop myself up, awkward.

"Shut up, Vinnie."

I scratch at my knee in rhythm to his movements. I feel outside of my body and oppressed by it at the same time. There's ointment mixed with blood on my fingertips. The TV is talking about the Centers for Disease Control and I reach up to Vinnie's shoulders and pull my bloodied, oozing fingers across his skin, into the scratches I made.

TWENTY-SIX

When Vinnie leaves, I drive back to Jesse's. The house is completely dark. I sleep in my car that night, parked across the street. I fling the driver's seat back and slump into the gap between the top of the seat and the bottom of the head rest, stretching my feet out on either side of the pedals. It's almost as good as lying down.

When I wake up in the morning, the sun is bright and high in the sky. Jesse must have long since left for work. I try to remember if I've ever seen him leave for work. I wait to feel sadness or disappointment for missing him, but nothing comes.

At home, Vinnie is in the courtyard. He's doing something to a pair of glass eyeballs.

"Were you keeping your business a secret from me, or something?" I say.

"What?" he asks.

"I mean, I've lived here for two years and didn't know you were a taxidermist. And then just days after you tell me, all of a sudden you're painting eyeballs out in the light of day?"

He laughs. "Well, I suppose it looks that way, doesn't it?"

"It's a shameful profession," I say with a smile. "You should be ashamed of yourself."

"Are you just now getting home?" he asks.

I don't have to answer to him, I remind myself. I've never had to.

"Nah, I just had to run some stuff over to my mom's." The lie feels good.

"Hey," Vinnie says. "Don't worry about explaining anything to me." He's smiling.

I smile back. "Okay."

"And," he hesitates. He picks up the eyeball and twirls it a little, squinting to see whatever it was he was doing. The edges of his skin around his fingernails are almost all split. "Thank you."

"Hm?"

"For last night."

"Oh."

"And the other night."

"Yes. Well," I say. I want to be inside. "Thank you."

"Well, okay, yeah, you're welcome," he says.

"Please don't ever thank me again."

"Right."

"Is it a real eyeball?" I ask.

"No, Sheila."

Inside, I lock the door, but then I open the windows. It still smells like sex in here.

Dear Rosamond,

I am pleased that you are finding the time to reply to me so frequently. Your letters bring me such joy. Unfortunately, I will not be able to respond for the next eight days. I was unable to tell you sooner because my travel plans have been up in the air, but I am going on a trip to visit my brother. He and I are quite close, and his wife just this morning gave birth to their first child. Despite having lots of young nieces and nephews, it still

*feels strange to be an uncle, but I am looking forward to seeing
my brother and his new family.*

    *However, I daresay I will miss you. I'm afraid that come
eight days from now, you'll have a hefty stack of letters pushed
through your fence, letters I wrote you while I was away.*

    *I saw you and your daughter playing in the backyard yes-
terday. Do you think of me when you're in your backyard, as I
think of you when I am in mine?*

Harold rambles the most in this letter. It's one of his longest. I
try to imagine him in this space between meeting her and professing
his love, between the beginning and the middle. He tests the waters
with affection. He tests the waters with familiarity, with anecdotes,
revealing things about himself.

I want more.

I'm asleep when Torrey comes home. She knocks on my door,
which is unusual for any of the now three residents of this tiny courtyard. There's not supposed to be any sort of inquiring. We just wait
in the courtyard, and someone will come out soon enough.

When I open the door, she steps forward, like she's coming in. I
remember that she is twelve. I remember that my house smells like
sex with her dad. I step toward her too, so that the both of us are
more outside than inside. I win.

"I want to read the letters again," she says.

"No," I say.

"Oh, come on."

"No."

"Well, just one? Please?" She looks so expectant, so pitiful, that
I almost consider it.

"Maybe another day."

"Now?"

"Torrey."

"Okay, okay."

"Come and sit," I say. I feel motivated almost (almost) entirely by a desire to make this other person feel good about herself. I wonder if this is what it's like to have a sibling. Then I wonder if this is what it's like to have a child. Then I wonder what it means that I considered someone twenty-three years younger than me more viable as a sibling than as a child.

"How's school?" I ask.

Torrey laughs. "Really?"

"Really what?"

"You're doing the 'how's school' thing?" she asks. She uses air quotes.

"Yes, I'm doing it. Since when do you use air quotes? Is this a new thing?"

"Nobody else I know does air quotes. It's not a thing. I probably saw them when I was little, watching old nineties movies or something."

"So you're, like, retro," I say.

"I guess I am," Torrey says. She kicks her feet up and she's wearing the exact same shoes I wore at her age, navy blue Converse low tops, faded enough to be mistaken for grey, and the black line along the toe is rubbed thin, some plastic shoelace aglets missing.

"You totally are retro."

"I've been thinking about that one letter," she says. She's not even cautious. She doesn't feel like she needs some sort of preamble. I love that about her. I love that about children.

"Oh, that one?" I poke her arm. "There are three hundred and eighty-two of them. Narrow it down a bit for me."

"The one where he is upset."

"He's upset from like, number twenty onwards," I say.

"The first one where he, you know. Where he goes a little crazy?"

———

Dear Rosamond,

It's been ten days. You've never gone this long without writing to me. Even a few months ago, when I visited my brother, I was so pleased to come home to eight little oilcloth packages, each containing an individually wrapped letter for each day I was gone. I was filled with joy! Despite the fact that we have no expectations between us, no commitment, no rules, I am finding myself afraid as each day passes. When I am the most selfish and the least paranoid, I worry that you have tired of me. When I am the least selfish and the most paranoid, I worry that something terrible has gone wrong, that you are ill or hurt. And when I'm somewhere in the middle, both selfish and paranoid, I worry that Mr. Baker has found my letters.

I've taken to sitting on the grass in the backyard, near my vegetable garden. I watch as best I can through the cracks in the fence but I can't see much. I know I'd be better off indoors, where I can at least see that people are in the backyard. Sometimes I can see the top of your head, the sun shining on your hair. I feel like a Peeping Tom. I feel like a scoundrel. I don't care.

My dear Rosamond, I just want to be closer to you. And that is why I sit near the fence in the afternoons after work and first thing in the morning. I feel slightly batty. I've considered moving my bedroom to the spare room, just so that when I sleep, I sleep one room closer to you.

Oh, my Rosamond. It would behoove me not to send this letter through the fence. I'm glad you are receiving my other ones. I worry that a growing stack would be too conspicuous. But this one in particular, well, it is not in my best interests that you be made aware that I am losing my mind over you.

Alas, sweet Rosamond, I will surely send this anyway. I seem to have a misplaced all sense of restraint when it comes to you.
   Sincerely,
   Harold

"So, you know, the first one where he goes mental?" Torrey asks.

I do know. "Do you have a photographic memory?"

"Not really," she says.

"Well, there's no *not really* about it. You either do or you don't. You seem like the type to have a photographic memory, that's all."

"There's a type?" she asks. She kicks back her chair so it balances on the back two legs.

"Yes. You. You're the type."

Vinnie's patio furniture is so old that I worry for her safety. The chair's back legs bulge a little as she slowly rocks, but they don't give.

She rocks for a while, minuscule movements on the chair. I'm suddenly desperate to try it, too, like a contagion, like a yawn. But I don't.

"What's the deal with your family?" she asks.

I kick back on my chair after all.

"What do you mean?" My chair falls forward and crunches back down on all fours. I suck at doing the artful idle thing.

"I mean, where are they? Why do you have the letters? Why not her own children? Why was this a secret? I need answers! Or whatever."

"Goddamn you."

Torrey laughs. Vinnie comes out. He sits on my step because he only has two chairs in the courtyard, the ones Torrey and I are in. He nods at us and lights up to smoke. Torrey hands him the ashtray.

"I can't believe you endorse his nasty habit," I say.

Vinnie grins.

"What are you ladies doing?" Vinnie asks.

"Talking," Torrey says. I'm not looking at her to see if she rolls her eyes but the nostalgia I feel for my own adolescence is heavy.

"Torrey asked me about my family," I say vaguely.

Vinnie laughs.

"What?"

"I hear your phone calls with your mother. Well, I think it's your mother," he says.

"Yes. That'd be her."

"Is she all you have?" Torrey asks.

"Jesus, where do you get lines like that?" I ask.

"Sorry," she says. "But is she?"

"Yes," I say. "She's pretty much all I have now that my grandmother died. I don't have any siblings. Neither did my mom."

"So is your dad dead?" she asks. "I can ask because I have a dead mom."

"Torrey," Vinnie says.

"I'm ready to joke about it like that," she says. "She's my mom. I decide."

"I thought it was awesome," I say.

"Well?" she says.

"No, my dad isn't dead," is all I say.

Nobody speaks. Vinnie extinguishes his cigarette.

"Have you heard about Sheila's grandma and her crazy affair?" Torrey says to her dad.

"Torrey!" I say.

"No," Vinnie says. He watches me carefully. I watch him back. "I don't need to hear about your girl stuff," he says. He gets up, messes up Torrey's hair as he walks by, and goes back in the house.

Vinnie is a good man.

The moon is high in the bright sky. "My mother always used to call it a Children's Moon," I say, nodding upward. "When it's out in the afternoon."

"So did mine," Torrey says, and her voice is quiet and small.

It takes a minute for me to muster up the courage. I don't even know what I'm feeling. Friendship? Maternal instinct? Sisterhood? It's something and it's strong and I just want Torrey to feel like she's not alone.

I reach over between the two faded green plastic lawn chairs and pick up her hand. She flinches at first, but quickly relaxes and lets me hold her hand. She's stubborn, and she's tough, but the first time I squeeze her hand, she begins to cry. She's a quiet crier. It's so tidy and gentle.

I can't remember the last time I cried. But I can remember the first time I definitely didn't.

"Sheila!" my mom shouted from downstairs. I'd once loved this house for the staircase. The decor was shitty but the staircase was magical, with a banister that seemed right out of the movies. But it's also where I sat the first time my dad left, where I sat when I felt like I was a balloon on a string, tied to the staircase, but the knot was loosening. All I could do was watch from my spot on the stairs as the stubby free end of the string slipped back through the loop. All I could do was feel myself untether.

It'd been three years since my father left us that first time, and he'd come right back. Three years of being back to normal. Three years, though, when every time I climbed up and down that staircase, I'd think of that day. I'd remember my worn-out jeans, an orange and brown striped tank top, and chipped pink toe nail polish, the cheap stuff from the drugstore down the street. I'd remember the ragged, fraying edges of my hair, bunched together at the end of a long, two-day-old braid. I'd remember the way that staircase made my stomach jump, a mixture of fear, worry, shame, sadness, and the unshakeable knowledge that I'd done something wrong. That I'd done the thing that made everyone not fit together. I felt it with each footstep on these stairs, every day for three years.

"Sheila," she shouted again. "We're going to be late."

I didn't hurry. I knew that as soon as I got downstairs she'd find something else she had to do and then I'd be the one waiting.

In the mirror, my dress looked so much worse on me than it did on the hanger. A bit too short. A bit too puffy in the shoulders. Too much going on in the floral design. In The Gap, it looked perfect next to the two different yet coordinating patterns and colors. I wished I could somehow include those other dresses in my look. My legs were too hairy because my mom had yet to let me shave them. I had a patch of eczema on my right knee, and when I noticed it in the reflection, I automatically reached to scratch the coordinating patch beneath my left elbow.

I decided, quickly, that I looked good enough for Jesus Christ. I wriggled my feet into the bridal white satin shoes my mother gave me, because "Confirmands always wore all white when I was a kid. You can wear whatever dress you want, but at least borrow my old shoes," she'd said, and it seemed important, that she had gone through this too. My parents supported me in this church stuff. My mother drove me to youth group events, to Sunday services, but she mostly just dropped me off, turned around, and went home. I clammed up every time the priest talked about family bible study or family prayer or all the lines in scripture about eternal life, because if my parents died, they wouldn't go to Heaven with me. And then I'd try to imagine it, the afterlife; with or without my parents, it all seemed so out of reach. Were we still human? Did we have bodies? What was the point, then, in dying, other than clearing out all the people who didn't think like us? What if someone you hated also went to Heaven? What if someone you were afraid of was there? What good is it to keep on keeping on if it's no better than this?

Downstairs, I asked her, "Where's Dad?"

Her face looked extra wrinkly and sallow. She wasn't old enough to look this old. Her eyelids were red. She closed them for just a beat longer than a normal blink.

"He's probably not going to make it to church," she said in a voice I'd never really heard before.

That night, when it was dark and my teeth were brushed and my skin was properly buffed with St. Ives Apricot Scrub, I asked her again. "Where's Dad?"

She didn't answer right away. I stood in the doorway of our upstairs bathroom, and she sat at the top of the stairs, on the top step, her head against the wall, her back to me. The staircase I hadn't forgiven yet.

"Well, Sheila," she said. "He left."

She didn't move. I was afraid she would cry. Nobody had taught me how to take care of a mother who cried. She didn't cry, though. Maybe she was done crying. Maybe she hadn't started yet. I stood in the bathroom doorway and stretched my arms up high, rolling up onto my toes, my fingertips grasping uselessly for the lintel. I thought about one day being taller, I thought about how small I still was.

"Don't say anything to anyone," my mother said, her cheek pressed against the wallpaper at the top of the stairs, her words slightly slurred. "Not yet."

I didn't answer. I didn't cry.

TWENTY-SEVEN

"SHEILA?" MY MOTHER SOUNDS confused when she answers the phone. Possibly because I never call her. She always calls me.

"Hi, Mom. Yes, it's me."

"What's going on? Is something wrong?"

Yes. She is doing this on purpose. She is not making this any easier on me. I want to hang up. I feel strongly that I should hang up.

"Not much. I lost my job," I say. I actually wasn't planning on saying this. I wasn't planning on self-sabotaging the phone call so soon. I was just going to say hello and talk. I don't know when I last called someone and said hello, talked, and felt great about it. I wanted to see if just saying hello and talking is possible.

Answer: no. It's not possible.

"Oh, Sheila. God. What happened now?" Her tone is indistinct. She is a master at this. Judgment, pity, panic, motherly support, all wrapped up together.

"Nothing happened, really," I say.

This could go one of two ways:

I could push it:	I could lie:
"Nothing happened, really," I say. "Well, I just called them and told them I wasn't coming in anymore."	"Nothing happened, really," I say. "The temp position ended and since it was just a project rather than regular staffing, they didn't need me anymore."
"Oh, honey. What on earth did you do that for?"	"Oh, honey. I'm sorry," she says. I can feel that she is pleased by this. Her daughter working on a project, even a vague and un-named project, is the best thing she's had to say about me in years. She's looking forward to it, to telling people about The Project.
"Well, I didn't feel like going in anymore."	
"Nobody feels like going to work, Sheila."	
"That's not true," I say. "Some people love their jobs."	"It's okay."
"Name one," she says.	"Are you sure? Do you need any-thing?" she asks.
Vinnie, I don't say. Vinnie loves his job.	"No."
"People who do different things than you or I do," I say.	"Are you sure?"
"You don't even do anything!" she says, and it's the meanest thing she's let slip in a long time. I cherish it, in a way. It's good to have something to pinpoint.	"Yes," I say.
	"How long since they let you go?" she asks. "And when do you think you'll find something else?"

She pauses. Her breathing right at the mouthpiece is annoying.	"It's been about a couple of weeks," I say.
"I'm sorry, honey. I didn't mean it like that. But surely you're making contacts or at least learning about different careers with all of this temping?"	"A couple of weeks?!"
"I guess."	
"When did this happen?" she finally asks.	
"A couple of weeks ago."	
"A couple of weeks?!"	

The call ends with rhetorical non-questions like "Why didn't you tell me sooner?" and not-questions-at-all like "I can't believe I'm just now hearing this." My mother is the one who is the most wronged by my unemployment.

I hate every minute of the phone call, but I feel better about myself. I feel valid. What if, in any given mother-daughter relationship, someone just has to self-sabotage once in a while to give both parties something to hang on to?

There's a knock at the door.

"Go away," I say, but I answer it anyway. The only person who knocks on my door is Torrey.

"What are you doing?" she asks.

"Nothing," I say. "Wait. What day is it? Why aren't you at school? It's not Saturday, is it?"

"Yes," she says. "It is. Wow, that's pretty pathetic. When I grow up, I hope I forget what day of the week it is."

"When you grow up," I say, "I hope you know a twelve-year-old who makes fun of you."

"What are you doing today?"

"Torrey, I didn't even know what day it was. Do you think I have plans?"

"I thought I heard you talking on the phone," she says.

"Like father, like daughter."

"Like neighbor."

"True," I say.

"That sounded like a super fun phone call," she says. "Your mom?"

"Yeah."

"Well, can we hang out today?"

"Hang out? Torrey. You don't need to be hanging out with me. I'm thirty-five."

"You are? I mean, I knew you were old, but not *that* old," she says. Amazed.

"I'm sure I'm not as old as your dad!"

"You're older than him. He's thirty-three."

"Shut the fuck up."

"Sheila," Vinnie says, at conversational volume, from inside his kitchen. "Don't cuss to my preteen daughter and don't act so surprised."

"I need to get my shit together," I say, staring at the midmorning sky, still not quite blue enough. I repeat it: "I need to get my shit together."

It's not very quiet in the courtyard, when I slow down to hear it. Cars pass in regular intervals; just beyond our rusty gate is a busy street and a stop sign. Lots of revving engines. Periodic honking. Cell phone drivel of passing walkers. Regular conversations of passing walkers. Shouted conversations of passing cyclists. Cyclists never talk to each other, they only shout. Our single-story places are dwarfed by two-story postwar apartment buildings on all sides, and I feel oppressed by all the chatter, movement, slamming doors, ringing phones: busy, endless lives. There are birds on the telephone wire, nondescript black birds. Are they crows? Smaller, greenish-brown birds populate the bushes and hedges in the courtyard. I bet Vinnie could identify every last one of them. He's washing dishes. The swish of running water and clanking ceramic and steel is louder and nearer than most anything else, but I notice it last.

I close my eyes.

"You don't have to start today," Torrey says. "Getting your shit together, that is."

I look at Torrey and can't stop the giant smile.

"Can we go to the library?" she asks.

"Lord Almighty. You want to go to the library?"

"Yes. I want to look up your grandma."

"You're so nosy about her," I say.

"Aren't you?" she asks, matter of fact.

"Well, yes," I say. "But I know a lot already. What's the library going to tell me?"

"Dad said—" she starts

"Were you talking to Vinnie about this?"

"She volunteered the information," Vinnie says from the kitchen. There are no secrets in this shared courtyard.

"It's not a big deal, is it?" Torrey asks.

"No," I say. I don't know why it's a big deal.

"So Dad said we could find deed records. And look up stuff like what year Harold bought the house."

"Oh."

"I mean, we don't know how long he lived there before he met your grandmother. Do we?"

"No, I guess not. I assumed he had just moved in," I say.

"Why's that?" she asks.

"Because he seemed so lonely," I say, not mentioning how lonely I was living here for two years before I made any sort of meaningful contact with my neighbors. Not mentioning how it hasn't made me feel any less lonely.

"Yeah," she says. "I think you're right."

I don't even know what time it is right now. I don't even know exactly how to get to the library. Three minutes go by without a single car passing through the intersection.

"Are you lonely?" she asks.

"I don't know," I say. I don't know. "Are you?"

She doesn't answer right away. She thinks, and she doesn't hide that she's thinking. I like that Torrey is a thinker.

"I don't know either," she says.

TWENTY-EIGHT

My darling Rosamond,

Seeing your letter through the fence this morning was a balm to my wounded soul. But when I read it, it was as if I were wounded all over again. I am sorry that you have been ill. I am deeply sorry. It makes my heart hurt that I was so close to you, so willing to care for you, but unable to. Unable to even know you were infirmed in the first place. Unable to help in the ways I need to help. I feel compelled to take care of you, I feel compelled in every inch of my skin. I feel it on a biological level. It's as if you are the other animal in the world I am supposed to protect from predators.

I must know. When can I see you again? When can I see your face and speak with you? I am not supposed to be a lonely man. My work keeps me very busy and engaged. My friends are sociable and loyal, though not as geographically near to me anymore as they used to be. But being so geographically near you but not being able to spend every waking minute with you feels incredibly lonely. I want to take everything I can get. You simply must find someone to take care of Ellen one morning and come over for a cup of coffee.

My friend called on me yesterday afternoon. His name is Artie, though ever since we returned from the war he has been trying to go by Arthur instead. It's been years and I have yet to hear anyone actually call him Arthur. I am telling you this only because, well, first, in the grand scheme of our lives we do not know too much about each other, and second, he pointed out my sunflowers. In jest! I was so close to telling him about you. I almost pointed out that if he knew of a woman like you who grew sunflowers, he would suddenly want to grow sunflowers, too. Suddenly more than anything, I wished to tell him about you. But I didn't.

Today, after I return home from work, I am going to walk in the park with Ripper shortly before sunset. I know that you will have Ellen, but it would please me greatly if I were to walk past a beautiful young mother playing with her daughter in the waning afternoon warmth. The fresh air will do you well now that you have regained your strength. I will not stop or speak to you, but I will walk by and cherish that moment of seeing you in the flesh, of smiling, of looking right into your eyes. Perhaps the edges of our fingers will brush as we pass.

Anxious to see you again,

Harold

TWENTY-NINE

THE DOWNTOWN LIBRARY IS strangely lovely. All these people all doing the same things individually, apart. It's my favorite type of community, the type where I can coexist but not have to look anyone in the eye. I never expected to love a library.

It's just so big. Floors upon floors of information. Torrey is as overwhelmed as I am.

"I've never actually been to a library before," she says.

"But you're *twelve*," I say. "Kids, they go to libraries. It's what they do."

"Yeah, but not in Virginia. We went to bookstores. And I have a Kindle anyway. My school had a library, but it was just a converted classroom."

"I don't believe you."

"Well," Torrey says, looking around. "There's a lot of crap here. Surely there's something about one Harold C. Carr."

The library doesn't tell us much about Harold and Rosamond. We get lots of information about that house, the date Harold left, and the buyer. It turns out the buyer is the current owner, though, and Torrey hatches a plan.

"No," I say.

"Why not?" she whines. I'm reminded she is a kid.

"I'm not doing this if it pesters people. That sounds like pestering."

"It's not pestering. People love a good love story."

"This is not a very good love story," I say.

"Why? Because it doesn't have a happy ending? The best love stories have sad endings."

"You know a lot about love for a twelve-year-old."

"You don't know very much about being a twelve-year-old, then."

"I was twelve once."

"Maybe I'm special," she says. She is. "I understand love already."

"You're wrong. Nobody ever understands love," I say.

"So we can't go visit Harold's old house?"

"No."

"Well, maybe I'll just go by myself." She tries to look petulant but she really can't pull it off.

"On your own? What would Vinnie say?" I ask. I try not to laugh.

"Well, when I'd ask him to drive me over there, *Vinnie* would say 'Sure.'"

"So, what's stopping you, then? Why did you even bother inviting me to any of this?" I ask. I realize that I actually want to know the answer to this.

She pouts, as best as she can.

"Torrey," I say. "You're a pretty pathetic kid."

"Dude. That sucks."

"No, I mean, you can't even do normal kid things like whine and pout. You're better at being a mature human than pretty much every grown-up I know."

"Well, thanks. So now will you take me to Harold's old house? Please?"

"Maybe later." Goddamn it.

"When?" Torrey asks.

"Maybe never."

"Pleeeease?"

"Maybe later, like a long time from now. I want to know more first," I say. "And I want to go home now."

I'm so weak.

> *Dear Rosamond,*
>
> *Oh, it was so lovely to see you in the park. Walking by you electrified me. I daresay I felt a true electric current pass between us our fingertips brushed. You must think I am so silly. But, I implore you: tell me if you felt it too.*

"I love that part," Torrey says.

"Which part?" I ask.

"The 'electrified' part."

"Yeah, me too. It's so cheesy. Now shut up, I'm trying to read."

> *Yes, let's meet again. I suppose I suggested it first, so I shall say that I accept your implied agreement on the matter. Tuesday may work. I do not have to work until the afternoon. You may stay all morning if you wish. I would wish for that, of course, but I understand if you either do not share that wish or if you cannot arrange it.*

"I love that," Torrey says.

"God, you love everything."

"Well, yeah. But I love how insecure he is."

"Nice."

"You know what I mean. He came across as such a poised and witty man in his first letter. Just all, 'Sorry about your daughter's mangled doll,' and stuff. But now he's kind of…I don't know. Adorable. Isn't he?"

"I guess my grandma thought so."

Torrey laughs. "Yeah. I guess she did."

Please reply as soon as possible. I'm not sure I can survive the wait until Tuesday morning. I suppose I have endured much worse. The war, nights in trenches, enemy fire. Perhaps there are tortures greater than having you live so close to me. It just doesn't feel like it right now.

Sincerely,

Harold

"Oh, man," Torrey says.

"Let me guess. You loved that part."

"And you didn't?"

"He's so dramatic. He's like a caricature."

"Well I love him," she says, as if I don't.

"You should go home. Doesn't Vinnie ever feed you dinner?"

"I think we're going to make pizzas together tonight."

I feel stupid, because I can feel it happening, and I'm powerless to stop it and powerless to step outside of my head. I feel an icy-edged tightness in my lungs, climbing swiftly to the back of my throat. My fingers spread, locked. I close my eyes. I try to focus on breathing instead of focusing on panicking about panicking. I have the wherewithal to identify what's happening to me but I don't have the presence of mind to do anything about it. All I can do is wait.

"Sheila?"

I was eleven and my dad stood next to me. I knelt on one of the barstools in the kitchen, the same one that I fell off when I was six. I needed four stitches behind my ear and it was the first time I saw that much blood.

So, from ages six through ten, I wouldn't use the barstools and I forget if this was a rule or a suggestion from my worrier parents, and my dad would put a tablecloth on the kitchen floor for pizza night prep, to catch our mess. Eventually we stopped bothering to make the dough ourselves; it was shitty Boboli but I didn't mind. This was our thing, me and my dad, whenever my mom went out in the evenings. It had always been just us two.

By ten, I was back on the barstool. My dad got more artful with the slicing of the toppings now that he was back at the countertop. Mushrooms, sliced thinly so they'd crisp in the oven. Olives, only on his side. Green peppers, cut into long strips to make a green mouth for pepperoni eyes.

"Sheila, you're making a mess," he said. He was always talking about the mess.

"Sorry, Dad," I said. "This cheese is sticky."

"It's okay," He said, and he exhaled loudly. "It's just mess," he said. His voice cracked. I tried not to look at him.

"Are you excited for tomorrow?" I asked.

"Hm?"

"Tomorrow morning? My confirmation?"

"Oh, yeah. Sure. I'm so proud," he said, and I could tell he was lying. Neither of my parents cared about the things I cared about: that I was the youngest person the church had ever confirmed. Neither of them cared about my significant and intellectual relationship with Reverend Jenny, the youth pastor I babysat for. She paid really well. She understood me. She didn't ask me questions about Jesus or salvation, and when I asked her the questions, questions like, "Isn't it wrong to believe in that?" or "Isn't it wrong to not believe in that part?" she told me: "Kiddo, it doesn't matter what you believe, it's just that you believe at all." She told everyone that same thing, but I felt like she made it up just for me.

"Are you going to go?" I asked. "To church tomorrow?"

"Sure, Sheila. Sure," he said.

We made the pizzas. I watched my dad clean up the cutting boards while the oven seethed. He picked up all the pieces of cheese and the dusts of flour and errant crumbs on the floor. He wiped down all the splatters of sauce, all the miniscule grease imprints left by the spilled shreds of cheese. But the pizzas turned out terrible, they were always terrible. I just wanted to pick up the cheese in clumpy, melty sheets and eat that plain. So I did. I peeled it off in one giant slice-shaped piece and rolled it into a little saucy cheese roll.

"Shelia, that's disgusting," he said. I was only eleven but I already knew that he shouldn't shame a child like this. My mother would stop him if she were home. "Just eat it properly, would you?"

I picked up the slice and took a bite.

I felt exactly as disgusting as I was told I was.

And then, the next day, he was nowhere.

THIRTY

"Sheila!"

It's Vinnie. He's shaking my shoulders. He's in my house. So is Torrey.

"What?" I say. "What are you doing here?"

"Sheila, are you playing dumb?" Torrey asks. She sounds apathetic. It's the way I like her.

"No?" I say. "I mean, I know you were already over here, but Vinnie just fucking appeared out of nowhere."

"I've been here for five minutes," he says.

"He's exaggerating," Torrey says. "It hasn't even been like one entire minute. Forty-five seconds max."

"Why are you so brilliant?" I ask her. "Why? You're so great."

"Sheila, are you drunk?" Vinnie asks.

"No, she's not," Torrey says. "I was with her all afternoon. She's just been reading with me."

"I'm not drunk. God."

"Dad, she just spaced out. Just like I said."

"She's acting drunk," he says.

"I'm not," I say. "You'd know if I was drinking. Believe me. And hey, it's pizza night," I say.

Nobody answers me.

"You should go," I continue. "Make sure she doesn't fall off the stool. She'll always have a scar. Never use Boboli crusts."

"Sheila…?" Torrey asks.

"Come to think of it, pizza night is a bad idea. Never make pizza with your dad, Torrey," I say. I know I sound crazy. I can hear the slur in my voice. "Pizza. Bad idea. Crazy idea."

"I love pizza," Vinnie says.

I open my eyes. I didn't realize they were closed until I open them. Vinnie is smiling, at least.

"I haven't had pizza since I was eleven years old," I say.

I watch Torrey look at her father. I envy her. She's twelve. Even if their relationship falls apart in thirty seconds, she'll still have at least one more year with her dad than I did. But that makes me think about all the years when Torrey's mother had primary custody and she lived hours away and then, I remember. Her mother.

"Oh shit," I say out loud. "Your mom. I'm sorry. I shouldn't think like that. How dare I envy a girl with a dead mother!"

Torrey smiles. "I like her like this," she tells her dad. "It's like, Sheila unplugged. I think she's having some sort of brain barf."

"No, I'm not," I say. "I'm totally fine. I guess I checked out for a minute. I was lost in my head."

"You still are," Vinnie says.

"Pizzaaaa," Torrey says.

I look at her. She is intently staring at me with a crazed look in her eyes.

"Oh my God! You're trying to trigger me!"

"Torrey," Vinnie says. A warning tone. I like him when he's being fatherly. It occurs to me at this incredibly twisted time that, yes, I am sleeping with him.

"Vinnie, you're a good man," I say. Vinnie's eyes flash to mine. "Torrey, did you really run and get your dad when I was…thinking?"

"Thinking?" she says. "About pizza?"

"Stop it, you."

"Torrey," Vinnie says. "Sheila is fine. I'm going back home now. I have dough to punch down."

Vinnie puts his scratchy fingertips beneath my jaw and lifts it just a teensy bit. It's such a Hollywood move, but it'd be more effective if he just said, *Look up a quarter inch, would you?* He slowly moves his head side to side, never breaking eye contact.

"Vinnie," I say in a stage whisper, my chin pressing down into his hand. "I don't have a goddamned concussion."

He flicks my chin up a little more, like he's some sort of Humphrey Bogart.

"Pizza'll be ready in probably twenty minutes," he says to Torrey, and walks out.

"Do you think people have soul mates?" Torrey asks from amongst the letters on my kitchen floor.

"Torrey, can we go back to pretending I'm having a mental breakdown? That was easier."

"No, you're fine," she says. "But look at Rosamond and Harold."

"Technically we can only look at Harold."

"Technically we can look at neither of them right now," she says. "But Harold's letters tell us a lot about both of them."

"Yes, okay, fine." I want to roll my eyes only because it bothers me when a twelve-year-old has more motivation than I do.

"And," she says, "we know your grandmother. Well, you do. You know what she was like before she died." She's speaking in a teacher or lawyer voice, all prompty.

"True. She had dementia," I say. Torrey glares at me. "And before that, she was, you know, nice and all, but she was always a bit distant."

"Exactly!" Torrey says.

"I don't mean to make it sound like she wasn't a good grandma," I say. "She was. She was always very sweet with me."

"Torrey!" I hear from across the courtyard. It's Vinnie's inside voice. "Pizza."

She runs out of my place. And then she runs back, just to pop her head in the door. I know exactly what she's going to say.

"We're not done with this. This isn't over!"

THIRTY-ONE

I CAN SET MY clocks by Torrey.

It's dark and dinner's over. And she's knocking on my door. I hide the evidence of my shitty frozen dinner because I don't want anyone to ever say anything they'll regret, like *You should come over and eat with us next time.*

"Okay," she says, as she walks through the door. "Hear me out."

"Come on in."

"I'm just saying that it is incredibly likely that everyone has a soul mate."

"No," I say. "No, it's not. That is such bullshit." I consider Jesse Ramirez.

"Harold and Rosamond."

"That's one example, not proof for everyone."

"Sometimes I wonder if I shouldn't exist," she says. She doesn't sound depressed or suicidal as she says it. She kind of shrugs a little. She sounds scientific.

"Go on."

"Well, my mom and dad were not soul mates."

"Oh."

I sit there in quiet. The only lighting in the room is the dim pendant lamp above the kitchen sink and the flickery glow of PBS's News Hour.

"So, you see, if we are to only seek out our true soul mate, and only have children with them, then there are a lot of people out there who are shirking responsibility."

"Shirking responsibility?" I laugh. "What are you, sixty?"

"I'm well-educated," she says. "And I have no friends yet. I have lots of time for vocab."

"I'm your friend," I say, even though I didn't mean to say it out loud.

"And what about you?" she continues, undaunted.

"What about me?"

"Well, your grandmother wasn't supposed to have your mother."

"I think you're being presumptuous," I say.

"Listen—not only should your grandmother have been mating with Harold C. Carr, your mother doesn't seem to have found her soul mate, either."

"Torrey, you're worse than, like, a pope. Divorce is okay. Divorce does not render a child worthless."

"But do you think Rosamond regretted having your mother?"

I'm supposed to reply very quickly here. I'm supposed to say: absolutely not! A few months after her mother's death is not the time for a kid to be wondering if her mother regretted her. But there's something about Torrey. Something that drives me to be as real as possible. I want to do the right thing.

"Well, possibly only logistically," I say.

"Logistically?" she asks.

"Like, a pesky child meant it'd be harder for her to walk away from my grandfather."

"I wonder…" she starts, but she looks down. It occurs to me that she's prettier than I ever noticed. It's an unassuming, sneaky pretty.

"Your mother never regretted you. Neither did your father. That's totally impossible. Your mom probably thought things like, 'Wow, that marriage was terrible. The only good thing that came of it was my sweet baby girl.'"

Torrey smiles and for some reason I feel triumphant. I try to remember a time when my life didn't revolve around a twelve-year-old's state of mind.

"It's not even what I'm worried about," she says.

"Don't worry about *any* of this stuff, is what I'm trying to tell you. Nobody loves anyone in the exact same quantity and quality as that person loves them back. It's impossible."

"That's depressing," she says.

"Look at Vinnie, for example."

"What about my dad?" she asks. Her voice is slow and cautious.

"I think he was still in love with your mom."

She looks surprised. "Are you in love with my dad?" she asks.

I laugh. "No, Torrey."

"Well, is he in love with you?"

"No, Torrey."

"So you've never, like, kissed him?" she asks. Her cheeks are red.

"No, Torrey," I lie, and in a split second I realize I'm not lying at all. "I've never kissed your dad."

I reach for the remote. Gwen Ifill is on and I love Gwen Ifill. I turn it off. The silence hurts. There are too many spaces in the room.

"Torrey," I say. "You know, I have no fucking clue what you know about sex and reproduction. I actually am wishing I never started this conversation."

"Go on," she says in a fake bored tone.

"Well, the probability that you end up being *you* is so small, minuscule. One in billions. And that's just, like, that your DNA gets crafted a certain way. There are so many ways by which you either do or do not exist."

"Ugh."

She lies down on my couch. She puts her feet up with her shoes still on. I consider how Vinnie recently fucked me on that couch. I'm ready for the television to be back on again. It was only a minute ago when I realized that my happiness hinged upon this girl, and now I'm so tired of everything, so tired of having her in the house, so tired of her being happy, so tired of me being happy, so tired of me being unhappy.

"Rosamond and Harold might have been infertile. If my grandparents hadn't been married with a child, they likely wouldn't have moved from their apartment downtown into that house. And then Rosamond wouldn't have even met Harold."

Torrey closes her eyes.

"The only things we have going for us are our skin and our bones. Our ancestors, the shit we live in, the world—none of that is ours," I say. I feel incensed. "It's not something we can control and it's not something we'll ever benefit from. The only inheritance I have is me."

I close my eyes and lean back, propped halfway up on the bed. My head hits the wall behind me.

"Sheila?" she asks. The room is dark. The sun must have set. How long have we been sitting there?

"Hm?"

"If the only things we have going for us are our skin and our bones, what happens to us when we die?"

I pinch my eyes shut tight again, furrowing my brow and scrunching my nose. My eyes sting for a split second, but I squeeze them closed even more tightly. It passes.

"I don't know," I say. "I don't fucking care."

THIRTY-TWO

It's probably for the best that I'm alone when I finally realize I want to find Harold. I've read this letter three times already. This time, it gets to me.

It's dark and silent outside. There's no oceanic traffic coming and going in waves, no birdsong, no Vinnie, no Torrey, no pedestrians on cell phones or the clacking whir of skateboard wheels. Without looking at the clock, I know it's something like three in the morning.

I'm naked. I've been naked for hours. It's been hot for days, but I'm starting to shiver. My mind is racing and I can't get away from any of it.

In the bathroom, I scrape out a horrific clump of soap scum and filth-blonde hair from the bathtub drain, and then I fill the bath. I can't remember the last time I took vitamins, so that's probably why I'm losing so much hair. Am I even losing *so much* hair, or is it just that I haven't cleaned the drain in months? I think: I should go to the kitchen and take a multivitamin. I think of a girl online who takes dozens of pills a day for her autoimmune disorders. I bet one of them is a multivitamin. I bet she eats lots of leafy greens. This is a familiar pattern, the passing recognition of solutions but the unwillingness to go through with them. And maybe an accumulation of slimy hair in a drain isn't the problem at all. It's all symptoms. The problem is me.

I don't get up. I don't take a vitamin. I lie flat on the bathroom floor with my arms flailed out beside me while the tub fills. The way the water moves through the pipes shakes the whole floor. I feel it in my belly. The cold of the tile makes contact with my skin in so few places: my scalp, my shoulder blades, the top of the swell of my bottom, my elbows, the backs of my hands, my calves, my heels.

I turn my face and press my cheek to the tile, too. I feel the movement of the water in my teeth.

With my fingertips, I reach for a letter from the small stack by the sink and inch it toward me. I curl my body to the side, fetal.

I think about my mother.

I lived inside of her for forty weeks and three days. I didn't breathe except for the oxygen she gave me straight from her blood. She grew a new organ just to feed me. I learned to move while curled toward her guts. I grew fingernails and hair before I ever left her body. I pissed and shit meconium tucked up inside her. While still in the womb, my own ovaries filled with six, maybe seven million eggs of my own—six, maybe seven million possible children of mine, my cells dividing and regenerating to the thrum of my mother's heart. Everything about me was finished while we were still together.

And where are we now? Nothing ever happened to make us like this, nothing beyond the relentless drain of being us, surviving my father, surviving my teenage years, surviving, surviving, surviving. I miss her, and it's all wrapped up in the fear of even trying to be close to her again.

My dear, sweet Rosamond.

I must start with gratitude. Thank you, my darling Rosamond. Thank you for being in my life. Thank you for your visit. It was remarkable to sit across the table from you. Everything about today was remarkable. I felt blessed by a God I don't believe in. It was as if the sunshine coming through my kitchen window was a sacrament. The way it fell upon the exquisite skin of your cheek, it was as if you were on fire, an angel. Your beauty makes a zealot out of this hardened, unbelieving soul. I must laugh, however, to think of the horrifically decapitated doll that brought you into my life.

I could sit across from you and listen to you speak for days on end, watching the way your mouth moves, the way it forms vowels and the thing your lips, tongue, and teeth do together when you say "the." It's such a simple word, but my God if it is not my favorite word in all the languages of all men on this entire fragile Earth. I have never, ever had a friend like you, someone who can make me feel peace and happiness, but also get me thinking, get me talking, get me interested in the vastness of the world. My friends are dear to me, and I enjoy my time and cherish that we will always be incredibly loyal to each other, but I talk to none of them like I talk to you.

My sweet Rosamond, when can I see you again? Let us go to the park again next Tuesday. Still, as wonderful and electric as it is to encounter you in public, I crave privacy with you. I hope that does not sound untoward. I do not intend to. I just want to be free to speak with you. Please make time for me as soon as possible. Until then, write me. Write whenever you can. Write everything you can. Write me a hundred letters a day. I will read each a hundred times or more.

Sincerely,

Your Harold

There's a line in the Book of Common Prayer, 1979 (written decades after Harold and Rosamond shared their letters) that I will never forget, and if I hear any combination of these words, my memory fills in the rest: *At your command, all things came to be: the vast expanse of interstellar space, galaxies, suns, the planets in their courses, and this fragile earth, our island home.*

It's exactly everything I hate and love about religion. I absolutely do not believe that some sort of divinity sat there waving a finger. I always imagined a scene with a conductor's baton. There's a music stand, and God is standing at the podium, conducting. Would creation be in three-quarter time, a waltz?

But, "this fragile earth, our island home." I adore that. I imagine Earth on a little stem, like a volcanic island, a little broccoli planet. I imagine myself on a little stem. I am fragile. I am an island.

And that is the part that makes me want to find Harold. He says my grandmother made a zealot of him, but I know he's being hyperbolic. He wasn't a religious man in a time when almost everyone was. I want to crawl inside his head.

I fold up the letter and put it back in the pile. I'm shivering again. My hands feel disconnected from the rest of me. I touch my chest, letting each breast fill each hand, but I hardly feel a thing. I lift and push them until the skin scrunches up and wrinkles and I'm not young anymore. I climb in the water and it's not hot enough, it's never hot enough, but I feel the pressure as I lower all the way in, all the way under, eyes shut tight and water leaking into my ears. In this watery static, I marvel at the weight of the water, its solidity, its deadly comfort. My lungs begin to burn. Eyes open, mouth closed, cheeks puffed with the air I need to exchange. It's loud, the splash and the gasp as I emerge. Out of the open window, once-slumbering birds take flight from the trees, their wings a drumline in the quiet night.

I'm ready to find Harold.

THIRTY-THREE

"HONESTLY," I SAY. "IF that squirrel fell off of the telephone wire, I'd just leave it."

"Just leave it?" Torrey says. She's horrified. I'm sitting on my front step, and she's sitting on theirs. If we both stretched out our legs and our toes, they might touch.

"Yeah. I can just imagine its mangled body. I'd probably have to touch it or something to clean it up."

"God, you are so selfish," she says, plucking the green leaves off some tall, stalky weed. I don't know the name of it, but Vinnie would. Vinnie would know the name of it but still not pull it.

"I don't know," I say. "I mean, yes, I'm selfish, but I don't think that's what's at work here."

Torrey looks up at me. She squints with her whole face and blocks the sun with her hand.

"You know what?" she says. "You make me feel so much better sometimes."

"Yeah?"

"Yeah. Like, however weird I'm feeling, I know you're weirder."

"My point is, I think I'm helping along the social order," I say. "I'm stepping into certain roles and stepping out of certain other roles."

"Or copping out," she says.

"Well, take you, for example."

"What about me?"

"If a squirrel fell off a wire, you would absolutely race to it."

Torrey laughs.

"Yes, you would, you'd race through traffic if necessary. I say that with certainty. You'd even pick it up. You wouldn't give a shit about getting blood and squirrel guts on your shirt. You wouldn't even give a shit if it was almost in two pieces, held together by stringy squirrel tendons. You'd gladly contract rabies for its sake."

"You're gross."

"But I'm right," I say. "You see? I *can't* go near the squirrel. I need to make room for the people like you who don't know what they're capable of. Plus, I would rather it die than have to sift through tiny, freakish, furry squirrel guts."

Torrey doesn't say anything for a while. A car slows on the street, windows open, the bass in the speakers shaking all the nuts and bolts of the vehicle, more rattle than music. I watch Torrey as it dopplers away. She's looking out toward the street, beyond the bushes and the rusted gate, her eyes a bit darty. I wonder if she's looking for squirrels. I wonder if she knows I'm right, that she'd run to a wounded animal. A wounded anything.

"But, these letters," she says.

"Letters are cleaner than squirrels."

"Well, okay. But this little project dropped at your feet. And you have to pick it up and nurse it back to health."

I consider this.

"You're such an idealist," I say. "For one thing, I'm not nursing anything. This is dead. Nothing can be fixed, nothing stitched up. The only thing this will achieve is something selfish."

"Like what?" she says.

"My own, I don't know, flair for the dramatic?"

Torrey chokes on her laugh. "You, lady, do not have any fucking *flair for the dramatic*," she says, waving a finger at me, mimicking my tone.

"Torrey! Your language! Who taught you that?"

"You, obviously."

"Well," I say finally. "I don't know what I'm getting out of this. I just need to tie up these loose ends. I'm not saving any goddamn squirrels. I will stop this whole endeavor in its tracks if I get any furry guts on me."

And here's where I absolutely want to adopt Torrey as my own, when she says: "Such a loving and beautiful tribute to your late grandmother."

I look at Torrey and she tilts her head, smiling, but she keeps her eyes on the street.

"Don't you need to go to school soon?" I ask.

"Yeah. What are you doing up so early?"

I lift my shoulders. I don't tell her I'm still awake.

"Did you even sleep last night? I'm worried about you," she says. She laughs. "That sounds dumb."

It does sound dumb. It sounds preposterous. A girl, a kid, worrying about a thirty-five-year-old. I feel burdened by this, the fact that I burden her, but I feel powerless to change it. Not that I do not want to change it, but that I have no idea how. I don't know how not to burden a twelve-year-old girl.

"You don't need to worry about me, Torrey. I'm fine."

"Are you?" she asks. The school bus pulls up across the street.

"Yeah," I say. I don't even know if I'm lying. "Have a nice day at school, kid."

She's at the gate when I say, "And when you get home, let's go to Harold's old house."

Her smile could launch ships.

THIRTY-FOUR

I CURL UP ON my front step. Despite the morning chill, I drift off to sleep until the click of Vinnie's door startles me awake.

"Hey, you sleeping out here now?" he asks. He lights a cigarette.

"I'm tired," I say.

The courtyard and my lungs fill with his smoke. I try to surreptitiously take deep, swallowing breaths.

"Why'd you quit smoking?" he asks.

I laugh, a bitter noise. "Everyone quits smoking."

"I haven't."

"Why haven't *you* quit smoking, then?" I ask.

"I can't," he says with a grin. He takes a drag and leaves it between his lips a little too long. My mind swirls. I want nicotine and sex.

"I want nicotine and sex," I say.

"You're dangerous before breakfast," he says.

He fucks me outside, in the courtyard, at eight in the morning. I'm cold and nearly naked, but Vinnie keeps all his clothes on. It should feel like he's being overly controlling but I don't care. If passersby turn their heads at a precise point on the sidewalk and look between the rusted iron gate and the variety of bushes our landlord carves into giant bush balls twice a year, they'll see me pressed against the concrete steps, raking tiny scratches down the small of my back and my elbows, with Vinnie on top of me, Vinnie sucking at the skin beneath my collarbone, Vinnie sucking my breasts, Vinnie pulling out just to suck between my legs for a minute before going back in. I wonder if this is how it feels to be wanted and what it means to want, free from obsession. I'm quiet, the quietest I've ever been, but it's the best I've ever had.

Vinnie, coupled with the plan of driving to Harold's old house, makes me think of Jesse Ramirez. I'm just on the wrong side of finding this problematic, of finding this disturbing. I would love to just enjoy Vinnie, to just walk away from him and bask, but it's out of my hands. I can't handle going back to Jesse's house, so I drive to the church where I used to work. The place we met. The place he spoke to me. If only he'd never spoken to me, if only I'd never needed him to speak to me. Maybe then I'd be able to lie in a sunny spot on my front steps, warm inside and out, a little tired, a little happy.

St. Peter's Episcopal Church has changed a lot in the last few years. There's an entirely new building where the lawn used to be. It's massive. I think of all the old widows who struggled by on their fixed incomes and gave all their extra money to the church's capital campaign, to fund a building that hardly does anything. I know this because I've seen it all before. It's sparse and modern, whereas the original church and adjacent office are unassuming and brown, relics of the 1970s. I've actually never been to any of their services, even when I worked here. Everyone assumed I went somewhere else. I went nowhere. Since the morning of my confirmation, the morning I lost my father, the morning that something passed between my mother and I, the morning I was supposed to declare faith in a God I didn't ever know was real, I go nowhere. I don't know what I believe in, and with alarming clarity in that moment, as a child, I realized I never knew.

I sit in the parking lot. It's deserted. No signs of life, no other cars. Jesse used to show up for deliveries midmorning, so I have an hour to kill. I don't even know if he's still on this route. I wonder if they spent any of their capital campaign money on the tricked-out lock on the back door of the church. It's worth a try.

It's fussy, but I can tell the staff still uses this point of entry from time to time. It only takes me a minute to get it. Thankfully, none of that new money went toward a security system, either. The church smells like old carpet and older books. It never smelled like frankincense, warm and sharp, like the church of my youth did, and because of this I never saw this place as a real church.

It's almost dark inside. There are so few windows and they're all stained glass, so the light in the sanctuary is muffled and dim. The church is small, but I feel overwhelmed choosing a place to sit. The childish part of me wants to sit in the priest's chair. The childish part of me wants to try everything, the organ, the communion wine, the host. To sit on top of the altar. To turn on the sound system.

I laugh. The sound of my laugh does this strange thing in the small, stuffy church. It partly echoes, but mostly just disappears into the walls.

The real childish part of me is the part that's still afraid of doing the wrong thing, of making the wrong choice. The real childish part of me would never try out organs or sit atop an altar. That's me now. Maybe I just want to find the place to sit that makes me look the least guilty.

I decide on the back pew. I don't really know what made me want to come in here. I don't know what I'd hoped to achieve but this is all wrong. I feel the strange sinus headache first, then the bubble-like feeling at the top of my nose. And then the trickle. I suppress the normal human instinct to stop the bleeding. I think of the teacup full of blood on my nightstand. It was never really full—only half an inch max, diluted with mucous and old tea. The trickle touches my upper lip.

It's not exactly a decision. It's not a conscious effort. I'm just suddenly walking up to the altar with a nose full of blood. A drop lands on the old, dark carpet, lost within decades of stains. I know I won't get much out of this. It's not like I'm trying to stage an act of carnage. I don't know what I'm doing. I'm just *doing*.

The altar is covered with a crisp white tablecloth and a silver, gold, and green embroidered chalice burse and veil, the small, stiffened cloth covering the holy vessels. I'm eleven again and Reverend Jenny is amazed I can remember any of the terms for this stuff. I'm thirty-five and amazed I ever knew it at all. As I run my fingers down the ugly satin chalice veil, the next drop of blood lands on the bright white altar cloth. It spreads slowly, each drop expanding as it hits the altar, the stain growing larger and darker. I can't seem to move. It's ten o'clock in the morning. I hear a loud truck, a door, footsteps, a heavy cardboard box hitting the ground, footsteps, truck door, engine roar.

Jesse.

Sixty seconds later, the nosebleed stops. I stare at the bloodstain until my vision blurs and the entire altar cloth seems bloodied in my fuzzed peripheral vision, the entire church, everywhere. I breathe through my mouth, my nose clogged, and I close my eyes. I want to feel holy and I want to go home.

THIRTY-FIVE

Dear Rosamond,

These letters soothe my soul, whether it be writing them to you or reading yours. I have had a troublesome day. I did not sleep well, for one thing, on account of the shouts coming from your house. I heard your husband slam a door and come into your moonlit backyard, where he stayed for what seemed an hour. I held my breath as I sat in my bedroom, wondering if he could see right through me. I had to remind myself I have not done anything ungentlemanly. I am simply corresponding with my neighbor. My neighbor who is the delight of my life.

After a restless night, I reported for work quite early. Because I was home early, Artie and some of the fellows came over to have coffee and sandwiches, and I mentioned you. I mentioned you as my neighbor, a new friend. We spoke briefly on the matter, and I suppose I had been discreet about not mentioning that you were a woman, and certainly not a married woman with a small child underfoot. Then I mentioned you again, this time inadvertently by name. Oh, the teasing. At first, it was charming. I basked in the feeling of a gentleman discussing a new romantic interest. But then, as I myself realized the futility of the idea, it saddened me.

I read all of your letters after they left. I do not care about futility. I do not care about ungentlemanliness. I will take what you can give. I will give what you can take. I will have you just the way you are. Reading your letters makes me feel I can bear anything.

With exceptional and beautiful futility,
Your Harold

"This one is sweet," Torrey says. "I'm glad this is the one you picked to bring. I always love it when Harold mentions his friends."

"It's also one of the biggest downers," I said. "I feel like this is show and tell, like I'm in kindergarten again."

"Well, it kind of is," she says. "And you eat like a kindergartener."

"Shut up." I rip a sliver of sliced turkey right out of the resealable deli bag. "Want some? We need to eat it all or it'll spoil."

"We should go in," Torrey says.

"Not yet. I need to finish my turkey."

I chose this letter because, above all else, it makes me want to spend an afternoon in Harold's kitchen reading all of Rosamond's letters. It all comes down to one thing: Rosamond's letters.

"So…" Torrey says. "This is where it all happened."

"Yeah."

"It's smaller than I imagined."

"Well, he was a single, childless thirtysomething man in the fifties. I think this is the perfect sized house for someone like him."

"That's because your perspective is your own single, childless, thirtysomething shack."

"It's not a shack."

"It's a shack," she says.

"Then your place is almost as shacky."

"Our place is much nicer."

"I wouldn't know," I say. "I've never been inside."

"I think you're stalling," she says. "I think you don't even like sliced turkey. Let's go in, please?"

"Okay, but I'm doing the talking."

"Is that why you're wearing such a nice dress?" she asks.

I don't answer. There's no answer to that. I wore it today for so many reasons and none of them make any sense, not even to me.

"This was my grandmother's dress," I say, as if that's a reason. I think of my mother and half expect Torrey to clutch her chest and say *Oh, honey*. She doesn't.

"Let's go then," she says. "Let's not waste such a fancy old lady dress."

When a small, round old woman answers the door, I try to summon a pleasant face, at least a smile.

"Hi," I say. But I pause too long. The woman starts to rear her body back into the house. "I'm Sheila. My grandmother used to live in the house behind this one." She relaxes. "Mrs. Baker?" I offer.

"Yes! Oh, it was Roselyn, or Rose something, wasn't it?"

"Rosamond."

"Rosamond," she repeats. "She was a lovely lady."

"She just died," Torrey blurts out. "Oops, sorry."

"Oh, dear. I'm sorry to hear that. Is this your daughter?"

"No, this is my friend. My neighbor's daughter."

"She's kind of babysitting me," Torrey adds. I turn to her. She is fighting a smile, dimples blaring.

"Yes, I suppose I am," I say.

"Well, I'm sorry for your loss," the woman says.

"It's okay. That's not really why I'm here. I suppose it's related, though. Do you know anything about the previous owner of this house?"

"Are you on some sort of murder investigation show? Is this *CSI*?" she asks, and she looks behind us like she's checking for a camera crew.

"Oh, no, it's nothing like that. I just have reasons to believe that Rosamond and the previous owner of this house were friends." I choose my words carefully. "That they might have corresponded?"

"Oh, well, I don't know anything about that. I barely knew Rosamond."

"Did you ever meet the previous owner? Do you remember where he moved?" I ask.

"Come to think of it, I do. He moved to just a few houses down from my old house, where I lived with my parents before I was a bride. My husband Jim and I used to joke that we should have just swapped houses," she says. "So I suppose that's why it stuck in my mind."

"So…" Torrey says. I can tell she is trying so hard to play it cool. "Where?"

"Oh, not even a mile away. On Juniper."

I turn to Torrey. She is grinning a mile wide.

"You don't remember which house, do you?"

"I'm sorry, sweetheart, I never knew. Let me think of my old house number. You can go from there. Goodness, it's been over fifty years since I moved. My husband and I came straight here on our wedding night. He carried me over the threshold, like we all used to do. I was just barely in my twenties."

She looks distant. She looks sad. She's old, but not as old as my grandmother. I want to ask her if her husband is dead.

"You must have lived in that house with your parents for twenty years, then," Torrey prods. "Do you remember the number?"

"Yes, I did. It was just around the corner from the streetcar station. 3012 Juniper. That's the one."

It's hard to stand on her porch and continue the small talk. I just want to be back in the car. Torrey is practically bouncing and I'm loving this about her, she's almost infectious, but I'm overwhelmed by it at the same time. I suspect she wants to go straight to Juniper Street. I want to get home. I want to be alone. I want to deal with this another time.

Maybe I've been right all along. This should be Torrey's job. She's the caretaker. She's the one who dives into a problem and fixes it, guts and all.

THIRTY-SIX

"STOP TRYING TO GIVE me the silent treatment."

"What?" Torrey says, in that way teenagers do. She doesn't look up.

"You're pouting."

"I'm not *pouting*."

"I might be more than twice your age, but that doesn't mean I don't remember being twelve. I know about the pouting."

"I'm *not*," she says. If I squint when I look at her, she's five years old and stamping her feet.

"Sure. Well, I'm going to go inside and watch *Antiques Road-show*."

I wonder if I have to invite her to join me, or if it's unspoken. I wonder if this is okay, this official next step. All we've done together is read letters and sit in the courtyard. None of it has been social for social's sake. It's easy to talk myself out of this. She's twelve years old. She is not exactly my equal, though she may be intellectually superior to me, socially superior to me, basically superior in most of the ways someone can be. She's my neighbor's daughter, a grieving child. I'm fucking her father. She's not exactly an ideal friend. But it's been forever since I've had a comrade stick around as long as Torrey has, since someone overlooked my inability to be a good friend as well as Torrey has. The girls in high school, did they really stop bothering with me or did I stop looking at them and just never see it, never see that they were trying at all? That became my social coping mechanism: Assume the worst. Nobody wants you. It's easier that way.

"You can come over if you want," I say, finally. I feel triumphant.

"Yeah, okay," she says. "Maybe after dinner."

There's quiet. The moon is rising before the sun says goodbye. Another Children's Moon, and I never asked my mother why she called it that. I love the way it looks, the white of the moon almost see-through against the blue sky.

"What's *Antiques Roadshow*?" she asks.

I laugh. "Never mind. We can always just read your favorite letters," I say.

Except Torrey doesn't come over. I wait, though. I wait the whole night.

I sit outside the next morning from seven on. I don't remember what time the bus comes. I don't remember what time she comes outside.

Vinnie comes out at seven fifteen holding some sort of canine jawbone and a jar of fluid.

"Sheila, hi," he says.

"Where's Torrey?" I ask.

"Hi."

"Sorry, hi," I say. "But where's Torrey?"

"She's moving a bit slow this morning."

"What's with the skull?"

"I'm putting on some sealer. A little varnish, if you will."

I watch him apply the varnish with a small brush. He is incredibly meticulous. I desperately want him to get a much larger brush and just slosh it all on.

"How long does it take?" I ask.

"Does what take? Putting varnish on?"

"The whole shebang. Stuffing an entire animal."

"Well, Sheila," he says, not looking up from his jaw project, "it all depends on the animal. And let's not use the word 'stuffing.'"

Torrey comes out and sits down next to her father. She has a Pop-Tart. It's strawberry, with icing and sprinkles. I could identify it by the smell alone.

"And," Vinnie continues, "of course, it all depends on how much decay there is."

"How much decay?" I repeat.

"How dead it is," Torrey says, picking at her Pop-Tart. "You're up early."

"Yeah. Can't resist a little death in the early morning."

"I like to work early in the day," Vinnie says. "I don't eat while I work, so I like to get it over with."

"I suppose this is why it took me years to find out what you do for a living."

Torrey makes eye contact. She looks so old this morning, like she has so many more secrets than I ever gave her credit for. Maybe I should stop sleeping with Vinnie. I feel insecure in this moment, like Torrey intentionally chose not to come over to my house to hang out. But I catch it before it spirals any further. This is why I don't have friends. This is why I stopped having friends. This is why it's not worth it. Nobody is ever worth getting close to if I second guess myself all the time. Nobody is ever worth getting close to if the night before my Confirmation he'll just walk out of our house and never return.

And then it occurs to me: if Torrey walked right out of my life right now, never to return, I'd be crushed. I'm already in too deep. It's not like she is a normal friend. She's not a sister. She's not a daughter. She's something else—someone I don't have to care about, but I do.

And then another thing occurs to me. If *Vinnie* walked right out of my life right now, never to return, I'd be devastated.

"Fuck," I say to no one in particular.

My sweet Rosamond,

Yesterday afternoon, did you feel it, how close we were? I was sitting in the backyard, near the fence. I was complete-ly still, perched on the large wooden chair with my feet up and Ripper slumbering on my knees. I was close to dozing off myself. But then I heard Ellen's small voice over the fence. I haven't heard her speak much. I hear her plenty—squeals, cries, shouts, and the other clarions of early childhood—but I think this was the first time I heard much from her linguisti-cally. That small voice of a very small child is such a thing of wonder.

Have I told you about my siblings? I was the youngest for a long time, many older brothers and sisters, some of them well into their teenage years when I was born. I was raised with many mature minds and hands in the house. But then, when I was eight years old, my mother became pregnant. She gave birth to a very tiny girl, my new sister Delilah, the apple of my eye. Tragically, my mother passed away that day; the birth, her ninth, proved too traumatic for her. It was on that day that an eight–year-old boy became a mother.

Certainly, there were many people in that home to care for the child, but with the loss of my own mother, to whom I was very close, I channeled all of the love we had shared into that tiny baby. My older brothers and sisters, sometimes even my fa-ther, would often turn to me for the final say regarding Delilah. Your daughter reminds me a lot of her, from the brief bits and pieces I have seen. She speaks almost exactly like my Delilah did at that age, the same missing "r," the same trouble with double consonants.

When I was away at war, Delilah was married and moved up the state to San Francisco. I'm afraid I haven't seen much of her since. She is very happy in her new life. I suppose it's always easier on the baby bird. I don't know if she knows how important she is to me. She had a baby very young, and named him Harry after me.

But this is all inconsequential to what I wanted to write to you about, my dear Rosamond. Did you know? Did you know I was there, outside with you? Mere feet away? I sat there in my dreamy state, inches from sleep, when I heard your voice, your sweet voice singing to Ellen. My heart raced. I felt I was soaring. You sang "Oranges and Lemons," which my own mother always called "London Bells." It's such a silly and detailed song. I could never remember all the different church names and what the bells say. I was impressed with your memory as well as charmed by your editorial skills. "And here comes your mother to tickle your head" is so much sweeter and less sociopathic than "And here comes the chopper to chop off your head."

I have always wondered if I would ever have children. It didn't seem like the inevitability for me as it always seemed for others. Raising Delilah gave me a taste of unconditional, unfailing love and unconditional, unfailing worry. I am not entirely sure I could have a child of my own without being overwhelmed by the proper, grown-up versions of that love and that worry. And this is a strange and curious thought, a new layer: I cannot ever imagine having a child since I cannot have a child with you.

I'm not entirely sure this type of longing is welcome to you.
I'm not entirely sure this type of longing is welcome to me.
My sweet Rosamond, till we meet again.
Sincerely,
Your Harold

THIRTY-SEVEN

IT'S BEEN THREE DAYS since I met the woman who lives in Harold's old house. I wonder if one day she'd let me sit in the backyard, against the fence. I want to meet the family that lives in my grandmother's house, and at the same time I don't want to meet them. I just want to sneak past them while they sleep and sit in their backyard. I want to feel dirty and creepy. I want to feel insane.

Rosamond must have felt insane. Rosamond must have known Harold was there that day and every other day they were both in their adjacent backyards, breathing the same air. No dog could sleep soundly through a toddler's play. Ripper would have made tiny ruffs and growls in response to my mother's childish noises. Rosamond knew. Rosamond felt him there. Did she feel dirty and creepy? Did she return Harold's longing?

It's dawn. The low light spills into my single room, faint but thick. I don't remember another time in my life when I slept this little. I let the pages get out of order; it's his longest letter, many small sheets of tissue-thin writing paper. I've never before let them get out of order. I turn on my side and release the letter, allowing it to flutter to the ground, page by page. I'm wearing my grandmother's dress again and by now it's wrinkled and has some crusted dirt on the skirt. An onlooker would mistake this scene for devotion, for grief. I reach for my chipped teacup on the nightstand. I made this tea eight hours ago, after I watched NOVA, but I would still drink it. It's just water and leaves and honey. There's only a tiny bit left, strong and sweet and cold.

But my fingers, they are tired, my eyes, they are tired. The teacup is not quite where it looks like it is. I fumble and it falls to the ground, splashing and shattering. Tiny slivers of gold-rimmed china fly across the floor, under the bed, over the letter, the tea-soaked letter. I close my eyes; I squeeze them shut until my forehead hurts. I sleep.

Eight years old. Technically the same age I was two weeks prior when my father walked out on us for the first time, though I felt like I was a new person. I felt so much older. I felt like I'd had a hundred birthdays, a hundred cakes, a hundred party hats, a hundred things my dad hadn't been there for. My mother and I were doing the dishes after dinner: hot dogs, no buns, steamed broccoli, Rice-a-Roni. I was washing and she was drying and the water was running, a tinny whoosh against the stainless-steel kitchen sink, so we didn't hear the rattle and twist of the key in the lock. We didn't hear the click of the door opening, the muted creak of the rusted hinge, or even the click as it closed. I heard my mother first—her gasp, the way she dropped a cutting board onto the drying rack as she stared into the blackness of the kitchen window. Reflected, behind us, was my father, standing with his arms at his sides.

I spun around. I didn't know how to act. I was so happy to see him and so sad that he had been gone in the first place, but something else too. It was just brewing, bubbling beneath the surface, and it'd take me years to figure it out, but it was shame, more than anything. I felt like my emotions were wrong. I shouldn't be happy to see him because I was supposed to be mad that he'd left. I shouldn't be mad that he'd left because I was supposed to be happy to see him. I didn't know what to say to him. I didn't want to say something that would make him feel bad about leaving, although I wanted him to feel bad after all. I didn't want to say anything that would make him leave again. I wanted to look to my mother for help, but I was scared that I might see her crying and that might make me cry.

I was already crying, I just hadn't noticed it yet.

"Oh Sheila," my father said, taking a step closer, reaching, pulling me toward him. "Oh Sheila."

That night, when I brushed my teeth, I heard them whispering, the loud sort of whispering, so I tiptoed to the top of the stairs. They were in the living room and I couldn't see them. But I heard bits and pieces. "I don't care," said my mother, and "I'm sorry," over and over again from both of them, but not in the kind way, not in the really sorry way. It was the *I'm sorry but* way, the *I'm sorry you feel that way* way. The *I'm right* way. I heard my father say "I don't know" a lot. I heard my mother say "I don't care," followed by "I don't fucking care where you were," which made me cover my mouth with my hand, absolutely shocked.

And then they were quiet. I wondered if they remembered themselves. If they remembered me. I hurried back into the bathroom and flushed the toilet to make them think that's what I'd been doing, and then I remembered I still needed to pee before bed. What if they asked me why I flushed twice. What if they asked me what I was really doing. What if they asked me if I overheard. This was dumb, because they never asked me anything.

My father read me a few pages of *Matilda*, my favorite book, which felt awkward at times because Matilda had such a shitty home life with shitty parents and nobody wanted to mention how my father had just disappeared for two weeks. But it also felt good, because my dad was back. My dad was back and he wanted to read to me from my favorite book.

"It's almost nine o'clock," my father said, closing the book. We were only a few pages into it. We hadn't even met Miss Honey yet. Matilda didn't even know what she could do yet. All we had was the parent hate. "Time to go to sleep."

He left the room. For the next few years, until it finally happened, each time he left a room I'd wonder if that would be the time he left forever.

My mother tucked me into bed and sat there, silent, when my father came back in to kiss me goodnight. He looked at her, but she looked away. When he left, she lowered her head next to mine on my pillow, pale yellow with an eyelet ruffled edge, and stretched out next to me. "*Oranges and lemons, say the bells of St. Clement's,*" she sang. "*You owe me five farthings, say the bells of St. Martin's.*" She didn't sing the rest. I made my breathing quiet, which I now know is not how breathing sounds when someone is asleep, but at eight years old I wasn't yet well schooled in the art of faking. My mother was silent, but she wasn't asleep either. I wanted to tell her everything, but I didn't want to make her any more sad.

In one night, a happy reunion, a family stopped saying the important things to each other. A family stopped talking.

The next morning, my parents were both in the kitchen when I came downstairs.

"There's not enough milk left for cereal *and* for coffee," my mother said. "Can you have toast today?"

My father sipped his coffee, milky.

"I'll drop you off at school today, Sheila," he said. "But you have to hurry. It's late."

My mother handed me a slice of toast on a paper towel as my father ushered me out the door.

"You're getting crumbs everywhere," he said, halfway through the drive. "Can you not?"

And then, not even a minute later, seconds really, his voice soft: "It's okay," he said. "Hey, it's Friday. Let's have a movie night tonight, kiddo. Okay?"

"Okay," I mumbled, my mouth full of toast. I panicked, afraid to get in trouble for talking while eating, and pulled the wadded-up paper towel to my lips. A piece of crust I'd pulled off fell onto my lap, and then onto the floor. I heard my father sigh. I felt like a failure. I wished I'd had cereal. I wished I was tidier. I wished I was on the school bus instead. I wished he was still gone. I wished he was still sitting with me, on the edge of my bed, reading for hours, all the way up to the part where Matilda makes chalk float in thin air. I wished he'd never left so I would just be upset about the toast mess, that it wouldn't mean all these other things too. I wished he wasn't the kind of dad who had left and who might leave again.

It's not that we all stopped talking. It's just that we only said the things that didn't matter.

Torrey's been just as friendly as ever, but she seems to be giving me space. I overanalyze. I worry. I'm not even sure what I'm worried about.

"Sheila?" she says through the door. "Let me in."

I turn to my side. I don't know if it's morning or evening. The blinds are closed and the light is low but I can't tell which direction it comes from. My eyes are too crusty and blurry to focus. I'm very hungry and my bladder is uncomfortable. I wonder how long I've been lying there. I wonder how long it's been since I got out of bed. I don't want to move. I don't want to speak.

"Sheila?" she calls again. "Are you in there?"

Above all else, I don't want Torrey to suffer. I don't want her to worry.

"I'm here. It's open," I say. I really only lock my door when Vinnie is over.

The door clicks and creaks.

"Whoa, Sheila. What happened here?"

I realize I never cleaned up the spilled tea, the shattered teacup. I don't even feel like lying to her.

"I was sleepy and knocked the cup off the nightstand. I was too sleepy."

She stands in the open doorway for a while. It's cold out there. The breeze is too cold to be late afternoon, so I assume it's morning. I assume I did not sleep an entire day away.

"By the way," Torrey says. Her voice is curious and amused. "Your mom is outside."

I snap up. I swing my feet to the floor and stand up. A sliver of teacup wedges between my toes, sharp and stinging. The teacup. I remember now, how I knocked it to the floor last night while surrounded by letters, sleepy, out of it, and then left it there, shattered beneath my bed. I don't let myself think too much about how disastrous this must look to Torrey. The shard of china between my toes aches. I think of the medicinal properties of tea leaves, the medicinal properties of honey, and try not to panic.

"Outside?" I repeat, slowly, doubtfully.

"Yeah, she's talking to Vinnie."

I take a step and it presses the piece of teacup further between my toes.

"Shit," I say. Then I cover my mouth and switch to a whisper. "Shit shit shit."

Torrey closes the door and comes in.

"I'll help you."

She walks me to my tiny bathroom. I'm in there for barely a minute with a pair of tweezers before I realize.

"Torrey!" I whisper, running out to the main room before even finding a bandage, smudging bloodied footprints on the tile. She's cleaned up the entire tea mess and straightened out my bed. "We need to hide the letters."

"Done," she says, holding up the shoebox.

"Hide that, too!"

"Done," she says, as she drops it in her pink and white Jansport backpack.

"I want those back," I say. Maybe I'm being greedy, or maybe I'm just surviving.

"I'll leave them in my room," she says. "And you should probably change. You look a bit suicidal in a black dress first thing in the morning."

I change right in front of her. Torrey takes the dress and hangs it up, handing me some clean clothes, a grey dress—hardly an improvement, I want to say, but I feel helpless. Inside of that helplessness, I also feel failure. When did I become one more thing Torrey has to deal with? Now's a good time to thank her. Now's a good time to say I'm sorry.

I look at her, searching for something, some way of saying the right thing, but I can't do it. I can't say the things that matter. I must just look stunned, half asleep. I must look like someone who needs her to come in and clean up my messes, to dress my wounds. My shoulders sink a little.

"Okay, I think we're done," she says. She smiles at me and furrows her brow and I feel like maybe she doesn't mind this, that I can trust her with this, with my mess.

"Okay," I say. Okay. "Shit."

I follow her to the doorway and out into the courtyard.

"Hi, honey," my mom says.

There's a part of me that thinks maybe we could just do this out in the courtyard. Surely any conversation will be easier with Vinnie and Torrey there, too. They'd rescue me. We could just talk about them the whole time. But they get up, gathering their stuff, Vinnie his phone, Torrey a small bottle of black nail polish. Vinnie lifts his chin up in the air, a brief nod that makes me want to mock him, before they both disappear into his house.

"Come on in, Mom," I say.

As soon as I watch my mother sit down on the small couch, I see it, beneath the bed. The letter. The one I read last night. The long one. The one stained and wrinkled with old tea, and how did I not notice it last night or this morning? It's too far under the bed. Torrey must have missed it. It's *stained and wrinkled*. The *tea*. Oh God. It's ruined. I forget myself for a moment and squat down next to it. Some of the writing has smudged and run beyond recognition.

"Fuck," I say. "Hold on."

And while my mother watches, I grab my journal and skip past the first thirty pages where, over and over again, I've copied my favorite lines from Jesse Ramirez's unsent letter. Then I begin to copy the entire long letter from Harold, filling in the smudged blanks as best I can from memory.

She's quiet.

"Sorry," I say, five minutes later, the letter safely rewritten in my journal. "I spilled some tea."

It's a showdown, a total showdown. I stare at my mother and she stares at me. Either we're both too daring, willing the other person to risk speaking up first, or maybe neither of us has the courage to say anything at all. Maybe neither of us wants a showdown at all. Maybe we both just want it all to go away. Maybe we both just want to be friends. The saddest part is that I can't imagine it.

"Speaking of tea," I say. "Want some? I'm making some."

"No," my mother says. "No thanks. I just had coffee."

"I'm also going to scramble some eggs. Want any?"

"No thanks," she says.

"What did you come here for?" I ask.

In a way, the idea that a letter from Harold would be right out in the open between us, under our noses, excites me. It's not like she can assume anything. She probably assumes I saved one letter for myself. She probably assumes I wasn't lying about burying the shoebox with my grandmother, because who the fuck would lie about something like that?

She probably assumes that asking me about the letter would be awkward. She probably assumes I would blow up at her. Or maybe I'd just make her feel like shit. I cannot deny that these things would happen. I cannot deny that my mother is possibly afraid of me.

"Just to say hi," she says. She glances to the right. To my bed. She's checking for more letters.

I crack an egg. The cast iron is hot. There's a rush of crackling and splattering and the white cooks instantly. I decide against scrambled eggs.

"I need to get going into work soon," I say. I don't have a job. "I need a shower."

"Oh, gosh, sorry, sweetie. I didn't realize you worked on Saturdays!"

Oh.

This could go one of two ways:

One:	Two:
"I don't work on Saturdays, usually. I'm just a little behind and need to catch up."	"Well, you know. Retail."

She pauses. "What's going on? Why are you behind?"

I want to scream. Seriously?

"Well," I say. "The workload is intense."

"You'll have to learn to handle that stuff," she says. Her voice is overly kind, like she's trying not to be aggressive. "It's how business works."

Unbelievable, I want to say. But then I realize exactly how believable it is.

"Oh, goodness! How did I not know you're working retail?"

"I don't know," I say.

"Well, where are you working? When's your shift? Can I come by and see you? Wouldn't that be lovely, to come visit you at work!"

"Well, I'm kind of behind the scenes," I hedge.

She pauses. "Well, where?"

I scan the house, the kitchen, my teakettle. No inspiration. None.

Vinnie coughs.

"The pharmacy. At the drug store."

"Wow! A pharmacy!"

"Well, I just do paperwork in the back." She looks too proud and it annoys me.

"And janitorial stuff," I add. Just because she looked proud.

"I still don't understand why you left that perfectly good job at the Spike family's church. It's a far sight better than janitorial work on a Saturday."

Unbelievable, I want to say.

"Well, I suppose I'd better get ready," I say.

"Sure," she says. "It was good to meet your neighbors, finally. They seem nice."

Yeah. They do. They are.

THIRTY-EIGHT

MY MOTHER WALKS THROUGH the courtyard. Now's the time, I'm aware of this, to try to reconcile whatever has gone wrong between us. Now's the time to make things a little better between us. A little more vulnerable, a little more uncertain, but a little better. Now's the time to *not* widen the gap, the gap that came out of nowhere, a nearly untraceable gap, a nearly blameless gap. She's at the gate. And she's through it. And she's down the steps. And she's at her car.

"Mom?" I shout.

She pauses, her key fob in hand, her arm outstretched.

"Maybe I could come by tomorrow instead. That'd work better."

"Okay, honey," she says. She looks relieved, which makes me wonder what she thought I might say when I called for her from across the courtyard. "That sounds fine. Just come whenever. I'll be home all morning."

She drives away and by the time I'm back in the courtyard, Vinnie and Torrey are somehow already back outside the house, relaxing like nothing has happened. Torrey is painting her toenails and I wonder if they heard me lie about my job.

Vinnie goes inside and opens his fridge. I can hear the flump of the sealed rubber strips pulling away from each other. I can hear him slide a glass jar off to one side of the tempered glass shelf. Glass on glass, much lower in pitch than I'd imagine. I hear the soft pop of the jar lid. Maybe he's opening pickles. Maybe he's opening strawberry jam. Maybe it's kombucha and I'll never understand this man. But either way, I can hear a jar open from well inside their house, so I know, with certainty, that Vinnie and Torrey heard me lying about my job.

> *My darling, my Rosamond,*
>
> *I never imagined that you would reply to my last letter in such a way. I never imagined it in a thousand years. Or not even an entire year, which often surprises me, that just one year is all I have known you. It almost feels as if I knew you before I knew myself. It almost feels as if all of the things that happened to me before I met you, before Ripper lived up to his namesake and ripped a certain head off a certain doll—it's as if all of those things happened to someone else. I didn't hear my father wail upstairs when my mother finally stopped breathing in childbirth. I didn't see the horrors of the war. I didn't kill a man. I didn't kill more than one man. I didn't spend a night in the trenches, freezing, motionless, full of agony and misery, waiting for dawn. I didn't spend many nights like that. I feel new. I am not naïve enough to think this happens to everyone who meets a new friend. I am not naïve enough to think of you as just a friend. I am not naïve enough to think that we are commonplace neighbors.*
>
> *I know that this is special. We must guard it close to our hearts for many reasons. First, I do not particularly want to share you. And second, I fear for you. I understand how tumultuous your life would become if your husband knew of our growing friendship.*

Meet me in the park this afternoon, please. Rather, walk
past me. I will smile at you, and I will delight in your smile.
      Sincerely,
      Your Harold

Technically, I'm a better person than Harold. I haven't wished to
break up anyone's marriage. Technically, I'm standing on more solid
karmic footing. That doesn't stop his letters from making me feel like
a degenerate in comparison. He may be an adulterer, or at least a
hopeful adulterer, but he is so pure in heart. He isn't the one hanging
by the thread.

I imagine being Rosamond. I imagine being the same mess I am
now, but all vintage, nineteen fifties style. I imagine hanging by a
thread, fifties style.

I don't have a Harold. Jesse Ramirez is a scam. He doesn't even
know me; he just knew my dress once, for thirty seconds. Not knowing who Jesse is, or who the letter was for, is comforting. The mystery,
the fantasy. Having an answer would devastate me.

At the worst of it, the thick of my obsession with Jesse, I stopped
answering my mother and grandmother's calls for two weeks. My
mother drove by my house repeatedly, panicking at the constant lack
of my car out front. My car was parked outside Jesse's house. My
phone was off.

"I told your grandma that you had mono," my mother said,
when it was over, when I went home, when I snapped out of whatever I had snapped into, sitting in her living room with my eyes fixed
on the coffee table. "So she wouldn't know you just disappeared."

She wrote me a check. "Early birthday money," she said. Neither
of us wanted to admit it wasn't birthday money.

I used every cell in my body to thank her, to stop thinking about
the loss of something that was never mine.

"Thanks, Mom," I said.

"I wish you'd tell me what's wrong" is how she said goodbye to me that day.

Even now, somewhere in the dark places of my mind, the cold places, Jesse is steadfast and committed to *me*. Somewhere in those sick and sinister reaches, he has been steadfast and committed to me all along. He met me once. He wrote me a letter—surely he was thinking of me. He dropped it for me to find. And the rest of me? The rest of me is still sickened by longing and hope.

In the bathroom, I notice that there's only one thing in the laundry basket, a pair of my dirty underwear. One inanimate thing, that is. Hundreds of ants swarm from an invisible crack in the baseboard, into the basket, directly to the panties, directly to the crotch, and then they turn around and head back. They are feasting on the remnants of vaginal lubrication in my underwear. It's the first time they've ever come inside the house. I don't know whether I should throw the underwear out or what, but I toss the whole plastic laundry basket in the bathtub and turn the water on. The swarm turns into tiny black curled specs, floating in a sporadic layer on the surface of the water. Some of them struggle. Some of them are trapped in the lace edges of the underwear. I leave the drain open and the water running.

I wonder if an ant colony could survive only on my dirty underwear. I wonder if it could survive only on the crust of my cells.

I turn off the water, hoping that everyone is drowned and dead by now, but I just leave it all in the bathtub. It's time to get this out of the way. It's time to take Jesse out for a test drive.

THIRTY-NINE

Parked outside of his house, I read the Jesse letter again. It's so startlingly similar to Harold's letters. His longing, his sensitivity, but above all, his broken-heartedness. The penmanship and the language is far too modern for it to be some sort of mysterious missing piece of Harold's correspondence. But whomever this letter was meant for was victorious over my grandmother. This woman seemed to have a chance to say goodbye. Because he opened, he started with, "*By now you must be gone.*" She was the one who left. *She* left *him*. Poor Rosamond never had that luxury. Poor Rosamond never said goodbye.

As far as I know.

I take a deep breath. The dress is wrinkled and does not smell very fresh. I try to smooth my hands over it.

I have one memory of my grandmother wearing it. I'm very small, maybe six years old. My mother drives to pick Grandma up for Thanksgiving or Christmas, and Rosamond stands in the middle of the living room in a floral bathrobe, smoothing the iron over the fabric. "Just one more pass, sweet girl," she says to me. My mother waits in the car. Or maybe I'm wrong and she wears this dress every time she dresses up, all those memories stitched into it. Rosamond disappears into the bathroom and emerges with the dress on, red lipstick painted tidily across her aged lips, lips that I can never remember smiling, and her fragrance follows: rose oil, sandalwood, something orange.

My grandmother never kept anything around for long, especially after my grandfather died. She constantly purged her clothing, the objects in her life. Except, I realize now, for these letters.

I have only her dress and her letters, but I'll never forget the way she smelled. I wish I had that perfume. I wish I had something that beautiful.

I fold the letter and hold it close to my heart as I walk up the steps to Jesse Ramirez's house. It's a shame I have to do this. It's a shame I had to follow him for so long. I am shameful, this is shameful, he is shameful. No, I alone am shameful. I know this and I do not stop.

I knock. He answers.

"Hi…" he says. I don't wait for him to guess.

"I'm Sheila. I have your letter."

"Letter?"

"You dropped it. Here," I say, offering the folded pages.

He doesn't take his eyes from mine as he takes the letter, and even unfolds it from its perfect trifold before he glances down at the paper. He gasps. It's a scared gasp, it's fear.

"What the fuck is this?" He's angry, he's confused.

I close my eyes. I can be somewhere else if I close my eyes. I'm the one he wants. I'm the one he can't have. I'm the one who left him. Keep your eyes closed. Keep them closed and it might come true.

"What the fuck is this," he says again. "This is three fucking years old! Three years old!" I hear the pages shuffling over and over again, but there are only three of them and I wonder if he knows that stain on the first page is my blood. I have all three pages memorized.

"Stop it!" he shouts. "Stop that," he says again, and his voice is low and disturbed and I realize I'm reading the letter out loud, verbatim, from memory, a whisper, a ghost, with my eyes closed. I am halfway through the first page. It's wild, this combination of Jesse's presence and the deeply internal forces that bring these words to my lips. I am beyond my own control. I don't stop.

"*I could be in a room of a thousand people…*"

"Stop it," he says. "Now."

"*…I could be the loneliest soul on the planet.*"

"You are a fucking psycho," he says.

"*…I wouldn't have you.*"

"Don't ever come here again. Don't ever call me. Don't even think about me again," he says. He slams the door hard, the air lifting my hair and my skirt.

"I'm sorry," I say to the closed door. "I'm sorry I kept it for so long."

I wish I could cry. I don't know if Jesse Ramirez is an asshole or if I'm just out of my mind. That's really all I wanted to know, I realize.

"I'm sorry," I say again, a little louder. "I'm so sorry."

I walk away slowly, down the front steps. They're red, but must have been painted years ago. Now they're a chipped pink. I hear the door unlatch and open a little, but no other movement. Jesse is watching me from the front door.

"I'm sorry," I whisper without turning around. I didn't even realize how much I wanted to tell him about Harold and Rosamond until the opportunity had already passed.

"I could be the loneliest soul on the planet," I say. "The loneliest."

FORTY

THE SKY IS NOT yet fully dark, but the stars are already out. They're so bright tonight; they seem closer than usual. On my concrete front step, I lean my head back against the closed screen door, and I slowly lift my hand, wrist first, my fingers dangling. I feel like a ballerina, feline, as I straighten out a fingertip. I touch each one, each distant star. There's hope, I realize. On this planet I'm alone. On this planet I'm disconnected, I can't make sense of anything. Maybe the stars have my answers. Maybe the stars will help, an anchor at my fingertips and unfathomably far away.

"Connecting the dots?" Vinnie says as he sits down in his faded green plastic chair.

I close my eyes and lower my hand. "Something like that," I say.

"They're old news."

"Hm?"

"The stars," he says, lighting a cigarette. "They're no good to us. Billions of years old and trillions of miles away."

"I'm not even looking at the sky, then," I say. "I'm looking at the past."

"Tell me about the letters," he says. Casually. No big deal.

"What about the letters?"

I assume he has to know something. Sound carries. He's heard Torrey and I talk and even read the letters together. He has talked to Torrey about them.

"They're your grandmother's?"

"Yeah. Well, not her writing. Letters written to her."

"That's lovely," he says, like it's the first time he's ever said the word lovely.

I imagine a Vinnie years ago, a happy, amazed man with his new bride. I imagine him finding her lovely. I imagine him the day she tells him she's pregnant. I imagine him the day Torrey is born, all pink and wrinkly and shuddering lungs. Lovely. He'd find it all lovely. Would he cry? Would he cry the first time he laid eyes upon his baby girl, his only child, the only thing he has left? Did he cry?

"It's heartbreaking."

"I don't need to read them or anything," he says. "Don't worry. It's just, this old man is feeling left out. I was starting to get a bit of a complex."

"You're not very old."

"Figure of speech. But if you ever need any help with anything, let me know."

"Thanks, Vinnie."

I watch him as he smokes. He has a nice mouth and a nice jaw. He is a good man. I think about how I judged him. I thought he was the lowlife. But here he is, a good man. A good father. A hard worker.

It's me. I'm the lowlife.

"I need a job," I say. "I think I'm going to go check with the temp agency tomorrow."

"Oh yeah?" he says. He's smiling and I hate not knowing why.

I go inside and make some tea and toast. I consider vegetables. There's a carrot in the fridge, so I slice it into little sticks, and then halfway through, think better of it and make circles instead. My mother used to call them carrot coins. I wonder if she noticed that I didn't visit her today.

"Hey, Vinnie," I call out through the screen. "You want some tea?"

It seems dangerous, more dangerous than sleeping together. We coexist in this space without sharing much except the courtyard. I regret asking. I don't even know where the fuck that came from. I eagerly dread his reply.

"Sure, Sheila," he says. "I like tea."

I bring some teacups out, and a kettle and tea bags. My grandmother would use a teapot but it seems so unnecessary these days. I only have three teacups left. They're old china, nothing heirloom, nothing inherited. I bought them at a thrift shop when I was twenty and I've carried them with me for a decade and a half. I wonder if anyone else carried them for that long. Maybe someone held onto them for half a century. The broken one, my favorite, had a small crack in the handle and a chip in the edge, through the gold rim and into the china. I loved the rough of it against my lips.

"Look at you, all fancy," Vinnie says.

"Where's Torrey?" I ask. Is that all I ever ask Vinnie these days?

"She's inside, studying or something, listening to something terrible. I made her put headphones on."

"Every generation thinks the next one's music is terrible."

"That's an overgeneralization," he says. "I like some of what she listens to."

"Music makes me insane."

"You're already insane," he says.

"I mean, it makes it worse. It makes it all worse," I say. Why have I never had someone listen to me in my whole life the way that Vinnie and Torrey listen to me? "Sometimes I can't listen to it without feeling like I'm drowning. I guess everything just feels...stronger."

"So that's not entirely a bad thing?" he prompts.

"It is, entirely."

"Even when you feel the good stuff more strongly?"

I turn my head and look away. It's dark now, the crescent moon is rising, the clouds, the marine layer have all moved in and I can't see the stars anymore. I feel very young and very old at the same time, in the same body, in the same heart.

There's never any good stuff.

My dear Rosamond,

Oh, that knock on my door this morning. It is always a joy to see you or correspond with you, but to see you unexpectedly was such a pleasure. I failed to ask why I deserved such a visit. I failed to inquire as to how you orchestrated it. There was too much on my mind.

In the mornings, you are quiet and peaceful. There is much that I could feel about that, much that I could say about that, but I do not desire to let myself get started now. Mostly: I hope your husband understands how lucky he is. Does he recognize your peace? Does he feel grateful? If only there were some way to pat him on the back, to shake his shoulders, to ask him, "Do you know how lucky you are, my fellow?"

I find myself disturbed at my own thoughts. Would I like that? That he would suddenly realize how lucky he is, and step up as a partner and lover? Where would that leave me, the neighbor? What do I truly want? Do I want you all to myself, or as much to myself as I can get you? Do I simply want to make you happy? Or is that still too selfish? Shouldn't I just want you to be happy, however you get there?

The human being is, at its core, a selfish creature. I cannot deny my own desires and my own selfishness. But human beings are also granted compassion and empathy. And above all else, above my animalistic selfishness, I want the best for you. You are more important to me than my own needs. If your husband were to suddenly delight you, so much so that you no longer had any need for correspondence with your lonely neighbor, then my primary emotion would have to be happiness. I would be so happy that your life were richer.

But until then, I am here.

Sincerely,

Your Harold.

FORTY-ONE

The Ziploc bag is empty. The nightstand is empty. Just the bag, the empty shell. It's see-through, and it's not even zipped shut. It's regret, in a way, what I'm feeling. I wish I still had Jesse's letter. Jesse was a jerk, but I have to believe anybody would be a jerk to someone like me.

I take a deep, loud breath, in and out, through my nose. It's been three days since I last used my phone, and it takes me all morning to find it. It's dead. I consider leaving it dead. I consider that there might be messages waiting for me. From whom, I don't know. My mother was just here the other day, so it turns out we have the kind of mother-daughter relationship that includes stopping by unexpectedly. The temp agency stopped contacting me. It's my turn. And my father wouldn't call. My father doesn't even know my phone number. My father is nowhere.

When my phone is charged enough to turn on, I stare at it. Nothing happens. No notifications. No messages. I am nowhere.

"Hi, yeah, sure. My personnel number? Hang on, let me look," I say as I shoulder my phone and shuffle through the filing cabinet. I read it off, this number I used to have memorized, like my social or my passwords.

"Sheila?"

"That's me."

"You're interested in a placement?"

"Yes, anything really."

"Okay, well, we have a bit of a waitlist right now for general staffing, but something should come up in the next few hours."

"Hours?"

"Yes, we should have something for you by tomorrow at the latest. You have a pretty diverse history."

"Okay, well, thanks," I say. "I just wait for a call? Or do I, like, get ready for work tomorrow?"

I can hear a smile in her voice. Either a smile or total face-paralyzing apathy. "Yes, go ahead and get ready for work tomorrow. Whatever you need to do."

"Whoa. What are you doing?"

"I'm going to work, Torrey."

"Whoa," she says again. "I always thought you were, like, independently wealthy or something, and you didn't work because you didn't need to."

"If you were independently wealthy, would you live in my house?"

"Probably not," she says. "So, how long have you had a job and never mentioned it?"

"This is my first day. It's just a temp job."

"Oh, so you actually haven't been working."

"No. Well, off and on. I like to keep things off and on," I say.

"So, what are you going to do?"

"I don't even know. It's a bank. I hate bank jobs."

"Does this mean I won't see you much?" she asks.

"Nah, I'll be home by four," I say. I want to make some sort of joke about the fact that I just told someone what time I'd be home but I'm afraid to trigger some sort of mom grief. Torrey does it herself.

"Just in time to make me some milk and cookies."

I step through the bank's glass doors without taking a second to steel myself. I know, steeled or not, that this day will be insufferable. I know, steeled or not, that I will not last here. I know, steeled or not, that this time I'm going to try anyway.

"How was it?" Vinnie asks. It's midnight. Torrey's asleep. A dense marine layer lies over much of the city. A dense marine layer lies in our courtyard. A dense marine layer lies between Vinnie and me.

"Fine," I say. It's not exactly the truth but it's exactly as much truth as I feel like getting into. If I'm not fine when nothing terrible is happening, then how can I ever hope for anything beyond fine?

Vinnie kicks back onto two legs of his green plastic chair. They bend a little. It's barely noticeable, but they bend. I expect him to be smoking but he isn't.

"I can never read you," he says.

"I'm not for reading."

"Are you lying?"

"About what?" I ask. It's almost funny enough to crack a smile, toying with him. Except he doesn't seem to be toying.

"About being fine."

"I'm not fine," I say. Now I smile. "I never claimed to be fine."

"About work," he says.

Goddamn, his patience is annoying.

"Goddamn, your patience is annoying," I say.

"Thanks. Your annoyingness is annoying," he says.

"That was brilliant. What happened to irritated, impatient, angry Vinnie on Skype calls to your ex and Torrey across the country?"

"I'm not making those calls anymore," he says, and I'd feel like a jerk, but he sounds mellow. "How was work?"

I look up. There's no sky to see. I can barely see Vinnie.

"It was terrible," I answer eventually.

"Tomorrow is another day," he says.

The next morning, I don't go to work. By eleven, I feel so guilty that I go in anyway, and by eleven thirty I completely regret this. I'd have been better off blacklisted by the staffing agency than subjected to half a day of this negative cubicle energy.

At first, I feel triumphant. I somehow managed to craft myself as a martyr on day two.

"Are you feeling better, Shelly?" my new boss asks. She wears a lot of makeup and a lot of tight pants.

"Sheila. And, yeah, I'm feeling a little better. I didn't want to miss my entire second day at work," I say.

"Well, that's really good of you. It shows tremendous dedication," she says.

And here it is. Farewell, triumph. Welcome, shit.

"But we are an official Healthy People, Healthy Workplace site. We take illnesses very seriously as to how they affect our bottom line," she says. "One employee out sick has little to no impact on productivity. But a dozen employees out sick over a small period of time, well, that has a great impact on productivity."

"Oh, okay," I say. "I'm sorry."

"As long as you're feeling better?" she says.

I nod.

She walks off, but then returns to the shared temp cubicle and leans in.

"Now, I understand that your staffing agency does not guarantee sick pay. Or that perhaps you do not have health insurance?"

I fight the urge to roll my eyes. This close, it looks like she might paint in the mole on her cheek. It is a perfectly symmetrical circle, a shade of brown too dark and with edges too sharp to be natural.

I nod again. I'm not even sure what she's getting at.

"Well, I understand you're in a pickle. If you wish, you may go home early without any consequence. We'll mark you as having worked a full day. We take workplace health and the illness-to-productivity quotient very seriously here."

I'm home by one forty-five.

FORTY-TWO

I SKIP AHEAD IN the letters. I need some bad news. I need something to make me feel better about my shitty day, not something to make it seem like everyone else is having wonderful lives around me and before me and after me.

> *My dearest Rosamond,*
>
> *Today has been torturous. Saturdays are usually lazy days in the garden for me, but all morning I haven't been able to sneak a letter through your fence due to your husband's presence in your backyard. Even through my open windows (it was too hot, I couldn't keep them closed) could I hear the laughter of your little family, the three of you at play. As you should. It is your right as a family. I spent the morning with only the company of my own thoughts. Thinking about the new reality of our friendship. Thinking about the things I have somehow implicitly agreed to accept. About the things I never, ever imagined in a million years that I would concern myself with. Inconsequential things, like the life of a child, the life of a mother, the logistical differences between your life and mine. And things not so inconsequential. Incredibly consequential things like infidelity, like marriage vows, like the anger of a scorned man, like the broken*

heart of a child in a broken home.

Do not be mistaken. I came to no conclusions. I have no new wisdom on any of this.

You were so busy today, so occupied with your life. I considered the difference between you and me. You, happy, delighting in your perfect family. And me, sitting alone, festering in the shadow of this joyous morning across the fence.

There's a knock.

"Sheila?" It's Torrey.

"Come in."

"Oh, hey. I just got home from school. You okay?"

"Yeah, I came home sick."

"Reading letters?" she says.

"Yeah." I try not to laugh. I wonder: what if I told her I was actually sick. What if I told her to leave? I expect to like the idea, to revel in being alone, but I don't. I hate the idea.

She stands awkwardly in the doorframe.

"It's the one where he heard Rosamond's family playing in the backyard."

"Oh, shit. That one," she says, puffing out a breath.

"Yeah."

"I'm glad your mom never read these, especially that one."

"I'm still not convinced she hasn't."

"But to be your mom and know he was, like, totally tormented by your toddler happiness? That's gotta suck."

"Yup. Gotta suck," I repeat, smiling. "It's a good thing these are buried six feet down."

She sits down on the edge of my bed. "Read it to me."

"From the beginning?"

"No, from wherever you left off. I remember them pretty well."

The hardest part, I admit, was hearing him exchange words of endearment with you.

"Oh!" Torrey interrupts. "So he's already said the thing where he's afraid of the anger of the scorned husband?"

"Yes," I say.

"I love that part. It's so creepy. Kinda ominous. Okay, carry on."

When he mumbled anything, I imagined him putting his arm around your shoulders. Perhaps even a full embrace. Did you kiss? On second thought, you shouldn't answer that. Judging by my disposition this evening, I believe there are some things best left a mystery.

I do not feel any differently about our friendship. I have not changed my mind in any way. My day of tormented thinking has not solved any puzzles.

"Ooh," Torrey says. "I like this part. This next part is the thing about honesty, right? Such a glorious train of thought."

"Jeez, Torrey," I say. "Do you have these memorized? Why am I even reading this out loud?"

"I read everything more than once. Even things I know like the back of my hand."

"I'd blame it on your lack of social life since moving here, but I also have no social life. And I do not have your fervent reading skills."

"I have a social life!" she says. "Well. It's getting there?"

"Oh, that's good news," I say. "I'm happy for you. Want to tell me about your friends?"

I feel like such a douche, carefully spooning out these lines, like I'm reading some teleprompter on How to Talk to Kids About Their Friends.

"Can't we get back to Harold?" she says. "He's about to be really awesome."

"Awesomely hypocritical."

"I disagree. Well, on the surface. It's hypocritical to be in any sort of affair and then be all high and mighty about honesty."

"The end."

"What?"

"I mean," I say, "you've said enough. You can't rationalize it after you say that."

"Hear me out," she says. "It's no secret that I think Harold and Rosamond have something beautiful."

"Had," I correct.

"God, you're such a downer. Yes. Well, I think they are against the odds. They're the underdog. Think of them that way. The affair is a circumstance they can't control."

"Torrey, for a kid, you're awfully forgiving of grown-ups making bad choices."

"I'm hardly a kid. I'll be a teenager very soon."

"Let's just let Harold rant, hm?"

"Yes, fine," she says. "I still love him."

I smile. "You're a sucker."

"You love him too," she says. "Don't even try to deny it."

But I wanted to tell you about my strife, my torment, my torture. In a way, I think I need full and complete honesty with you. I'm not certain if that is some terrible way of alleviating the guilt of our one true dishonesty, or my own attempts at balancing it out. But I need it nonetheless. I simply have to tell you what I'm going through. What I suffer through when I'm apart from you. What I feel when I see you with your family. I hope you do not think I am telling you all of this to achieve some

underhanded goal. I did not write this to make you feel guilty
for your happiness, for your life that is separate from me. I want
you to be happy, however you may come about it. But you are all
I have to talk to about my torment. You alone are my torment
and it must forever go unshared, unaired, except with you. And
please, do pander to my need for honesty between us. I feel so
dishonest in all other ways. The least we can do is be honest with
each other. I believe it might be the one thing I have to cling to.
    Missing you terrifically,
    Your Harold

"I love it when he customizes his greetings," I say.

"Yeah."

It takes a minute before I realize why I chose this letter to read. The bad mood, the terrible work day, the shitty boss. I wanted to feel better about myself with a reminder that other people had shitty lives too. But instead, my shitty life was completely forgotten.

"Hey, Sheila," Torrey says. "Let me see it." She scans the first page. "I've been thinking," she says.

"About?"

"You know how you once mentioned that their affair is uncon-summated?"

I panic. *Don't ask about sex. Don't ask about sex.* "Yes?"

"Well, I think you're wrong," she says. "I think they kissed or something."

"What?"

"That's what it means, right?"

Shit. "Uh, basically," I say. "I'd definitely consider kissing to be taking the affair to the next level."

She nods and I'm incredibly grateful that she seems satisfied with that answer. Torrey is not naïve. I assume she already knows at least a little bit about sex. I just do not want to discuss it with her.

"Well, I've thought this before," she says. "That they, like, did stuff, but later on in the stack of letters. I think a year or two from this point? But this part, about the 'new reality' of their friendship, the 'one true dishonesty'? That makes me wonder if it had already happened."

"Wait. You think they did stuff later? Show me!" I point to the shoebox.

For some reason, the order and the tidiness of the letters soothe me. Order and tidiness in general soothe me, but it's not dependable. I could very well be listless, prone on my couch for days, dust crusted around me, dishes piling up, whiskey the only thing cutting my cottony mouth, musk caking the spaces between my breasts and my legs, and not care. The letters, though—I'm dependable with the letters. I'm curious how Torrey will treat them when given unbridled access, because the first time she read them I micromanaged the whole thing. I'm curious if she knows this about me, and if she'll be hyper-vigilant about my fucking shoebox. Or if she'll dig into them with childish glee. It fascinates me that she has a different relationship with these letters than I do. I'm willing to surrender my obsession, just because she fascinates me.

In a way, it makes me think, yeah, maybe having children wouldn't be so goddamned terrible.

I get up to make some popcorn. I just saw a thing on News Hour about microwaveable popcorn. It was pleasantly surprising that all they warned against was feeding a child microwaveable popcorn and pumping their immune system full of PFCs the day before they get a vaccine. I was expecting much worse. I press the popcorn button and lean down to watch it spin. My mother always used to tell me to stand back from a microwave.

"Don't irradiate yourself," she'd say.

"I don't think they sell things at Sears that leak radiation, Ellen," my father would say, and even I felt like he'd properly made her seem like an idiot.

The pops space out. I count: one, two, pop. One, pop. One, two, pop. One, two, three, and I press stop. There's a minute thirty-eight left on the popcorn cycle and I wonder what kind of sturdy popcorn brand takes up the entire time.

I consider my childhood immunization schedule. I consider all the fucking popcorn I ate as a child. It was the wave of the future. I wonder if I'm truly protected against smallpox.

"Sheila," Torrey says. "Come and see."

She hands me a letter. I hand her the popcorn bag. Then I think better of it and take it back.

"Don't get my bed all buttery," I say. "Butter flavor-y."

"I'm pretty sure it's this one that first made me think it. You have to read slowly. I almost missed it the second time," she says.

"You're a regular Harold C. Carr scholar, aren't you?"

"Just read it."

Torrey takes the popcorn and hoists herself up onto my kitchen countertop, her gangly legs swinging and banging on the cabinet door. I read. And then:

"Oh. Oh shit," I say. "You're right."

FORTY-THREE

My sweet Rosamond,

"This is taking too long," Torrey says. "Skip to the middle of the second page."

> *Well, I do not mean to get so poetic and flowery on you, but sometimes I cannot help myself. Sometimes the devilish mixture of torture and exquisite pleasure renders me incapable of speaking like a man.*

"I love that. That 1950s crap," she says.

> *But, my dear, the world must forgive me. The world does not know the torment of having you so near to me but at arm's length. The world does not know the torment of knowing what your skin feels like against my fingertips but not being able to chase that sensation at will.*

"Yeah," she says, through a mouthful of popcorn. "That."

"Possibly, but he could just be talking about shaking hands or whatever."

"Do you have a boyfriend, Sheila?" Torrey asks. She's put the popcorn down.

"What? No."

Silence with Torrey is usually a beautiful thing. In contrast to time spent with my mother, where quiet is judgment, imagined or real, it's nice to know someone exists with whom I can be quiet, no expectations. Except for right now. The space between us is awkward. The silence is annoying. I realize that I always want Torrey to leave the room when things get difficult, and I realize this is a shallow, weak response to conflict. I couldn't even say whether I'm just worried she'll name my loneliness, or whether she'll ask me if I'm boning her dad, or whether she'll somehow know that I once parked my car in front of a man's house, a man I didn't know, for two weeks straight. I'm about to ask her to leave when:

"I think I have a boyfriend," she says.

"Oh, God."

"Don't tell my dad."

"It's not like he can't hear us."

"I'm trying to talk quietly!" she says. Her face is flushed.

"And, you're, like, going to girl talk with me about it or something?" I say. I'm painfully aware that the panic in my voice comes through loud and clear.

"Um, no," she says. She laughs. "I'm not going to girl talk. I don't even know what girl talk is."

"Me neither," I say.

"Your phone is buzzing," Torrey says, nodding toward the edge of the counter where my phone is plugged in. "It says Mom."

"Ah shit," I say. "I need to take this. I've missed a few calls."

I pick up the phone and look at her, but she doesn't move. It's a face-off. Torrey is not leaving. It's the fourth ring now. I have to answer.

"Hi, Mom," I say.

"Sheila?" she asks, predictably. "It's Mom."

"Uh huh," I say, because I don't trust myself to say anything nice.

"You didn't have a chance to come by on Sunday?" she asks.

"Oh, sorry, I couldn't make it," I say. "I was feeling sick. I only worked a half day today, too."

There's victory in the sense that I'm not lying.

"Oh, honey, I'm sorry. Are you feeling better?"

I contemplate. I could go for maximum pity, tell her I still feel pretty sick, but that might mean she'd step up her mothering into the "feeling needed" category and I really do not want that.

"I'm feeling better," I say.

I'm about to make a tedious gesture to Torrey, but when I look up, she's watching me, expressionless. It's the face of a girl who has lost her mother. A girl who has lost her mother listening to a mother and daughter treat each other poorly, listening to a mother and daughter perpetuate the cycle of manipulation, of dysfunction. She may not even be aware of what she's hearing. She may not even be aware of what she's missing. But I am. And that's enough. It's not even that I'm worried Torrey will think I'm callous, it's just that I'm suddenly struck by this need to keep Torrey safe. I'm suddenly struck by how I'm remembering how to feel things.

"My neighbor's kid, Torrey, is over," I say. "Well, technically she's my neighbor too. And she's not really a kid. She's smarter than I am," I add, with a smile and a wink to Torrey. She rolls her eyes. Success.

"Oh, that's nice. She seemed very lovely," my mother says. "What are you guys doing?"

"Nothing much," I say, snatching a letter out of Torrey's butter-flavored fingers. "Just eating some popcorn and hanging out."

"Is her father out somewhere? Are you babysitting?" she asks. I want to respond harshly, but it's best that Torrey not know about this question.

"Vinnie's fine, too," I say. "I think he's working from home tonight."

"Okay," she says.

Neither of us say anything. The silence is laced with judgment. Decades-old, recurrent judgment alongside fresh, minutes-old stuff. The space between us, radio waves and wires and data parcels, swirls with uncertainty and mistrust, with fear of intimacy and affection, with thick, thick resentment. I'm not above any of it. I'm not better than this. If Torrey weren't watching me, I think I'd hang up.

"Well, I'm sorry about Sunday," she says, and I hate that I was about to say those exact same words. It occurs to me that my mother would love that. She always thrived on that stuff, clinging to whatever she could that proved we were mother and daughter. Really, she raised me well enough, even when she was alone. I was well fed. I was loved, if only a little smothered. I was clothed. I was never hurt. When nobody explicitly makes a wrong move, how do we end up off track anyway?

It occurs to me that getting out of this silent resentment is only as difficult as I make it. I don't feel very good about this revelation.

I force a laugh. "I was just about to say that exact same thing."

"Oh, honey," she says. Her voice is light. It was the right move. "Don't worry about it."

"All right, I'd better get back to my guest," I say. Torrey smiles and takes the popcorn to the couch. "I'll talk to you soon."

"Sheila," my mom says, and her voice is slow and tentative and I worry.

"Yeah?"

"I've been meaning to ask you about that thing you were writing when I was last over."

"What thing?" I say, and then it hits me. Harold's letter.

"Some sort of letter. You had spilled your drink on it. You were copying it down in your little book."

I look to Torrey, who has no idea what's taking place on the other side of the phone. She's lying on her side on the couch, supine. She licks the popcorn grease off her fingertips and then picks up a letter from the floor. I know her fingers weren't dry or even completely clean before she picked it up. Torrey does not respond to my tele-pathic plea for advice.

"I can't even remember," I say. I need her to talk more. I need to gauge her tone. I need to know how much she knows.

"It was just the other day," she says. Her tone is blank.

"Oh," I say. "That. It was something I'm working on. For, like, a craft project. I'm making decoupage."

I want to accuse her of being stupid. Like, if I were hiding some-thing from her, why would I have it out, actively working on it in plain sight? I never take the time to ask the same question of myself.

"Well, then," she says. "That's interesting."

"Yeah, I'm thinking of taking a class," I say. I've never really been capable of a non-elaborate lie.

"I'll let you get back to your guest," she says.

"All right, Mom. I'll talk to you later," I say.

The phone is barely on the counter before I say, "Fuck, Torrey. I think she knows."

"Knows?"

"About the letters."

"Oh," she says. "That could suck."

"At least one of them. The one I spilled tea on. It's my own fucking fault."

Torrey doesn't answer. She's reading.

"Tell me again," she says. "Why are you hiding this from her?"

For as much as I know the exact answer to this, I really have no idea how to answer that. It started as an instinctual lie. It snowballed.

"It's too late now," I say.

"No, it's not," Torrey replies quickly.

"Yes, it is. She'd be so pissed."

"What if it were your daughter? And this happened? You'd want to know. I mean, even if you were pissed at first, you'd respect your daughter for confiding in you, right?"

"That argument is invalid because I do not have a daughter and never will and this is precisely why."

Torrey nods to the doorway, and I turn around to see Vinnie standing there, leaning against the frame. His T-shirt has a smattering of tiny holes near the collar.

"Tell your mother," Vinnie says. His certainty is stunning.

Nobody speaks until Torrey jumps up from the couch.

"I finished all your popcorn. Sorry," she says. She skips to the door and squeezes past Vinnie.

"Tell your mother," he says again, but he's grinning.

FORTY-FOUR

When I get in the car, I mean to drive to my mother's house and tell her everything. But somehow I'm standing in front of 3012 Juniper. It's not the house Harold moved to, but the old lady said it's just a few houses away. There's a café down the street, still in view of the houses, so I buy coffee and a scone and sit outside, at a small wooden table on the sidewalk, and watch.

It's one of those evenings where the sunset barely shows up at all. The sky turns from bright grey-blue to grey to darker grey with little ceremony. The sun is gone and the houses are dark. Nobody is home.

What would I do if I saw him? What would I do if Harold came home and shuffled up one of the short paths on a walker or with a cane? I don't know what I would do, and the thought terrifies me. As does the chance that I could find out Harold is long dead.

I wolf down the scone but the coffee is awful. I've never liked coffee. It's time to leave.

"Mom?" I say, against the door as I knock. "It's me."

No lights are on. The house is dark, though her car is parked out front. I press my face to the small window in the door, straining to see any slivers of light, a blue flicker of a television.

"Mom!" I say, louder now, and I try the doorbell. I have no plan. I don't know why the fuck I'm trying so hard to get her to answer. It's survivalist guilt. It's something.

"I'm coming!" she shouts. It's faint, from upstairs. I check my phone but it's only eight o'clock.

"What is it? What's wrong?" she asks, all frantic as she opens the door. And then, as if it's her prescribed right and privilege as a parent, she adds, "Do you need something?"

"Can I come in?" I say. "Nothing's wrong."

Yet, I want to add.

I sit in the living room. It's the same as it's always been, but I notice two new picture frames with my grandmother in them. Mom never used to have pictures of my grandmother up while she was still alive. I consider pointing this out.

"What's the matter, then?" she asks.

"You know you asked me about the thing I was writing?"

"Yes," she says. She looks at her knees.

"Well, it was from Grandma's shoebox," I say.

She has this horrifying mixture of tight-lipped calm and pre-explosion. She might explode. She looks like she is about to shout.

"I kept one. I saved it, as a memento," I say. It's so easy how the little lies stack up again. I'm here to come clean, but five minutes into the visit and brand-new untruths bubble to the surface, slick like oils.

She stands up. "I see."

"It's kind of ruined now, from my tea. Almost illegible," I say, too fast.

"So, you read it?"

"Yes, of course I did."

She hasn't really been looking at me this whole time, but now she stares. She's waiting for something. She's waiting for my statement. I cling to this expectation because right now, I am surrendering my power to this woman. I'm not only dishing out a major confession, but I'm also opening myself up to a lengthy discussion about Rosamond and her probably-lover. In this small moment, though, I'm in control. I control the silence. The most she can do is to cut in and say "And?"

She does. "And?"

"And what?" I want to laugh. It's absurd. I'm absurd.

"Well, what do you think of it all?"

"I don't know," I say. And as much as it's an avoidance tactic, as much as I want to deflect her question, I am telling the absolute truth. I do not know what I think of it all.

She sits down again, but this time on the raised edge of the fireplace. She's always looked so young, my mother. Her skin is smooth, kind of glowing. Her hair is nice, not too long, not too short. The honeyed color is not startling or noticeable. She seems timeless, like a generically aged grown-up.

"Have you read them?" I ask. And with that it's out there, in the space between us. The letters. They exist. I've read them. I know about them. I want to know if she's read them. It's almost like trust. It's almost like sharing. It's almost good enough. It is probably good enough.

"Yeah," she says, with a big, theatrical sigh. "A long time ago."

"A long time ago?" I repeat. "How long ago?"

"I found them when I was a teenager. Thirteen, I think, just before my fourteenth birthday," she says. "I was snooping around in my mother's closet when they were out. Looking for birthday presents."

I think about Torrey, having her world turn upside down. I think about the incredible presence of mind and capacity for intellectual grief she has. I think about myself, about my eleven-year-old Confirmation ceremony, the day my father left. I was already strikingly aware of human pain and suffering. Of relationships. Of fear, of failure, of disappointment. This awareness only got stronger as a teenager. I retreated into it, a gulf, a force of nature, warm and dangerous and it feels like only right now is it all crashing down around me. It feels like only right now am I trying to emerge.

I pity my mother. I pity her unearthing this secret at thirteen. I always default to being annoyed by my mother, but when I think about her like I think about Torrey, it's different. Despite my obsession with the shoebox, I've managed to stay detached from the reality of the situation. Not just the reality that someone in my family kept an intense secret for so long, because that charms me. That excites me. That makes me want more secrets in my life. The reality that this made my own mother question her family, how she understood her life—that's what I am having trouble processing. That's what I pity. My mother, the human. My mother, the girl. My mother, the me.

Torrey is better at this stuff. I wish she were here.

"Honey!" my mother says, completely alarmed. "You're scratching your elbow raw! It's bleeding!"

I didn't realize.

"Did you, um, ever tell Grandma?" I ask.

She leans back, restless, unsettled by the blood.

"Do you want a drink?" she asks. "I have some Prosecco."

"No," I say. "I quit."

"Oh, really?" she says, all offended. "Why didn't you tell me this sooner?"

"I just decided right now."

My mother gets up and walks to the kitchen. She's dressed like someone out of a fancy old lady J. Jill type of catalog. She always dressed this way, even when she was twenty years younger than all the models. She moves slowly. I try to remember how old she is. When she returns with her wine, I ask again.

"Well? Did you tell Grandma?" My inclination to refer to her as Rosamond makes me smile.

"This isn't funny, Sheila," she says.

"No, it's not that. But did you tell her?"

She sighs. I know the answer already. For as distant as my mother feels, I can usually read her every action, her every tone, her every sigh. I'm cut from her cloth.

"No," she says. "I didn't."

"Ever?"

"No."

"Huh."

"I guess everyone has their secrets," she says, and takes a delicate sip of Prosecco. It smells sweet. Fuck sobriety. I take the glass from her hand and finish it.

"Yeah," I agree. "Everyone has their secrets."

"I would check every year," she says. "Right before my birthday. Like some sort of messed-up tradition."

"Check what?" I twirl the empty champagne flute in my hand. It's crystal, etched and carved, with violent-looking angles and tiny triangular crevices. "Were these glasses Grandma's?"

"Yes, they were. I've had them since your father and I got married. And I mean I'd check the shoebox."

"Oh," I say. "Like, to see if there were new letters?"

"Yeah. To see if there were new letters."

"Wow," I say. Processing. Processing my mother. "Well. Was there? Anything new?"

"No," she says. "Never. But get this," she says, and suddenly it's as if we're co-conspirators. We're in this together. It feels more right than anything I've ever felt with my mother. "The box had *always* been moved. The letters were in a different order every time."

I've only possessed the letters for a few months now, and I've read them in some way every day. It doesn't surprise me that Rosamond moved the shoebox, or that she read the letters in secret, but it still makes me feel something like butterflies in my stomach, something like a chill. Until this moment, I've never fully put myself in my grandmother's shoes. I've never wished for a love like Harold's, or a box full of letters like Harold's, daydreams, remnants of a sweeter life. But I can imagine being Rosamond in this sense, in the sense of possession, obsession, compulsion. I'd have to ration my time with the letters. Months would turn into sixty years. There'd be more at stake having someone walk in on me reading them. More at stake leaving one out beneath the bed. Did Rosamond ever get tired of them? Did she ever forget about them? Did she ever forget about Harold?

"I can understand that," I say. "Re-reading them."

I want to dare my mother to ask me if I've read them all. I just kind of want to tell her. I'm still waiting for the fallout from lying about the shoebox for so long, and for all the little lies and big lies along the way. She still believes they're buried with my grandmother. Her wrath (or maybe it's heartbreak) may not be inflicted today, but it will come. It's not that I fear this, it's more that I just don't want to have to deal with it. My mother is the kind of person to forgive total strangers for much larger transgressions, but she will always hold a grudge for me for lying about decoupage.

"So, uh, where is that letter now," my mother asks. She has that forced casual tone again. She's nervous as hell. "The one you spilled on?"

Is this what it all comes down to for her? It's not how much I know, it's not what I read, it's not what I've lied about (or at least, it's not *yet* what I've lied about). It's about discretion. It's like when I was young and my dad left, and that same day, she asked me not to tell anyone. I think she just didn't want me to disappear into the bedroom and gossip with my friends, but I never told them.

"It's at my house, Mom," I say.

"Take care of it," she says.

"Like, make sure nobody finds it? And finds out about Rosamond and Harold?" I'm dredging this up. I sound so angry.

She stands up and picks up the crystal. She doesn't look at me.

"No," she says, quiet and shy. Her voice breaks on the words. These are her losses, too, all along. "Because it's all we have left."

FORTY-FIVE

A GOOD DAUGHTER WOULD not have lied to her mother about burying the letters with a dead woman in the first place. A good daughter would not have perpetuated this tale several times already. A good daughter would understand that right then, with her mother on the edge of tears, would be the time to come clean.

I am not a good daughter. But I know without question that my mother is a good woman.

Driving home, it starts to rain. My windshield wipers are old and useless. One flaps off to the side with each pass. It's that Southern California first-rain-of-the-season type of rain, not enough volume to do much except make cars filthier than they already are and fill the still-warm evening air with the fragrance of wet petroleum asphalt. My windshield is obscured for the remainder of the drive home, almost illegally so.

I wonder if my mother started crying or snapped out of it when I left. I wonder if it was all manipulation. I realize something: it doesn't matter. She's an island. I'm an island. This fragile earth, our island home.

My dear Rosamond,
I eagerly looked forward to seeing you today. It was such a
pleasure. To touch your hand from across my kitchen table, it

made me feel at home. It might be fair to say that my life has become bookended between anxiously awaiting our appointments, our rendezvous, and immediately following those appointments with incessantly asking, "When can I see you again?" It's a cycle I do not find unwelcome. Everything about you is enticing, even when you're not around.

But especially when you are around. I become such an animal. I mean that in so many ways. Of course, the obvious, the flesh. I desire you in such tangible ways, and it tends to be my first thought when we are together. Perhaps also when we're not together. But I also feel animalistic in the very sense of our human nature. Sex, loyalty, protection, devotion.

Today, as you sat across from me, I was entranced by your opinions on development, on politics, on health, and on our postwar zeitgeist. You are an exquisitely intelligent person. But all the while, I watched your lips move, your brow furrow, the delicate edge of your jaw flex and move, and your fingers lift and gesture. I wanted nothing more than to run my lips across all of it. Your lips, your forehead, your jaw, your fingertips. Do not mistake me: I did not want you to stop dispensing your ideas. I wanted you to keep talking. I wanted to feel your jaw move against my lips. I wanted to listen to you and touch you at the same time. I want a reality, a universe, in which that is possible all the time, twenty-four hours a day, seven days a week.

It has been so long since I have had a sweetheart, and I have never lived with one or had the kind of time and space to get to this point, but I wonder: is there a point in time when one would tire of that kind of freedom, the freedom to talk and kiss and touch at all times, without hindrance? I suppose you would be a perfect candidate to ask this question, but I cannot bear to think of you and your husband in this intimate way. I do not

wish to consider whether he has recently touched his lips to your
cheek or the soft part of your neck beneath your jaw, or, worse,
your fingertips.

I suppose I am rambling. My point of this letter: I am now
free from the "eagerly awaiting your visit" frame of mind, and
am now squarely back to "when can I see you again?" So, pray
tell, when can I see you again?

Sincerely,

Your Harold

There's something about the idea of someone putting their mouth on jaws and fingertips that makes me want sex, badly. It's complicated, the way my dead grandmother's ex-lover turns me on. It's conflicting that before I started fucking Vinnie I never wanted sex with another person. I'd just deal with it alone, the television on, my mind nowhere and everywhere at the same time. I'm beginning to lose track of whether I want sex or whether I want Vinnie. I'm beginning to forget that I do not want someone to have sent me a letter detailing how they'd run their mouth across my jaw.

I no longer have Jesse Ramirez's purloined letter in my nightstand, but that doesn't stop me from opening the drawer to check. The empty Ziploc bag is still in there.

Torrey is still awake; I can hear her talking to Vinnie. They're discussing after-school tennis. Tonight I momentarily forget how much I like having Torrey around. Tonight I wish for that freedom (the freedom I never took advantage of when I had it) to march the few steps across the courtyard and bring Vinnie back to my place without any consequence.

Instead, I hatch a plan. I open my journal to what I think of as the Jesse Ramirez Pages. The pages are softer from frequent use, they're dirtier, and they're obvious from the outside of the book. They make me think of the Sunday Pages, the Dirty Pages, in the Episcopal Book of Common Prayer, the ones the parishioners open to every single Sunday, oils and filth thickening and yellowing the pages with each use. The church has dirty pages of ritual and tradition, of rite and faith, but I have dirty pages of stolen devotion, of freakish obsession. The entire text of Jesse's letter is in here, piecemeal. With a small piece of writing paper, I begin to recreate the letter. The letter that I honorably returned to its rightful owner. I feel proud about being honorable and it lessens the blow of all the other times when I haven't been. It lessens the blow of what I'm doing now.

I know it's wrong. I know it's creepy. That doesn't stop me. And when it's done, I wave it in the air slowly, blowing cool breath toward the drying ink, then fold, a perfect trifold, place it in the Ziploc bag, expel the air against my stomach, seal, and put it away in the night-stand drawer.

Future generations, I fantasize, might one day discover this well-preserved letter in my handwriting and wonder: Who was she writing to? Who was Sheila's love, her one and only? The deception is exciting. I close the drawer.

FORTY-SIX

I'M READING A BLOG about fibromyalgia. All of these conditions are so much more desirable nowadays, with the pretty banner graphics and endearing stories and perfect fonts. Twenty-five years ago, when I first started wanting diabetes, all I had to go off was a character in *The Baby-Sitters Club*. Soon thereafter, I met a girl with childhood arthritis, someone with celiac disease, and someone with lupus. I never told any of these people that I was jealous. I didn't really comprehend it myself. I just wanted to feel special, unique, and have problems that other people would never understand.

When I first discovered fibromyalgia, it was little more than a word on a pamphlet in a student health clinic, but this blog is written by a hip twentysomething with an eye for design. She dresses well, quirky enough to be unique but not alarming, as if to say, *Hey, I am living well despite my condition, look at my boots.*

As an adult, I can acknowledge the desire to have some concrete pain to fill the spaces where my twisted mind expects it, but even that feels shitty. Like I'm objectifying people less fortunate than me, but this girl seems a hundred times more fortunate than me or anyone else I know. She has her shit together. She has purpose. She *blogs*. Sure, she takes dozens of pills a day with dire consequences if she misses one, and sometimes she can't get out of bed, but I have felt that way for far less clinical reasons. I have felt that way for no reason. No reason but that the insides of me are unbearable.

There's nothing wrong with me. This has been medically proven, once. My former insurance company stopped honoring my requests for more diagnostics and labs. A therapist gave me medicine but I didn't take it because she didn't even run tests. She based her diagnosis on my answers, on the things I told her, and I bullshitted so much I couldn't even remember which parts were genuine. How could I take a pill based on that? And what if it worked? What if my bullshit was the right-sized hole for a pill-shaped fix? I felt helpless in the face of someone helping me.

The blogger, her doctor gave her medicine, twenty-five drugs, each with a little slot in a twenty-five-pill sorter she keeps on her vintage vanity in her breezy bedroom, and each of those was linked to a result on a printout on a clipboard. A result that someone found when looking at a drop of her blood beneath a microscope. What if they took the way I felt and put it beneath a microscope, a slice of this untetheredness, smashed between a glass slide and the little plastic cover, glowing beneath a tiny golden light, and what if they saw absolutely nothing there?

I go outside. Vinnie's standing by the gate with a cigarette. Perhaps the presence of his daughter has made him more self-conscious of the plumes of secondhand smoke his lungs express into the shared courtyard. I watch him. He's stopped wearing so many stained tank tops and T-shirts. It could be the weather cooling off, or it could be Torrey. Or, I acknowledge without spending too much time on the thought: it could be our casual sex arrangement. Maybe he's motivated to not be undesirable all the time. *Well, Vinnie*, I want to say, *obviously you were desirable in the first place*. He was at least more desirable than undesirable. I watch him, the way he leans against the fence, the strength in his back, and I can't seem to remember ever thinking ill of him.

Torrey is seated at the green plastic patio table. She's working on some homework, a large textbook spread open and some math problems in her three-ring binder, but she also has a phone out, and it keeps buzzing. This is new. She picks it up periodically and punches something out quickly before setting it down. She is indifferent.

"Is someone texting you?" I ask. I realize as the words come out that I sound betrayed. "Cute," I add.

"Shut up," she says.

"Cute," I say again, in a singsongy voice. "Aren't you way too young for a phone?"

"You're just jealous that I have friends and you don't," she says.

"Vinnie, I thought you said everybody liked Torrey."

"Usually," he says.

"And anyway, I have friends," I say.

"Name one," Torrey says. Her phone buzzes and she ignores it, staring at me, arms folded across her chest and a mischievous smirk on her face.

"Vinnie?" I say. "Vinnie's my homeboy."

"Fine," Torrey says, rolling her eyes.

"Torrey's made friends with another kid who also just moved here at the start of the school year."

"Oh, how handy," I say. "Sorry, that sounds shitty but I actually meant it, like, genuinely."

"I know," Torrey says. "It's okay. I feel the same way."

"Circumstantial friendships are underrated," I say, acting like some expert on friendships. Once upon a time I had friends. Once upon a time I had friends and lovers and once upon a time I could never be who I imagined they wanted me to be. Once upon a time

I sabotaged every intimacy before it even really started. Now I have Vinnie and Torrey, my neighbors. I have a mother, the ultimate circumstantial friendship. "They're no different than anyone else's friendships. All those people who have been friends forever, well, at the beginning of that forever, they were circumstantial friends first."

Torrey's phone buzzes. She picks it up almost instantly, fusses her fingers and thumbs over the screen for barely a few seconds, and puts it down.

"I know," she says. "I don't mind. He's nice."

He.

My eyes lock with Vinnie's. I grin. He doesn't.

> *My darling Rosamond,*
>
> *Your written reassurances make my heart sing. I do understand that sometimes it takes more than a day to write back. You have more demanded of you than I, living alone. And also, I can write with abandon, out in full view. You, I understand, cannot. You must not only find time to steal away with your own thoughts, but you also have to find the time to steal away without anybody watching you.*
>
> *And in that sense, I appreciate your correspondence all the more. I acknowledge the great lengths to which you go to communicate with me and to continue our unexpected friendship. I appreciate you so much.*
>
> *But also I beg the same of you, the appreciation and the acknowledgment. I hope that you acknowledge my childish impatience when it comes to you. I hope you acknowledge my torment as I wait for days to receive a message from you, a signal, a lifeline. I am not angry. I am just making a statement. I am just declaring my state of mind.*

My state of mind, in case you have not figured this out yet,
is that I am in love. I am deeply in love. With you, my dear
Rosamond. With you.
     Sincerely, lovingly,
     Your Harold

Without even thinking of the love, I want to show this to Torrey
with all of her instant gratification, instant communication with her
new friend, her new *boy* friend. But I know she remembers it perfectly anyway, just from the one read-through weeks ago. And this is
the first time I've seen Torrey act her age. She should have a pass to
be a preteen girl, for once. Torrey cleaned up my mess, my late-night
broken teacup. Torrey has taken me to visit the old woman who lives
in Harold's old house. Torrey has taken me to the goddamn library.
All of that is too much responsibility for a twelve-year-old.

A tiny, quiet part of me wishes I was not the type of person who
mandates help from anyone. That I was not the type of person who
left messes to clean up. That I was not the type of person who was so
much of a mess herself. I'm aware that I'm too selfish to stop. To stop
being a mess seems unfathomable.

It's a cool night, crisp with a clear sky. There's a bright star close to
the moon. My mother always knew when the planets were visible.
If she were sitting next to me on the step right now, she'd point and
say, "Look, Sheila, Venus is out." And I'd be disappointed that it just
looked like another star, instead of a moon-sized ball in the corresponding mustard yellow of all the textbook illustrations.

I watch Vinnie. He's playing Tetris again.

"Turn that down," I say.

"I actually don't know how."

"Then turn it off. Just for a minute."

He complies so easily, but leans back on the wobbly legs of his green plastic chair and watches me. He even puts his hands behind his head, elbows splayed.

I pull my phone out. I realize that Vinnie also probably knows everything there is to know about astronomy and constellations. Vinnie seems to know everything about everything and has all of that everything filed in perfectly accessible pockets in his brain. Like father, like daughter.

"Hello?" the voice in the phone says.

"Hi Mom," I say.

"Sheila?" she predictably says. I am her only child. I am the only person who calls her Mom.

"Go out on your porch," I say.

"Are you here?" she asks, hesitant. Perhaps my drop-in confessional caused a little post-traumatic stress.

"No, just go look at the sky."

"What?"

"Mom. God," I say. Vinnie stifles a laugh. I attempt to shoot him a glare, but I end up grinning. Why is this woman making mother-daughter intimacy so difficult? "Just go look. I'm sitting on my front step, and when I looked up at the sky, I thought of you."

"Oh, that's nice, honey," she says. "Hang on."

I hear shuffling. I hear the phone drop to the floor with a thud. I hear her voice in the distance say, "Shit."

Then, after an awkward pause, during which Vinnie and I stare at each other, almost daring someone to comment on this ridiculous phone call:

"Okay, I'm outside. Oh look! Venus is out."

"Thank you!"

"What?" she says, puzzled.

"That's why I'm calling. I wanted to know if that was a planet."

Vinnie scoffs.

My mother's pride positively drips. "Well, I'm so glad you thought of me."

"Anyway, I'd better go. Just thought I'd call. Enjoy the sky," I say, and I hang up before she says anything to ruin my finest moment as a daughter in the last twenty years.

"Shut up," I say to Vinnie. "Save it."

"I'm not saying anything," he says.

"Exactly," I say. "But hey, look! Venus is out."

It's hard not to smile, stupid big. This is the happiest I've felt in a long time. I feel completely in control of the feeling and at the same time like it hinges upon the galaxy, upon the planets being lined up just so. Upon the Big Bang. Upon dark matter. Upon astrophysicists. A man once fell in love with his married neighbor. A man once told her so. A man once let his heart and everybody's heart get cracked wide open and crushed into thousands, millions of tiny, splintery pieces.

Nobody is ever in control. I'm not in control at all. I'm probably not even really happy. I'm not happy at all.

FORTY-SEVEN

I ENTER HIS NUMBER again. Jesse. I want to call him so badly, and I hate myself for this. It's beyond my understanding and control. The only thing that works is to remind myself that it's too soon, and I'll be more likely to maintain my very limited access to this man if I space things out. It's satisfactory. It's not even that I'm all the way crazy. It's that there's a crazy person who lives inside me. Sometimes she's bigger than me. Sometimes she's all there is. Sometimes it's all I have.

I put the phone down.

Frontline is on PBS. I'm not even interested. I haven't changed the channel in years. I turn the television off instead and sit outside in the cold. It's a nice feeling. Tomorrow I'll need to show up to work. Tomorrow I'll need to somehow make a life for myself. Rosamond managed to show up for her life. She managed to keep going, to continue being a mother, to continue being a wife, despite everything being upside down inside.

"You're up late," I say to Torrey as she comes out.

"Yeah, I can't sleep."

"Me neither. That's a lie. I haven't even tried."

We stare at each other.

"Sheila, can I ask you something?"

"Sure," I say. I hate that question. It's never a good thing.

"Why won't you go visit Harold's next house?" she asks.

"I don't know," I say. "Well, I've driven by it."

I wasn't expecting to admit that.

"I wasn't expecting to admit that," I say.

"You're weird," she says. "I mean, you're like this perfect mix of mysterious and secretive and then also? You're always such a fucking oversharer."

"Oversharer," I repeat.

"Oversharer. You say the weirdest shit."

"I like to be honest with you," I say, smiling. "You're my Rosamond."

"Oh, great," she says. "For the record, next time I want to be the successful, decorated war veteran doctor, and you can be the stay-at-home mom."

"I'm never having children," I say. "But whatever. A mother is a noble profession, too."

"I like that dress," Torrey says. "That's the one that was Rosamond's, right?"

I look down and smooth out the skirt. I hadn't realized I was wearing it.

"Try to get some sleep," I say.

"No, tell me. Why won't you go find out once and for all?"

"Find out what?"

"If there are other letters. Rosamond's letters. The match."

"Oh, Torrey. You're such a romantic for such a young person."

"It's not romantic. It's physics," she says. "For every letter there is an equal and opposite, you know...letter."

I laugh. "I'm assuming for every three of old Harry's letters, there's one from her."

"I think I would put money on that bet," she says.

I don't say anything for a while.

"We should just go visit them," she says, eventually.

"Them?"

"Harold. Maybe he has a wife."

It had never occurred to me that Harold might have moved on. He is so genuine in his correspondence. His love seems completely unfailing and pure. He might be the only person in the entire universe capable of such love. He might be the only person in the entire universe who actually means it when they say they'll never love again.

"He doesn't have a wife," I say.

She kicks back in the chair. "Now who's the romantic?"

"It's not romantic. It's stupid, actually. Harold could have been really happy."

"What?" she says, slightly offended.

"I mean, it was almost purely accidental that he befriended my grandmother in the first place. It was *her* luring him into a friendship. She could have cited decorum and walked away. He could just as easily have latched his ripe little heart onto another woman."

"Ripe little heart, that's adorable," Torrey says.

"You know what I mean, though?"

"Yeah. If he had never met Rosamond, maybe he would have just loved the next woman."

"Yeah."

I get the sense that neither of us quite believes it.

"How old do you think Harold was?" she asks.

"I don't know. Well, I have my theories. I have an age range."

"Oh yeah?" she says.

"Well, he served in the war. If he was drafted, he'd be between eighteen and twenty-six in 1943 or so. So that puts him somewhere between twenty-five and thirty-three when he met my grandmother in 1950. Rosamond was…" I count with my fingers and I don't try to hide it. "She was twenty-two in 1950."

"Jeez," Torrey says. "Young mother."

"Everyone was a young mother back then."

"So, he was a bit older than her."

"It would have been socially acceptable, even if he was on the old end of my spectrum. Let's just say he was thirty."

"My mom was thirty when she had me," Torrey says.

"Oh yeah?"

"Yeah. My dad was way younger."

"Really? Wow. Vinnie was a really young daddy. And a young groom," I say, with wide eyes.

"I know. My grandma on my mom's side gave me their wedding album after she died. I'll have to show you one day when he's not home."

I laugh. "He's always home. Go to bed, Torrey."

"Promise me you'll think about going to see Harold. Or, Harold's house. Maybe tomorrow."

"Fine, I'll think about it."

"I don't believe you."

"Me neither," I say with a grin.

Torrey, to her credit, laughs with me.

My dear Rosamond, my love,

Thank you for your letter. I will treasure your correspondence for the rest of my life. These letters will always bring me joy, even when I feel frustration, too. The joy will always be stronger.

I must see you again. It seems dishonest not to tell you that, while writing to you is cathartic and pleasant, it's increasingly not enough for me. I'm spoiled, my hunger ever stronger.

My sister Delilah and her family are here visiting. Have you heard the extra noise coming from my side of the fence?

Have you heard the baby's squeals? It makes me miss you, having
a full house. Having a child in the house. Having a woman in
the house.

> *Ever yours, increasingly mad,*
> *Harold*

His remaining letters degenerate quickly. All brief, all clingy, somewhere between sweet and insane. I wonder about Rosamond's replies.

I wake to a knock on the door.

"Sheila?"

"Torrey?" I ask. I have no idea what time it is. I'm still dressed. I must have dozed off reading. "What time is it?" I say, my throat croaky.

"Can I just come in? It's freezing out here."

"Yeah, it's open."

She bursts in. She's dressed. "It's six, chill. I'm just getting ready for school."

"I don't need to chill," I say. Which is sort of true. I'm lying down on my bed already. I'm wearing a dress I've been wearing for days. Weeks. Sometimes I wear other things.

"Sometimes I wear other things," I say out loud.

"You don't have to explain yourself, lady. And I can tell you need to chill out. You're panicking about the time."

"Not really panicking," I say. "More of a curiosity. Okay, I was panicking, but more about being the kind of person who never knows what time it is."

"Don't worry, it's a gift," Torrey says. "To not worry about the time."

"What do you want?" I ask. I realize after it comes out that it sounds mean.

"I just saw your lights on, figured you'd been up all night," she says with a smile. "Glad to know you got some sleep for once."

"Thanks for ruining it," I say.

"My pleasure."

"So?" I say. I want her to leave, but I also want to cook breakfast for her.

"Whatcha reading?"

"My God, Torrey. What do you think?"

"Which ones?" she specifies.

"The mad ones."

"Mad-angry?"

"Mad-crazy."

"The short ones?" she asks.

"Yeah, the last ones."

She makes a noise like the air leaving her, like an "Oof."

"How's your boyfriend?" I ask. "Want some breakfast?"

"No and yes."

"No isn't an answer to 'how,' Torrey."

"I don't have a boyfriend! Jesus Christ."

"I mean your friend. The friend. The boy," I say. I open the fridge. "Fried egg?"

"Sure. My friend is fine. It's only a matter of time, though."

"What's that?"

Lids fall out of the cabinet as I pull out a skillet. The noise is deafening and I'm sure if Vinnie wasn't awake yet, he is now.

"Before he makes other friends. Boys."

"You think he's just using you?" I ask. "Until he finds something better?"

"Well, not necessarily better. Just more gender appropriate."

"Come on. This is the twenty-first century. There are no gender *in*appropriate friends anymore. Chin up," I say.

The eggs crackle. Toast pops.

"This is basically the only food I have in the house right now," I say. "You came over for the right meal."

"Can we go today?" she asks. She seems nervous.

"Go?"

"To Harold's."

"You know what?" I ask, turning quickly to look right at her. She glances quickly to the side before matching my stare.

"Um," she says. "I actually have no fucking idea what you're going to say. I never do."

"Watch your language, kid," I say. "And yes. Let's go."

"What?!" she squeals. "No fucking way!"

She jumps up from the couch and rushes toward me. It doesn't take long in my tiny house, but she's suddenly right next to me, and her arms are around me, and she's hugging me, like really hugging me, and I think I'm hugging her back.

"Oh God," I say.

"I'm excited," she says, defensive.

"It could suck."

"I know. It could also be great."

"Yeah," I say, and I can't hide my smile. I hand her a plate. "Now eat your fucking egg."

FORTY-EIGHT

IT'S NOON NOW AND Torrey is still at school. I can't explain why, or even identify what is happening as it's happening, but I'm putting on shoes and walking out to my car. Surely I'm not going to Harold's house without her. This is a dick move. I should stop.

I turn on the car and drive. If I breathe deep enough I can still smell the dead sunflower from my grandmother's funeral.

It's alarming how close the house is to mine. I don't stop. I keep driving, home.

When I get home, Torrey is already there, and when she sees me return she seems to have the same faith in me that I had. That I'd pull a dick move.

"Well? Did you go?" she asks.

"No. Not really. I drove over and then just kept driving."

"Come on," she says. She takes the shoebox from my hands. The instinct to pull it away from her is strong, but the truth is I am very, very tired and there's a chance I don't have the energy to move at all. "We're gonna try again. At least you know how to get there."

We stand on the sidewalk in front of Harold's next house, the place he fled to, the place he went to escape my grandmother. "It's nice," Torrey says.

"Yeah," I say.

"What are you afraid of?" she asks.

"I'm not afraid," I say.

"Look at you, you're shaking."

I look at my hands. They're trembling. I stare, slowly rotating my hands. I stretch my fingers as wide as they will go and the trembling subsides, but only for a split second.

"I don't know why they're doing that."

I think of my grandmother, of her hands, purplish and pale, as she held the shoebox close to her body on her last day alive.

My feet are stuck, like they're weighed down by iron and steel. We stand there for a long time, on the sidewalk in front of a small but well-kept house. People walk around us with their dogs. A nanny has to push her stroller down the driveway and into the street.

"How long are we going to stand out here?" Torrey asks.

"I don't know," I say. I don't know.

One minute later, the front door opens, just a little.

"Come on," Torrey says. She tucks the shoebox under one arm and reaches for my hand.

As the door opens, a man steps out and stands in the doorway, watching the two of us. He looks to be my age, give or take ten years. I'm never very good at telling that kind of time.

"Hi," Torrey says.

"Hi?" he says.

Torrey nudges me.

The man is attractive. He has nice eyebrows and a scruffy jaw.

"Sheila, you need to talk," Torrey says.

"I'm looking for a man named Harold Carr," I finally say. I look at my feet before looking up. The man looks surprised.

"Harold Carr? That's my great-uncle."

I smile. I can't help myself. "Really?"

"Yes," he says. He smiles, too, and he has nice straight teeth. "Unfortunately, he is no longer here."

"You mean, he's dead?" Torrey says.

"Her mom just died," I say. "She's allowed to have no tact."

"Yeah, he died."

It takes a few seconds to sink in, but suddenly I feel like I'm crumbling. I feel the cement of his front porch scraping my knees and I realize I actually am crumbling. I'm falling to the ground.

"When?" Torrey asks.

"Well, not even a year ago now," he says.

I'm *crying*. I can't even comprehend what it feels like to cry. I touch my cheeks and they are wet and maybe this is what the robot feels when it becomes sentient. My throat hurts, my eyes sting. If only I'd been able to see him. Just once. To tell him. To tell him *something*. I think the most important thing that he'd need to know is that Rosamond kept his letters. That she cherished his letters, so much. But I don't want to be the one to tell him. I want Rosamond to tell him.

He'll never know.

"Harold knew her grandmother. Sorry, I don't know why she's doing this. I thought she didn't actually know how to cry." Torrey's voice sounds kind, like she's smiling.

I wish I were more like her. I wish I had the poise and maturity of a twelve-year-old girl.

The man kneels down in front of me. "I'm sorry. I'm sad too. He was my favorite relative. You would have liked him. Everybody liked him. He practically raised my grandma, his baby sister."

"Delilah," I say. "The baby."

I look at his face.

"This was Uncle Harold's house for most of his life," he says. "But he left it to me. I've been working on renovating it to sell it. I'm sorry you didn't get a chance to meet him."

"It's not that," I finally say, and the words feel like choking.

Torrey sits down next to me. I sit too. The man sits.

"I just wish my grandmother had seen him one last time. Before she died."

A little sniffle escapes Torrey. I look over at her and she is crying, too, her quaint, tidy Torrey tears.

The man looks uncomfortable.

"I'm Sheila," I say. "This is…my neighbor. My friend, Torrey."

"I'm Simon," he says but he still looks uncomfortable. "What's the shoebox for?"

Then he looks at it again, more closely. He stands up.

"What's the shoebox for?" he asks again, and he looks kind and threatening at the same time. "Tell me, who was your grandmother? She wasn't Rosamond, was she?"

I stand up. "Yes," I say, amazed. "Yes!"

We stare at each other. We stare at each other a long while. Neither of us are smiling.

"How did you know her name?" I ask.

"Come inside," he says. "We should sit down and talk."

"No," I say. My voice is low and I'm a little afraid of it. "Tell me. How did you know her name?"

I try to remind myself not to frighten this stranger who, standing across from me, forms some sort of ancestral mirror of two tormented soul mates. We're descended from the same sad souls. Sad for the same reasons. I want to touch him, I want to reach up and put my hand on the side of his face, and it takes a moment before I realize that I am, I'm touching him. My hand is on his face.

He puts his hand on top of mine.

"I know her name," he says. "Because I have some of her letters."

"Holy shit," Torrey says.

"I'm sorry I don't have them on me," Simon says. "They've been packed up."

I'm mostly incapable of speaking, but I manage to say "Oh."

"Don't worry," he says, and my hand is still on his face. His hand is still on top of mine. I'm suddenly really aware of this, but I'm not sure how to take my hand away.

He squeezes my hand a little and that's it, that's the cue. I lower my hand swiftly. It hits my dress with a whoosh.

"I know where they are in storage," he says.

"Oh."

"Come back," he says, and there's a plea in his eyes. I don't understand why, because I probably look desperate enough for the lot of us.

"Okay," I say.

"Tomorrow," he says.

"Tomorrow," I say.

"Or even tonight. I can go get them now?" he says. Maybe he's trying not to act too eager.

"Yeah," Torrey interrupts. "Go get them now."

He laughs, Simon, and I wonder if there's the same sort of mania in his house as in mine.

FORTY-NINE

IF ANYONE HAD TOLD me fifteen years ago that today I'd be sitting on the trunk of my car, age thirty-five, wearing a hand-me-down dress and eating Twizzlers with somebody else's kid in the late afternoon sunlight, I would have laughed. I never imagined myself getting *less* cool as I aged.

"He likes you," Torrey says. "My dad."

"Your dad likes everyone," I say.

"No, I mean," she trails off. "Ugh. This would be so much easier if you weren't so impossible to talk to."

"Sorry."

"You're not sorry," she says. "You're clueless."

"Probably," I say, bringing my knees to my chest. "But I really am sorry."

She doesn't answer. She jumps down and picks up fallen eucalyptus leaves, shaping them into the letters in her name.

"I like your dad, too," I say. I wish I sounded more sincere because, it occurs to me, I am sincere.

"And you *don't* like everyone," she says.

"Correct."

"But I mean," she begins, and she rustles up all the eucalyptus leaves into a scattered mess on the sidewalk: fallen leaves in a city without a fall. "He *likes* you."

I take a big breath.

"Vinnie is the best human being around," I say. "You don't even know how lucky you are to have him as your dad."

Torrey laughs. "You sound like you're letting me down gently."

I laugh a little. "What I'm trying to say is that Vinnie is really, really nurturing. If I were to venture a guess, I'd say he sees me as someone in need."

I smile when I realize that I'm not at all lying. Then I realize I basically said that Vinnie fathers me and my smile drops.

"Well, you're probably right. But I'm still saying he *likes* you."

"And yeah, you're probably right too," I say, on the edge of being too tired of this entire thing, on the edge of feasting on it all.

"So what are you going to do about it?" she asks.

"Nothing."

"Nothing?"

"Torrey, what do you want me to do?" I say, frustrated.

"I don't know!" she says, all defensive.

"I don't think you'd like it."

"Don't *not* go for my dad just because I wouldn't like it," she says. She kicks the back tire of my car. "Ugh."

"There are so many reasons why your dad isn't going to go for me and why I'm not going to go for him, and only one of them is that you wouldn't like it."

She climbs back on the trunk next to me.

"I do like your dad," I say, my voice this quiet, alien thing. "I do. He's the best man I know."

"Yeah."

We're quiet for a while.

"Do you like this guy better?" she asks.

"What?"

"Simon."

"Harold's Simon?" I laugh.

"Well, he's really handsome," she says.

"Oh, do *you* have a crush on him?"

"No! He's like, middle aged, like you."

"Fuck you," I say, flicking her knee with a Twizzler.

I try to think about what she's saying. Simon is an attractive man. Simon comes to me with this sort of built-in ancestral soul mate business that I'm not entirely sure I can wrap my brain around. Simon carries with him the agony and love that Rosamond and Harold inadvertently bequeathed to us both.

"It feels like incest," I say, and I shrug but it's a bit pantomimed.

"Yeah," Torrey says.

"Incest," I say again.

I look over to Torrey, and she looks toward me, and it's hard to stop ourselves. We're cracking up. I laugh so hard that my stomach hurts, my cheeks hurt, my jaw hurts. None of this changes anything important, but in this moment I am so free. My heart sings.

"It's almost time to go," I say. "Simon will be back from his storage unit any minute."

"Do you think he'll let us take them home?" she asks, her words muffled, her mouth full with Twizzler. "Rosamond's letters?"

"That's a good question." I wouldn't.

"You wouldn't," she says.

"Come on. We can wait on his front steps."

"That's awkward. You have no shame," she says.

"I know."

Moments later, we're back at Harold's old house. Not his house behind Rosamond's, but his new house, where Simon lives. It wasn't that hard for us to find it, and I wonder if Rosamond ever looked. The painful truth of their tragic romance is that he only moved a few miles away. The new tenants of the house behind Rosamond's knew exactly where he moved to. If it were me, if I were Rosamond, would I be content with his final letter, his goodbye? Or would I ask around? Would I try to find him?

Not even all that long ago, my answer would have been such a clear yes. I've spent weeks in the car watching Jesse Ramirez. Isn't that sort of obsessive thing genetic?

"I don't think he's back yet," Torrey says.

"Let's go in the backyard," I say.

"Sheila!"

"Come on," I say. "I want to see something."

"This isn't *the* house, remember?"

"I know. I still want to see something," I say, walking between the fence and the side of the house.

"You're looking for sunflowers, aren't you?"

I spin around. Torrey is right behind me and we both flinch a little.

"No," I say. She stares. "Yes."

"Sheila," she says, and her voice is quiet and a little insistent. She grabs my elbow.

"What?" I say, feeling attacked. I don't like feeling attacked. I don't like feeling attacked by a twelve-year-old. I don't like feeling stupid.

"Sheila, I get it."

"No, you don't."

"I get it enough. But I think you should wait and ask Simon to show you or something."

It's true. I can find out another day if Harold planted some sort of weird shrine to a sixty-years-gone maybe-fling here. And I already know. Maybe not in his old age, and maybe not right away, the year he moved in, the year he left Rosamond. Maybe he hated sunflowers for a little while. But he planted sunflowers in his garden at some point. Certainly.

"Or I could just look right now."

"Ugh, don't," she says.

She's still holding my elbow, and I like the way it feels. I like someone needing to touch me. I don't know if she's trying to protect me in some really saintly way or if she's just not eager to watch me make a fool of myself. It doesn't matter.

"Just be friends with Simon."

"Friends?"

"Friends. Like with me. Like with Vinnie."

"I don't need any friends."

"Sheila," she says. "Everyone needs friends. Just don't sabotage this from the start."

"I'm not going to sabotage it. I'm going in the backyard. There's a world of difference."

"When you put it that way, sure. But what if that guy comes home and thinks you're a weirdo."

"I am a weirdo," I say.

"I mean, what if it makes him not want to talk to us because you're so weird?"

Torrey is so wise. I've known this all along. I'm not immature enough to ignore that I could ruin my chance at seeing my grandmother's letters, at seeing the things she wrote to Harold. But there's something about my volatile relationship to this shoebox that just sends everything to shit.

"Fine," I say. "Fine."

We walk back to the front porch and sit down. I notice a small rip forming at the seam in the skirt, between some of the pleats. The tear only opens up to more of the pleat, but it makes me panic nonetheless. This dress. I don't want it to tear. I pull at the pleat, smoothing it out.

"I don't want to put up a wall," I say. "I guess I didn't know I didn't want that."

"You're doing fine, Sheila," she says, and smiles up at me.

"You know what?" I say, patting her knee. "You're doing fine, too."

We look at each other and there's so much I could say to her.

The front door opens. "You guys ready?" Simon says.

"You've been home the whole time?" Torrey asks.

He doesn't answer, and I'm pleased about this. I don't want him to say anything, because knowing Torrey, she would tell him something about the conversation we had in the side yard. She'd ask him if he heard it. If he said he had heard, maybe I'd lose control a little. If he said he hadn't, I'd assume he was lying. And maybe I'd lose control anyway.

"Come on in," he says, fanning out his arm and pushing his back against the door, a half-smile on his face. "We've got some reading to do."

FIFTY

"I HAVE TO CONFESS," Simon says. "I haven't really read all of the letters."

I quickly look over at him then and try to gauge what he feels. How could he own these letters for a whole year since his uncle passed away and not read them? How could he not spread them on his bed every night? How could he not wake up on the floor in old, inherited clothing, cheek pressed against the floorboards, letters spread around him like shed skin? How could he still be okay?

"Why not?" I ask.

"Well, I mean, most of them are pretty similar. And I don't really think I have them all."

I feel it in my gut, the disappointment, like a hope I didn't even know I was allowed to have has been crushed.

"How many do you have?" I ask carefully. I'm afraid. I suddenly don't want to be here, in the place Harold lived with a broken heart, the second of the two houses in which Harold lived with his broken heart. I want to be home. I want to smell Vinnie's cigarette smoke from outside, I want to hear the noise of his fucking phone, fucking Tetris. I want to surround myself with Harold's letters and go back to just imagining what's on the other side of them.

I want the letters to never have happened to me in the first place. I want Harold and Rosamond completely purged from my life. I think of my mother, and how I once thought that's what she wanted all along: a normal mother herself, with a normal marriage, but it's more than that. I think it's something we share now, whether it be a burden or a treasure. Rosamond didn't die with sixty years of heartbreak on her frail shoulders alone.

"Hm. Quite a few, actually. Like a couple dozen, I guess?" Simon says. "Here. Count them."

They're still in the envelopes, pinched together with a massive black binder clip. It's an optical illusion, I'm aware of this, but the stack looks tiny compared to the three inches of black steel.

I breathe in, the smell of old paper, the smell of the house, something woodsy, dusty, a little bit like an open canister of ground coffee, and I wonder if this is a Simon smell, or if this is how Harold's house has always smelled.

"You haven't read them all?" I ask.

"Sheila." Torrey whispers through her teeth. "Can we just read them already?"

"Well," Simon says. "I've read these ones."

"What makes you think there are more?"

"Well, there was one empty envelope, but also there were huge gaps in time and, I don't even know—" he trails off.

"No lines like, 'Hey, Harold, sorry I haven't written in a while'?" I offer.

"Yeah," he says. "Yeah, I guess that's it."

"You're probably right. I have hundreds," I say, nodding toward the shoebox under my arm. The shoebox I'm making no gesture to offer. I'm aware of this in a painfully cold way. I'm going to have to take baby steps.

"Go on, then," he says. "Have a seat. Read them."

"But," I say. I don't finish.

"Sheila wants to know if she can bring them home."

"My uncle was really special to me," he says and he takes a deep breath. "Though I do think they belong to you more than they belong to me. I just think we should be careful with these, treat them as relics, I guess?"

"She wants to line them all up in order, like the ones she has," Torrey says. I didn't know this until she said it out loud. I didn't know that this was what was unsettling me. It doesn't help, though, because now I'm unsettled by the fact that he is not going to allow this.

"Let's make copies," he says, and he's brilliant, because that has never occurred to me. "I can get you copies made."

"Okay," I say, grinning. "That will do."

"Now," he says. "Read."

It hasn't been long since I've known Harold and Rosamond. Since they've been somewhere between real and fictional characters to me. I haven't known about them for long. But this moment feels so important, like the kind of moment someone awaits their entire life. This doesn't feel like it's supposed to feel. I'm scared. I feel like I've put too much into this and I just want to go home.

"I just want to go home."

"Oh for fuck's sake," Torrey says. Simon looks between us, back and forth a few times.

"It's okay," he says. "I understand. But they're really nice letters. She seems very kind."

That word does it. It snaps me out of it. Because I was expecting "tortured." I was expecting "adulterous." I was expecting, at the very best, "star-crossed." "Kind" doesn't seem to fit the places Harold's letters went to as the time progressed.

I slip open an envelope. The letter is tiny, the paper thin. I look at the date and it's toward the end.

Dear Harold,

It's so nice of you to write so much. I'm always so happy to hear from you. It's nice to have a friend. It's nice to be friends with a neighbor, especially in this day and age. You never know when you could need something.

Today we went to the art museum. It was a lovely outing, even though Ellen does not have the same sort of patience for the exhibits as my husband and I do. Even I sometimes feel like I do not have enough patience for it, but I find myself persevering for decency's sake. Do you ever go to any museums? Which is your favorite?

I wish I could write to you as much as you can to me. I'd love to hear more from you about your work or your family if you have time.

Sincerely,

Your neighbor,

Rosamond Baker

And just like that, the bubble is burst. There's no date but it's in the middle of the small stack. If this stack is in order still, Harold was regularly professing his love and their shared chemistry, their shared agony in his letters. Rosamond acted like they were new penpals. He thanked her profoundly for replies like that?

"Sheila." It's Torrey, and her voice is full of concern and curiosity. "Is it bad?"

I look up, and I try to hide whatever is written all over my face. I try to hide what I can barely name as my own heartache. Harold's agony, which I've swallowed all along as my own, must have been so much more than I could imagine, if he only ever received letters like this.

I probably should offer it to Torrey to read, but I don't. I fold up the letter and put it back in the envelope.

"Want to go get copies now?" Simon asks.

"No thanks," I say.

"Oh," he says, sounding confused. "I can always just bring them by another time?"

I just don't want to be mean. I don't want to say anything that would hurt Torrey, or even Simon, but I just need to be away, I need to take flight and I need to bury myself under the floorboards, both at the same time. I use everything I have to keep myself together.

"It's okay. I don't need copies," I say.

"What?" Torrey says. "No."

"Torrey," I say, trying to sound steady. "I don't want to read any more."

"Well, I do," she says. "Let's go get copies, Simon."

"You know what?" Simon says, and he sounds like a teacher, a teacher on that constant tightrope between patience and frustration, and I don't blame him. "Just take them."

"Really?" Torrey asks, gathering up the bundle.

"Yeah," he says. "You know, as soon as I said it out loud, I felt shitty anyway. She's your grandmother. They're yours."

"Great," Torrey says. "I mean, she wasn't my grandma, she was Sheila's, but I'm kind of Sheila's family anyway." She's talking really fast, too loud, too much. "I'll make copies and get them back to you. And maybe you can read Harold's letters to Rosamond too, one day."

"They're mostly buried with my grandmother," I say. I don't look at Torrey.

Simon comes really close to me, like we were on his porch, and I realize we're in the same formation: him crouching before me, me crumpled to my feet, and again I don't remember crumpling. A person this close to me is so safe and so dangerous at the same time. This person with his ancestry of heartache in this house with its ancestry of heartache, of grief for my ancestry: safety, safety, danger. I want

Torrey to hold my hand like that time when we talked about our mothers and the Children's Moon, when she cried in our courtyard, because Torrey is all safety. If could find the words I could ask her right now to hold my hand again, right here in Harold's new living room, but there are no words. Simon touches my face. I don't know what it feels like. I can't name this. It's not relief, it's not sadness, it's nothing I've ever known.

FIFTY-ONE

I DON'T RECALL DRIVING home, walking up the steps, or saying goodbye to Torrey. I'm in my kitchen, and both sets of letters are on the countertop. One set bulging in its ragged old box. The other, tiny, in a neat bundle with a binder clip.

"Torrey?" I say out loud.

"Yeah?" she calls from the courtyard.

"Did you read them?"

"What?"

"The Rosamond letters."

"Are you kidding me?"

"What?" I ask, defensive. "Did you?"

"They've been in your purse the whole time."

"Oh. Yeah, that's right," I say. "Well, come and see."

Torrey walks in. "God, I don't know what to make of your moods, lady."

"I'm not moody," I say, but then I can't hide my smile, big and crazed. Moody feels like a compliment. "Torrey," I start, thinking I might be able to explain myself. I take a deep breath. I can't.

"That's all right," she says. "Lemme see."

"Wait," I say, stilling her arm as she reaches the bundle. "It's a bit unsettling."

"How can it possibly be unsettling?"

"Fine. Go ahead."

She picks a different letter than the one I read, and I'm not even curious. I know I'll read them all. I know I'll line them up, calls and responses with Harold's. I know I'll do this eventually, but my disappointment for what these letters do not hold is heavy and unrelenting right now.

I put a glass Pyrex jug of water in the microwave. I have no patience.

"Tea?" I offer.

"No thanks," Torrey mumbles without looking up.

The microwave beeps in time with her first, "Shit."

"Yeah."

"So, Harold?"

"Yeah," I say again. "Harold."

"Apparently wasn't getting what he gave."

I laugh out loud.

By the time Torrey speaks again, I'm down to just a lukewarm, honeyed drop of tea at the bottom of the cup.

"What if she just didn't want to get in trouble?"

"You're too optimistic," I say.

"Well, I think it would have been a good idea for her to not get in trouble."

The night before my grandmother died, she told me: *History always repeats itself.* What if she'd been obsessive, if she'd walked past Harold's new house, if she'd crept in his new backyard at night, reciting her favorite letters under her breath? Because it had to start somewhere. What lives in me had to start generations ago. And when Torrey says "get in trouble," it occurs to me that maybe my *grandfather* was the obsessive one and I have as much of his DNA in me as I do Rosamond's. Maybe my grandfather was the freak, the manipulator, the one messed up in the head. Maybe I am linked to these letters, but not in the beautiful ways I'd imagined. I'm just the trouble, two generations old. History always repeats itself. Who fears me, I wonder, and I think about my mother. I think about my father.

"Get in trouble," I say. "I know." I take a deep breath. I don't know how to explain any of this to Torrey. I don't even know if I properly understand it or if it's just a cop-out. "You're right. If she were not at all into Harold, she'd have asked him to stop with the ungentlemanly conduct in his letters, right?"

"That's what I'm thinking," Torrey says. "I'm wondering if they're code."

"You're so full of shit. There's no code." I laugh, but I hope she's right. I laugh because I'm the trouble.

"What! There could totally be a code," she says. "I just need to reread them all."

"My grandmother," I say, but I can't say it, I don't know what to say. "My grandmother—" I stand up and carry the teacup back to the kitchenette.

"What about her?" Torrey asks. "You don't think she was capable of carrying out some coded top-secret business?"

I sigh and lean over, my elbows on the counter, my fingertips against my temples.

"I don't know," I say. "I really don't know what anyone is capable of."

"See?"

"But it doesn't matter," I say. I push up and walk toward the door. I hold it open for Torrey but she doesn't move. "It doesn't matter because they're both dead. Even if they held a candle for each other their entire lives, what do we accomplish, digging into it? Nothing. We just get sadder for them. Is that worth it?" I'm talking fast and my voice is shaky but I'm trying not to shout.

"I don't know," Torrey says quietly.

"I don't think it's worth it. Do you someday want someone to honor your life in a way that makes everyone sadder?" I nod toward the door.

"Remember when you told me what my dad said about my mom?" she says. She walks toward me, and we're both standing in the doorway. I'm fully aware that Vinnie can probably hear us from his house.

"What about your mom?"

"That once upon a time he was, like, madly in love with her, and that doesn't just go away? That she would always be special to him?"

"Yeah," I say. "I loved that."

"Well, it made me sad."

"You seemed to like hearing it," I said.

"I did! But I had this special thing to think now, about my mom, and it ultimately made me sadder, thinking about my dad and her, thinking about how my dad feels. And I still think it's a good thing. I'm glad you told me."

Torrey walks out. She's made her point.

I have no sense of time, or how long we spent at Simon's. I turn on the TV and PBS has a kids' show blaring, so it must still be early evening. The voices and the sound effects are gratingly loud, and not like old-fashioned cartoons, with boing noises and full-orchestra soundtracks. It's just loud and constant, voices at full-sass, full-tilt. I turn it off.

Outside, it's cold and empty. Nobody is out there. I relish the feeling of being cold, as nowadays it's the only sign of the season we get in California. Cold evenings and mornings for a few months, then back to hot all the time for the rest of the year. I do not relish the emptiness of the courtyard. I want Vinnie and Torrey to be out here. I want us all out here like some terrible competition of awkward and nosy people.

I sit on the step outside until night falls, and when it happens, I'm surprised by it. After over an hour of the darkening sky going easy on me, doing it gradually, then suddenly, I blink. When I open my eyes, I'm alarmed by the darkness, just for a second.

"Evening," Vinnie says, and sits down in one of his green plastic chairs. The legs widen slightly and scratch across the cement. "How are you doing?"

"Hi Vinnie," I say.

We stay like that, wordless, as the moon rises and takes its place in the sky. I don't know how much time has passed but I always used to wonder how long it took the moon to make its arc across the sky. Finally, I stand up. I nod goodbye to Vinnie and go into my house. I close the door. It must be nearly twenty degrees warmer inside, the chill outside not yet seeped through the thin walls. It amazes me because my insulation is so useless. I know I'll be cold in the middle of the night, but for now, I open a window and speed up the process.

"Too hot for you?" Vinnie says through the window.

"Yeah," I say.

"Won't be long before you're freezing, unless your shitty place is somehow better insulated than ours," he says.

"I doubt it."

"Where'd you and Torrey go today?"

"Vinnie, you're not the type of dad to let his kid go off all day and not know where she is."

"Yeah, I guess I'm not. But you don't count. It's not like she's gonna get in any trouble with you. Let me guess. The records floor in the library? Some old woman's lover's house?"

"Hey, I've taken her other places."

"Hardly."

"Well, we went to see a man," I say, not intending it to sound as pointed as it did. "Harold's nephew."

"Wow," he says, after a moment. "So, any news about Harold?"

"Seriously, Vinnie?"

"What?"

"Don't pretend like Torrey didn't come home and gush about this to you."

"Well—" he starts.

"I didn't even overhear it. I'm just guessing."

"She told me a little."

"Did she tell you about Simon?"

"Oh, he has a name, does he?" Vinnie asks, and the way his words twist I can tell he's smiling.

I lie down in my bed. I place the shoebox and Rosamond's bundle of letters at my hips. I'm still not ready.

"Are you in bed?" Vinnie asks.

"Just lying down."

"It'd be a bit early for you to go to sleep, not even morning yet."

"Real cute," I say. "Mock the insomniac."

"You're not an insomniac," Vinnie says, and I hate him for being right. "I've seen you fall asleep on concrete steps."

"Simon is nice, and he had these letters," I say, feeling sleepy. "And it's all kind of weird."

"Have you read them yet?"

"No, just one. Torrey read them all."

"I heard."

"So what did she say?" I ask. I pick up the bundle and turn it around in my hands. It falls onto my chest, then tumbles to the floor with a quiet thud.

"Nothing much," he says. "I didn't pry."

We don't speak for a little while. I hear him unsheathe a cigarette, flick the lighter, and the smell of the smoke sneaks in the open window. A man walks by across the street, shouting nonsense and obscenities, tweaking out. Eventually, I hear Vinnie stand up, the plastic chair scraping against the concrete again. And then I hear the creak of his door and the click of his lock.

"Goodnight, Vinnie," I whisper.

FIFTY-TWO

IT'S NOT EVEN FIVE seconds after I settle down on my bed with both stacks of letters and a cup of tea that the lights turn off. It's silent, no satisfying click or shutdown noise like on TV. I check my phone, and it's half-charged, so I turn on the flashlight app and search for circuit breakers.

They're all fine. I test every light. Every appliance. Nothing.

I call the electric company. This could go one of two ways:

If it's an unscheduled outage:	If it's my fault:
"Hi, my power just went out?" I'd say, uptalk and girly curiosity turned on full throttle.	"Hi, my power just went out?" I'd say. I don't really nail the uptalk.
"Sorry, ma'am," they'd say, paying no heed to my uptalk and calling me ma'am anyway. "There seems to be some trouble in your area. We have crews on the ground right now trying to determine the scope."	"Ma'am, we're showing your account is in delinquency," they'd say.

"What do you mean?"

"I mean, you haven't paid your bill in over two months." |

"So…" I say.

"Ma'am, there's nothing we can do."

"When will we get power back?"

"Our system says, let's see, possibly by 6 a.m. in your area."

"What time is it now?" I'd ask.

"It's midnight, honey."

"So it's not my fault?"

"No, but it is showing that your bill is past due. Do you want to pay that over the phone?"

I hang up.

"What time is it?" I'd ask.

"It's just after midnight, ma'am."

"Isn't that kind of fucked up? Shutting off my power in the middle of the night? What if I had an alarm set to get me to work?"

"I'm sorry for the inconvenience, ma'am," they'd say. "Do you want to take care of paying the bill over the phone?"

"I can't fucking see anything," I'd say. "How can I pay anything if I can't see?"

"Ma'am, you have had plenty of notices. Do you have any flashlights or candles you can light?"

"I can't believe this."

"Ma'am, your last notice was supposed to be forty-eight hours ago. Did you get a notice on Tuesday?"

"Yes," I'd say. "Probably. I've been preoccupied."

"I'm sorry, ma'am, but we cannot restore your service until you pay your past-due amount. Do you need payment assistance?"

> "No. I have enough money. I just
> forgot. And I can't see."
>
> I hang up.

I hate that the stupid phone call drained my battery down to 45%. I shine the flashlight under the sink until I find candles and matches, and then I shut my phone off completely.

I light a match and hold it in front of me. I watch the flame elongate suddenly, then shrink back down, and then my fingers are hot and I have to shake the match out before I have a chance to light the candle.

I manage to get three small votive candles burning before the next match burns down. Another match, another three candles. A fourth match, three more. Suddenly my house is glowing, and it seems somehow larger. I carry a few big pillar candles to my night-stand and prop myself up until I have enough light to read.

By the time I'm done, which doesn't take long, I notice that one of the smaller votives has already burned out. I want to spread out the letters and line them up by date, but there isn't enough space away from the dozens of open flames, and there isn't enough motivating content in Rosamond's tight-lipped replies.

But maybe Torrey is onto something. Maybe there's a code. Maybe she's just making sure she won't look bad if she gets caught. Maybe her own sense of self-preservation is stronger than how much she cares for Harold.

It's well after midnight in a room aglow with candlelight and I feel *old*. Not old, but from another time. In the back of my mind, I feel a desperation and this is the perfect storm of things I want, badly, to believe in.

I've never had as much at stake as Rosamond did, in her maybe-romance and in her family, but it occurs to me that I identify with her selfishness on a base level.

In the kitchen drawer, I have a clothesline and a box of wooden clothespins. The line is basically just a thin rope, not the plastic clothesline they sell at hardware stores now. I step carefully over the floor to get them, winding a serpentine path around the candles, and climb up on my countertop, careful not to step on any candles there, either. I tie the clothesline around the pendant light on the kitchen ceiling. I remember my dad showing me knots, but not in a helpful way. He'd tell me how to do something, then make me watch him repeatedly tie the particular knot, and then he'd just hand me the rope and walk off. He'd never wait around while I tried it myself.

I try to remember a knot, any knot, but end up just tying five or six regular knots all in a row, a little appendage of stiff knots sticking out from the lamp. I climb down and tiptoe back toward my bed, letting the cord hang slack enough so I can reach it from the ground. I loop it around a few bunched-up aluminum horizontal blinds in the window above my bed, and then back toward the kitchen, to an upper cabinet knob. The rope zigzags across the small room.

And then, I fill the room. I get to work.

Letters dangle from every inch of the line. I'm incensed, focused, almost athletic about it. I love the determination mixed with the physical effort of navigating the candle obstacle course. I hang all of Rosamond's letters, and leave spaces for two of Harold's on either side of each of my grandmother's. Matching two of his for one of hers will still only use up a fraction of the stack of Harold's letters, but it's the best I can do given my small house and given Rosamond's unequivocal lack. Given: we might not have them all (given: that is an optimistic take). When I can, I find the Harold letter that I think might precede any specific Rosamond letter and peg it before that one. Then I find which letter I think he composed when Rosamond's lackluster, arms-length prose is still the most fresh in his mind, and peg it immediately afterward.

When I'm done, I sit on my bed and lie back. It's beautiful in here. It smells like hot candles and old books. It smells like church. The dim light makes each tired page glow. Some of them are translucent, like mica, like stained glass.

Rosamond. My grandmother. A sweet woman, kind, pensive. The most pensive person I ever met. She always seemed different from people who were just quiet. But the way Harold described her in his letters makes her seem warm, even chatty, and perhaps the last time she was that chatty was a morning visit to Harold's house, free of her daughter, free of her husband, free of that other life she'd never escape. When I'm troubled, I act. When I'm in a bad place, I do something—maybe not a good something, but a something. Rosamond seemed to do nothing except burrow inside herself. It frustrates me, even angers me a little. I suppose I even admire it.

Despite the dozens of miniature flames, it's cold now, a California November seeping in. I sit up a little and pull my knees up, beneath the skirt, letting my skin warm itself.

I want to sit back, to see all of this from afar, like glowing prayer flags for a sad remembrance. I don't want to study the letters right now, but I'm *compelled* to. I know Torrey is asleep, Vinnie too, and I want to do this on my own. I want to be alone, as alone as I was when I first read Harold's letters. It seems like an entire lifetime ago.

I walk slowly toward the clothesline, my bare feet heavy. There's no more athleticism, no more quick intensity. And then I start at the beginning, and read.

And it's unbearable.

How could they be like this to each other, for so long? I want to hate them both for doing this to each other, for not doing enough. If their love was so powerful, it would be powerful enough to uproot lives and still prevail. It's the first time I've properly let myself be upset by this and not just unmoored, and I'm acutely aware that I've stepped outside of the compulsive way I read and reread and catalogued the letters. I imagine my grandmother, holding that last letter, the one where Harold leaves. I feel like her, sad beyond words. Helpless. Lonely. I miss her desperately only because I want a chance to tell her that I understand and that I'll never understand. I want to hold her frail hands and tell her she was wrong.

I'm not touching the clothesline when it falls. I'm not even close to it. I've stepped back three paces, not even looking because by now I know where all the candles are. But I'm too far away, I'm helpless. The knots on the cabinet door must have given out—my father's failed knot lessons—because one of the lines sails, weirdly slowly, to the ground from left to right, all the way toward the window. It springs back a little at the point where I've wrapped it around the aluminum blinds, and then the line, the clothespins still attached, the letters still attached, sinks to the ground, the pages fluttering, feathers on a wing. My stare is glued to that point, to the blinds, when I hear the first rustle and crack of paper catching fire. The light swells in the room, golden, almost sweet. I lunge toward it, but I fall, and I cry out, and it's hot, I'm hot, and I'm tired, and I don't want to see any of this anymore.

FIFTY-THREE

"SHEILA!" IT'S VINNIE.

"Sheila?" His voice is thick and warbly. Maybe I'm inventing it.

"Come on, no. You cannot go back in. Shit," he says. I can't even think, never mind speak. "You're hurt."

"Shit. Sheila."

"They'll be here soon. I can hear the sirens. It'll be okay. God, I think you're hurt. Sit down."

I open my eyes. The letters are gone, the fire is gone. I'm in a hospital bed, not even in a room, more of a curtained-in cubicle. It's not any sort of gradual realization like in the movies, where I hear these curious beeps and slowly become aware of my surroundings. I don't try to tug at the tubes and wires attached to me. There aren't many, just some sort of blood pressure cuff on my fingertip and a clipped needle in the back of my hand, clear tubing to an IV. My head is tilted to the side, and that's all I see, that hand, and I don't move.

"I'm awake," I try to say but no sound comes out.

I go back to sleep.

There's smoke and tiny swirls of sparks, and I'm behind glass and can't get to it. I press my hands to the glass, then my cheek. It isn't even warm. I bang on the glass, as hard as I can, until it breaks. The fire rushes toward me, like it was sucked this way.

My eyes flick open and it's more dramatic this time, jagged breath and slight panic. My fingernails are digging into the loose sheet on top of the tiny mattress. My left hand and forearm are bandaged up. My breathing calms and I hold my arm up and rotate it back and forth. It doesn't hurt much. I try to lean up to see what else is going on. There's a blanket but I can move everything.

I close my eyes.

I can recite Harold's final letters, the crazy ones, from memory. I don't know if I'm saying them out loud. I don't know if I'm awake. I might be dreaming, or on drugs, or dead. I move my lips, my eyes are closed. I'm not here, I'm not here, I'm not here.

> *My Rosamond,*
>
> *I need to see you. It hurt me that you canceled our visit. Not that you canceled, per se, but because no matter how much we mean to each other, you cannot prioritize me the way I prioritize you.*
>
> *To be perfectly truthful, I actually cannot think of anything else to say to you in this moment. I have nothing to say.*
>
> *Yours, regardless,*
>
> *Harold*

When I grasp at the sheet, it lifts from the mattress. There's something in me, something in my veins.

> *Dear Rosamond,*
> *Please forgive my dreadful handwriting. You see, it is dark, it is early, maybe two o'clock in the morning, and I am so tired, and I have been drinking gin, and it is dark in my room. I do not want to turn the light on. With the light on maybe I will see myself more clearly, and my darling, I do not wish to see myself more clearly.*
> *I want to see you. Only you.*
> *Desperately, ashamedly,*
> *Harold*

I want gin, I want the dark. My eyes are closed but I feel so bright, it's too bright here.

> *My darling Rosamond,*
> *I want to throw away this pen. I want to burn this book of letter paper. I want to cement up the fence between our houses. I want to rip up the flowers. Sunflowers are such ugly, grotesque things. I want to be yours forever.*
> *Regretfully,*
> *Harold*

I try to roll over, to bury my face in my pillow, but I'm too tired, I'm too heavy, everything is heavy. I just want to be buried underneath it.

> *Rosamond,*
> *My dear, my Rosamond. Where have I gone wrong?*
> *Yours, always.*
> *Harold*

————

"Oh God, she's awake. She's awake!"

"Mom?"

"Oh God, Sheila. You're okay! You're okay. Jesus. You're okay. Thank God."

She sounds angry more than relieved, and I wish I had enough energy to hate her for it.

"I'm sorry," I say. My throat hurts so much.

"Oh, honey," she says. "Don't be sorry. It was an accident."

"What's with my arm?" I whisper.

"You're burnt," she says. "It's not too bad, it'll possibly just mean pain treatment. There's a patch on your hip, too. You've been sedated a bit."

I don't speak.

"All things considered, you made out pretty well."

All things considered.

"Hey." It's a new voice. A man. I can't place it yet. "You awake?"

I open my eyes. Brown hair, short, and for minute I think he's Jesse Ramirez and my heart skips because it *could* be Jesse, because he could have heard about my accident and remembered me, because maybe he cared all along.

"It's Simon. Remember? I'm Harold's nephew?"

"Oh," I say, and my voice sounds so relieved. It's a relief to be relieved. "Hi."

"You don't look so good," he says.

I sit up a little and try to squint at him.

"I'm sorry, I didn't mean it to sound like that," he says. "I just mean, you're in a hospital."

"I know," I say. I realize I'm fighting a smile.

"I mean, shit. I know you know."

"Why are you here?" I say.

"I just wanted to see if you're okay." He looks down.

"How long have you been here?" I ask.

He looks at his phone. "I've been here, like, maybe a few minutes?"

"How long have *I* been here?" I ask. I've been awake twice now. No, three times. Maybe I've been here all night.

"A night? I think," he says. "I'm not sure."

"I'm sorry," I say, and I don't say why, and he doesn't ask why, and he also doesn't ask me if I have his letters so I assume we both know what I'm talking about.

"I know. I'm sorry, too."

I lie back down and we stay like that for too long. We don't talk, because what is there to talk about? I feel weak. I'm a little hungry, and I'm so thirsty.

I hear nurses at the desk, and they're talking about *The Bachelorette*, maybe it was on last night. They have strong opinions on the girl and weak opinions on the men. Simon and I sit there in silence during their entire conversation, until they run out of things to have opinions about, and then the hallway is quiet.

"Can you leave?" I ask.

"Sure, God, I'm sorry." He sounds so awkward. I think I've upset him.

"Sorry," I hedge. "It was nice to see you. I just mean that I'm feeling really tired. I don't want you to be sitting here when I fall asleep. I'd feel bad."

"No, I totally understand. I'm sorry. It was kind of dumb to come here anyway. I'm sure you'd rather see a million other people."

"It's okay," I say. "I don't have a million other people."

I close my eyes.

He stands up, a scrape, chair legs versus hospital floor. I whisper "I'm sorry" to him and I mean about the letters, I mean about coming to find him, somehow pulling him into my mess. I don't open my eyes and I don't want him leave.

I think I'm asleep before he disappears.

"Torrey?" I say. I close my eyes again. "Is that you?"

"Yeah," she says. "Hi, lady."

"Hey, Sheila," Vinnie says. He sits back but Torrey leans forward.

I prop my pillow behind me. "I'm so happy to see you."

She's sitting in the chair with her arms folded. She looks annoyed.

"Did they just give up on giving you a room?" she asks. "Isn't it illegal to keep people in this, like, hospital farm?"

"It's perfectly fine," Vinnie says. "I think this is normal. Stop being dramatic, Torrey."

"I don't have insurance," I say. "That might be part of it."

"Ugh," she says. "You're so stupid."

"Thanks, I know."

"Seriously! How could you do that to me?"

I'm quiet for a little while. I don't really know what to say to her. I didn't do this on purpose. I'm the one who is hurt.

"I'm sorry," I finally say.

"How much longer are you gonna be here?"

"I think they'll let me go home in a bit," I say. "Nothing really hurts but I'm also on a lot of medicine."

"Oh good."

We look at each other. She hasn't unfolded her arms yet. Her lanky legs stretch out before her, all the way beneath the hospital bed.

"Well, you do realize you don't have much of a home left anymore, right?" she says.

I didn't realize. I didn't really think about it.

"It's not *that* bad, but it's definitely not livable yet," Vinnie says. "The landlord has been around, grumbling and cussing and fixing stuff up."

"You're so dramatic. I thought it burned down to the ground."

"Almost," Torrey says. "It would have if it weren't for my dad. And you'd probably be dead."

I close my eyes and lean my head back. I try to remember.

"I can't remember," I finally say. "I remember you, Vinnie, a little bit."

"There's not much to know. He went in, pulled you out, called the fire truck, the end."

He's so quiet.

She stands up and paces, slowly, in the tiny cubicle. I can't tell if she's awkward or angry at me.

"Some of the letters are still okay," she blurts out, like she's been holding it in the entire time. "Most of Harold's are fine."

"Oh," I say.

"Yeah." She sits down again.

"I don't really care about the letters," I say.

She slaps her hands on her thighs, stands up, and opens the curtain, but before she walks out, she turns back to me. In a small voice, not accusing, not judgmental, she asks:

"Did you do it on purpose?"

I take a deep breath, a long exhale. "No. Torrey. Of course I didn't."

I think that was a mistake, including the "of course." Because sometimes when I look at myself the way Torrey must see me, there's no "of course." There's just a live wire.

"I didn't," I say, and I reach toward her. She walks back to the bedside and I grab both of her hands with my right hand. "I swear. My power had gone out. I needed the candles to see."

"Okay," she says. "Okay, Sheila."

She squeezes my hand a little bit, then pulls her hands away.

"Torrey?"

"Yeah?"

"I'm sorry,"

"Don't be sorry. It was an accident."

"I mean, for everything. For being such a mess."

She looks at me for a long time, and it unnerves me. I'm glad that I'm no longer connected to anything that might beep.

"I really don't think you're a mess," she says, and she looks at me, hard, and then she leaves, and she's the strongest thing I've ever known.

FIFTY-FOUR

I WAKE UP AGAIN, not realizing I slept. Just Vinnie's here.

"Hey," I say.

I want to ask him so many things, but my throat is still sore from coughing, from breathing in smoke. I want to ask him what I was like when he walked in. I want to ask him if he saved any letters or if that was just pure chance. I want to ask him if he's noticed we haven't slept together in a while. I want to ask him if he's noticed we've never kissed. I want to ask him where my grandmother's dress is. I want to ask him if Torrey is okay.

Instead, we're both quiet.

"Where are you going?" he asks.

"Hm?"

"I mean, where are you going today, when you go home? For the time being, I mean?"

"Oh. My mom's. I don't know if I can go back to my house."

"Why's that? Is everything okay?" he asks, and he looks awkward. "Financially?"

"Vinnie," I start, and I feel this instinct to be mean but I also never want to be mean to him again. "Vinnie, I almost burned down my house."

The look on his face tells me I was mean.

"But you didn't."

"It doesn't matter. I almost did. And I'm not supposed to burn candles. It's in my lease."

"I'm sure the landlord could give you a pardon."

"I'm sure he won't. He probably had to pay my electric bills so he could use power tools to fix shit today."

"What?"

"Vinnie," I say. "I'm tired. My throat hurts."

"I'm sorry," he says. "I'm still going to talk to him."

"Why, Vinnie?"

"Because I'll never have a better neighbor than you."

I'll never have a better neighbor than you, Vinnie.

"My mom says she wants me to stay with her for a little while," I say, and I realize how childish it sounds. "That sounds bad."

"I understand. If I were a mother, I'd want the same thing, wouldn't you?"

"I don't ever want to be a mother," I say. "I don't want to think about that." But before I can finish the sentence, I'm already thinking about it. A girl, a daughter, burning down her house, lighting her flesh on fire, dripping blood from her nose into teacups. Into churches. Scratching her knees until the skin comes off. Stalking people, calling them, going to their *houses*. The way she'd disappear for weeks. The way she wouldn't be able to hold down a job. The way she'd treat me.

"Fuck," I say. "I want to go home."

"Sheila," he says, and he's looking down at his feet, at the sparkling clean vinyl floor. I miss our courtyard. I miss the green plastic chairs. I miss all the sounds I know, the smell of Vinnie's cigarette. "What happened to your father?"

I close my eyes.

"I'm sorry," Vinnie says. "I shouldn't have asked."

"Why did you?" I say, my eyes still closed, my voice thin and tired.

"Well, I guess I was just thinking about you thinking about being a mother. I was thinking about your mother. It was a natural progression."

"Oh God," I say, and I open my eyes. I laugh. It hurts. It feels good. I haven't laughed in a very long time. "Were you just imagining being my father? Because that's fucked up."

"No. Jesus. I was imagining Torrey, in a hospital."

The thought that Torrey could end up like this unsettles me. I feel nauseated. I feel like I could throw up. I clutch my stomach.

"Oh hell, are you okay?" Vinnie is alarmed. He's standing, reaching toward the curtains.

"Stop, don't get a nurse. I'm fine," I say. "I just didn't like thinking about Torrey like that."

"I know," he says. He sits back down. It's not a green plastic chair and the legs do not scrape against the concrete. "It tears me up to know that there's a daughter in a hospital and her father is out there somewhere, not knowing."

"My father is nowhere."

"He isn't," Vinnie says, and he's pissed. His eyes flash wild, angry, just for a moment, before he softens. He looks away. "He isn't nowhere. He's somewhere. Don't say that."

"My dad has been nowhere my entire life."

"What's his name?" Vinnie asks.

"Martin," I say. "His name's Martin. My mom always called him Marty, but he introduced himself to other grown-ups as Martin."

I suddenly want to tell Vinnie everything, all of it, even the good. The times when my dad and I had fun together. The times we made the best pizzas, and the times we made the shittiest pizzas, and it didn't bother us, it almost made it better.

I was happy when he was happy. It was a very simple formula.

"Vinnie?" I start.

"Don't worry," he says. "I'm not going to look him up or anything. That's your business."

"No, I know. I want to ask you something."

"Okay," he says, tentative. "Fire away."

"Which was worse? When your wife left you, or when she died?"

"That's a terrible question. Of course it was when she died."

"Really?" I say. "Think."

He does think. I'll never know if he's thinking about what I'm telling him to think about, or if he's thinking about how ridiculous this is, that I'm pressing him on this. But because he doesn't answer, I feel something like hope. I feel like in the tiniest way, he understands me.

"When someone leaves you," I say, and I'm staring at a spot on the metal bed frame. My vision starts to blur and the silver spot becomes the whole room and I can feel my eyes widen but I'm powerless to stop this staring. "Even when you deserve it, it's hard to, I dunno. Heal."

"People heal all the time, Sheila."

"But," I continue, ignoring him, "when you don't deserve it, but they leave anyway?"

"Sheila," Vinnie says, his face in his hands. "I know."

I don't keep going because I don't have the words for it. I close my eyes but it's still blurry silver everywhere, like the inside of my eyelids are molten steel.

"Do you remember," he suddenly asks. "When Torrey's mom died?"

"Yeah," I say.

"Well, remember, also, how I wasn't gonna go? To the funeral? And you talked me into it?"

I look down. I close my eyes. "Yeah."

"I'm a good father, you hear me?"

"Vinnie," I say, my eyes open. "You are. You're the best. You're the best man."

"And I still needed someone to talk me into showing up."

He touches my index fingertip, presses down on the nail. It's a weird kind of intimacy, like holding my hand would've seemed dumb right now, not enough.

"What if," he says, "this whole time, your dad hasn't had a friend like I had in you? Telling him to show up?"

I try to bring my other hand up to my face. I want to squeeze the bridge of my nose or something but the bandage is in the way. Vinnie is running his fingertip across the edge of my nail and I don't want him to stop.

"Maybe he thinks he's not welcome," Vinnie says.

I don't say anything because I don't really know if he'd be welcome.

"You could try, too. Instead. That's what I'm trying to say."

I look up.

"In case he doesn't have a crazy neighbor showing him how to be a better man."

He squeezes my fingertip again, his thumb on my nail, and I love the feel of it, the hurt, the way it's already normal for him to touch me like this.

"You could try," he says again.

It's so quiet between us. Even the nurses on the other side of the curtain, even the other patients, they're all hushed. All listening, all waiting.

"Okay," I whisper.

FIFTY-FIVE

I'M IN MY MOTHER'S house, my old home, sitting on our old couch. I turn the TV to PBS and it's Huell Howser and he is so excited about everything about San Diego. I put it on mute.

The shoebox must have sat in a puddle of water from the firefighters. Torrey saved it, but the box and the bottom layer of letters got really soggy. In the hospital, she told me she had the wet letters spread out in their warm kitchen, but the box fell apart when she picked it up. The dry letters are in one of those disposable Tupperware containers, resting on my knees. The rest are with Torrey.

I open the container and see the letters for the first time since that night. I wait to feel something, some sort of spark, but nothing happens. I don't care. I don't care that it's been weeks since I've seen these letters. I don't care that many of the letters from Rosamond to Harold burned to scraps in the fire. I don't care that the remaining letters are scattered all over town. Decades and decades ago, when these letters were born, when a man sat at his kitchen table trying to comprehend whether what he felt was wonderful or wretched—that was the biggest moment for these letters. That's when they shone, not now, not when they're just little exhibits.

That's the moment to worship, to light candles to, to light the world on fire for.

The one on top is the final letter. It's the one I've read the most. The one that takes the edge off my disappointment. That fills my grandmother with mystery again. It's the one that most makes me want to see the Rosamond letter he's replying to.

My dearest Rosamond, my dearest love,

I suppose you are right: It is unusual for you to send me letters without receiving a reply. Normally it works the other way around, and I'm the one who sends and sends again without waiting. But I have been withdrawn lately. I have been busy, you see. And I have been incredibly, incredibly sad.

I am leaving.

I need you out of my life. You need me out of your life. It's simple, really.

What we have, what we are, can never be decent. It can never be as pure as our love is. I do not wish that for us. You deserve a life much better than this. I deserve better than this.

When you came into my life, my world lit up in such a way that, while brilliant, meant nothing will ever be so bright again. The rest of my life will be a dim understudy to the life I knew with you.

But, in the last few months, the last year, really, I realized that I was becoming more and more unhappy. I witnessed you becoming more and more trapped in your horrendous life, but less and less comforted by me.

I've felt angry about this, betrayed. I have always felt like it's my right to be able to comfort you or bring you joy. Examining that makes me feel ill. Selfish. I shouldn't feel like I have any right to anything of yours, even if it's something as indefinable as being the one to make you happy. It all makes me feel unhinged.

You make me feel unhinged, ready to fall from the rafters. It is killing me to feel like this.

I am leaving. In fact, I have already left.

As soon as I finish writing this letter, I will fasten up my bags, load the boxes onto the truck, put the letter through your fence, and drive away. You will never hear from me again. You will never see me again.

Sincerely Yours, Always and Forever.

Forever.

Harold C. Carr

I fold it up and put it back in the container. At first, when I moved back in with my mother, I kept the letters hidden from her, because it just seemed like too much for her to take. Her daughter, the deadbeat, burns down her own house, moves back home, and reveals an elaborate ruse about burying letters with a dead woman. It's too much. It wasn't even that I was ashamed of having lied, or ashamed of keeping up the lie. It's just that I didn't want my mother to have to deal with it.

But now I set the container down on the side table, my mother's side table, in my mother's living room, and I don't even bother putting the lid back on.

I walk toward the mantel. It seems to have even more ridiculous stuff on it now than the last time I was here. From behind a family of small angel statues, I pick up the photograph of my mother as a child and her parents, my grandparents. I try to place the date based on my mother's age, but I can't even begin to guess how old she is. Four, maybe five? Rosamond looks so sad and alone, despite being surrounded by her happy family. I wonder, is this after she met Harold, but before he left her? Or after *everything*? Is she regretting never telling him how much she cared?

When my grandfather died a decade ago, if I had been Rosamond, I think I'd've rushed to see Harold. I wonder if she found him
again. I wonder if when he died last year, she knew. I want that for
her. I want her to have known.

What became of the letters Harold did not give to Simon? Maybe
Harold saved some, the good ones, the illicit ones. Maybe he had already burned them. Maybe he took them to his grave. I can picture
Harold being buried with them. And I can also picture him burning
them to the ground, an angry, unfulfilled man, incapable of ever loving
like this again.

I set the photograph down and run my fingers over the scarring on
my left forearm. It's rugged, almost bumpy. I try to pick at it with my
nails, but it's just skin, tougher than ever. The man on the TV is jumping
down from a rock onto the sand, near a pier. He's shouting something
into the microphone. I think of the coast, the beach, loud and windy,
and I realize I can't remember the last time I drove the fifteen minutes
to the ocean. My father hated the beach: the crowds, the heat, the sun-
screen, the danger. We rarely went when I was a child. I don't have the
ocean in my bones like other people raised in this town. The people who
raise us, not the places, lay out our futures for us, piece by piece.

There are no pictures of my father in this house. I wonder, before he left, did he tell my mother? Or did she find out later, like
Rosamond did, that he had left her behind. *By the time you get this*,
Harold wrote. *By the time you discover that I'm gone, I'll be gone.* My
mother had warning: years of unhappiness, of anger and disconnect.
Rosamond had warning: increasingly insane letters, his brief (and
probably exaggerated) withdrawal toward the end, the fragility of the
thing holding them together in the first place.

But I had nothing. My father left me without warning, without
notice, without deserving it. All I had was false hope, because he had
left one time before, and then came back.

"What are you doing?" my mother asks. Her voice is calm but I still flinch.

"Looking at this picture," I say. I stop scratching at my arm and pick up the photograph again. "Of you and Grandma and Grandpa."

She takes it from me, and she smells good when she's so close. Something orange and warm, something like home.

"Ah, I remember that day."

"No you don't," I say with a laugh.

"Of course I do! What makes you say that?" she says, one hand on her hip.

"It's like sixty years old. You've possessed this picture for sixty years. It's so much more scientifically plausible that you remember the picture."

"For such a know-it-all, I don't understand why you're not some kind of doctor," she says.

"Grandma is so sad," I say, ignoring her thinly veiled insult. She needs to come to terms with the reality that her daughter is a temp.

"Mmm," my mother says. "She does look a bit sad, doesn't she?"

I sit down, but my mother stays there at the mantel, staring at the picture.

"She was always like that, you know," she says.

"Yeah, I know."

"I never thought of her as sad, though. Just quiet."

"Do you think she's sad now?"

"Now?" she asks.

"After the letters." I try not to glance toward the box on the table. I suddenly wish I'd been more careful. I suddenly wish I had cared about lying to her. Right now, more than anything else, I don't want my mother to flip out. I don't want her to say something that cuts me, that cuts us.

"Honey, I've known about the letters since I was a teenager."

"That's what I mean. And you didn't think she was sad."

"Well, Sheila," she says, and breathes in and out, sharply. She puts the picture down, turns toward me, and folds her arms a bit. It's almost a hostile stance. Somewhere between hostile and at ease, and I feel like a soldier, in a battle, on a worn-down couch in my worn-down childhood living room, all our unhappy ghosts within arm's reach. "I never thought those letters were sad."

I want to laugh a little, because the letters are *tragically* sad, but I don't. Maybe she's right.

"Rosamond's letters back to Harold were almost anonymous. She never wrote the way Harold wrote."

"I know," my mother says. I glance up quickly. "Torrey told me about Simon."

"Well, so don't you think it's sad?"

She rolls her head on her neck, back and forth in half moon shapes, like a ballerina warming up. She's so graceful. And then her lips purse, and she looks so old all of a sudden.

"Have you ever had a love like Harold's?" she asks, except it's not a question. And I think, maybe it's just as bad when you *do* get that warning when someone leaves. I think maybe, if my dad is out there, and he dies, it'll be really, really hard on my mother, as hard as the day he left. I don't understand it, but something tells me it's true.

I think of what Vinnie said in the hospital, about how my father is out there somewhere, not just nowhere, and he doesn't know his daughter was hurt in a fire, he doesn't even know about the fire. I think of all the fires he's never known about, and all the fires I've never known about. I think about how maybe there's another fire that he walked into, willingly, to save someone. How many other burning places will it take for us to feel each other?

"Mom?" I say, and I look at her, and she is right here, she's always been right here.

"What?"

"Thanks for letting me stay."

"Oh, honey. Of course. You can live here as long as you need. It'll be just like the good old days."

"I don't know if I want it to be like the good old days," I say. "Do you?"

My mother looks at her feet, and then she looks at the mantel, and then she looks at me. "I'll take you however I can get you, Sheila," she says. "Now or then."

FIFTY-SIX

It's a Monday, the best day to come here. Nobody in the church biz works on a Monday.

I pick the lock, like I've done many times before, with and without permission, and open the back door to St. Peter's. It's cold in here, despite being sunny and warm outside. The cold nights linger in an old building like this.

"My dad will freak if he finds out I'm breaking into a *church*," Torrey says.

"Then don't tell him," I say.

"Aren't you supposed to be a grown-up? Setting a good example?"

"It's not like you're in a gang or something. We're sitting in a church. You're with an adult. You're totally safe. I'd probably kill anyone who tried to kidnap you."

"No, you wouldn't."

"It depends, I guess," I say. It really does. "And you're probably right. Let's tell Vinnie what we're up to."

I dial his number.

"Sheila! Don't really call him."

"Vinnie?" I say. "No, she's fine! We're fine. Listen, I just wanted to tell you we're at St. Peter's? Yeah, the church. Where I used to work. Uh huh. I totally worked at a church. Well, anyway. Torrey thought it was weird, so she wanted to be responsible and let you know we were somewhere unexpected."

Torrey rolls her eyes. She walks away from me and lets her fingertips trail across the edges of the pews as she moves toward the altar. She lifts her arm a little between each pew, like her fingers are bouncing from point to point.

"I'm fine, Vinnie," I say. "I'm not tired at all. No, I'm not on any medicine. Yes, I drove here. Yes. God. Okay. What time do you eat? I haven't ever eaten dinner with you guys before, do you realize that? Won't it be weird? Yeah. You're right, I am weird. So is your daughter."

"I heard that," Torrey says. She's behind the altar now.

I hang up without saying goodbye.

I don't really feel like being at the altar. I sit in the back pew, near the aisle.

"I wish I could have taken you to the church I actually used to go to," I say. "Back when I…"

"Back when you believed this shit?"

"Yes."

All but alone in a church, it's hard to remember I don't believe in it.

"My former church is way bigger. It's older, too."

"This place already seems really old. Let's go to your church, then," she says.

"I only know how to break into *this* church," I say.

Torrey leans back against the altar, and then bends her elbows and hoists herself up onto it. She lets her legs swing back and forth slightly, feet dangling, an arrhythmic *thump-thump, thump-thump* as her heels lightly bump against the table.

"Do you ever think this would be different if we met when things in our lives weren't as messed up?" she says.

"Different how?"

"I don't know."

"Do you think things are really messed up?"

"A bit messed up," she says. "A bit crazy."

I walk toward her and sit down on the raised step of the altar, leaning my back against it. Her feet hang inches from my arm, close enough that I feel her proximity like static electricity.

"I don't think I'd treat you any differently, regardless," I say.

"But we never would have met," she says.

Her shoelace is untied. I hold up a fingertip, and each time her foot swings forward, I swipe at the dangling shoelace.

"That's pretty fatalistic."

"Even if my mom had still died, I don't know if we would have talked as much if you didn't have those letters."

"Maybe," I say. "Maybe not. I don't know why I even talked to you about the letters, to be honest. It's not something I'd normally do. I've lived in that house for years without really talking to Vinnie, and just all of a sudden, one day, we talked."

"It wasn't all of a sudden. It was because of the letters. Don't you think?"

"That's pretty optimistic."

"First I'm fatalistic, now I'm optimistic?"

"So you're saying, if my grandmother never told me about those letters—which she only did a few hours before she died—then you and I wouldn't even be friends?"

"Basically," she says.

"Or if Harold had never fallen for Rosamond?"

"I can't tell if you're mocking me."

"Or if my mom hadn't throw her doll over the back fence sixty-odd years ago?"

"Exactly."

She hops down and sits next to me, graceful in spite of her lanky, preteen limbs.

I want to tell her that I think we'd have been friends anyway, that something between us, this weird age-defying understanding and peace between us, would have figured out a way. I want to tell her that I'm not glad her mom died and she had to move out here, but I am glad I know her.

The church smells stale and old, dust warmed over. I think I believe in something good.

"I feel like I should tell you about how I'm kind of at a rock bottom right now, like, this whole time you've known me," I say.

"I know. I understand."

"But the truth is, this isn't really rock bottom. It's basically how I've always been."

"I know. But," she stops, and exhales. She lowers her head to rest against my shoulder. "I know."

It's so quiet in the church, I can almost hear myself tell her she's the best thing ever to happen to me, the best thing.

ACKNOWLEDGMENTS

THANK YOU TO Monika Woods, for believing in me and this book (and for making me believe in those things too) and also for making me laugh a lot. To my editor, Michelle Dotter, for her brilliance, partnership, patience, and care. And to everyone at Dzanc for their love and hard work.

To the kind and brave souls who read early drafts: in particular Tessa Tinkler, Nelwyn Del Frate, James Tate Hill, Keith McCleary, Juliet Escoria, Jac Jemc, and Lindsay Hunter. To the writers and editors who held my hand, inspired me, or pushed me, especially Jessica Hilt, Matt Lewis, Jim Ruland, Zack Wentz, Lizz Huerta, Amy Wallen, Aaron Burch, Kevin Maloney, and so many more. To my womenfolk, my loves, who supported, loved, babysat, and cheered for me at every step. And to Ryan Bradford, thank you for tirelessly making this book what it is, and for giving me someone to write for (it feels like something between gratitude and life support). This is for you.

My undying love and admiration for the entire beautiful San Diego literary community, every last drop of you. And to Rory Kelly, who once upon a time assigned a fledgling writing group the prompt that birthed Vinnie and then birthed this book.

Last but really first: to my family, and especially to Erik, Oliver, and Edith. Thank you, for everything. You made this book happen.

Photo by Nelwyn Del Frate

ABOUT THE AUTHOR

JULIA DIXON EVANS lives in San Diego. *How to Set Yourself on Fire* is her first novel. Her work has appeared or is forthcoming in *McSweeney's, Literary Hub, Barrelhouse, Hobart*, and elsewhere. She is an editor and program director for the literary nonprofit and small press So Say We All and hosts The Foundry reading series.